POWDER TRADE

BLACK MAGIC OUTLAW
BOOK FOUR

Domino Finn

Blood & Treasure

Published by Blood & Treasure, Los Angeles
First Edition

This is a work of fiction. Any resemblance to reality is coincidental. This book represents the hard work of the author; please reproduce responsibly.

Cover Design by James T. Egan of Bookfly Design LLC.

ISBN: 978-1-946-00804-6

DominoFinn.com

POWDER TRADE

BLACK MAGIC OUTLAW

BOOK FOUR

Chapter 1

The man with the 9mm Uzi waved at me.

"Hey, you're Chucho, right?"

I nodded even though I wasn't. Chucho was dead.

He shook my hand and said, "I'm Manolo. I don't think we've worked together yet. They say you're solid."

I nodded again and hooked my thumb around the strap of my Uzi. We both had them. On the outside, we were nearly identical. Honduran mercenaries in Miami. Shady illegals working security for a Caribbean drug cartel. Not a bad gig for a homicidal psychopath.

But that was Chucho, and I wasn't him.

My real name's Cisco Suarez, and Manolo wouldn't believe it for a second, but I know magic. I'm an animist, a tapper of spirits, and right now I wore a straw mask. It's an intricate spell that involves, well, a straw mask, as well as other tokens of spellcraft. A beeswax candle, a little smoke and shadow, and boom: I had taken on Chucho's appearance. The real mercenary was facedown in a pool of blood in a cheap motel room.

I hadn't wanted to kill him, but he drew a gun. Wasn't that always the way? But I'd managed to interrogate him first, pick up his mannerisms, and confirm the final details of the drug deal. So here I was, an interchangeable mercenary in a nondescript parking structure before dawn. With Manolo.

"I'll clear the ground," he said. "You take the top two floors."

"Already did," I told him. "There's less activity here than in a nuclear disaster zone."

Manolo looked impressed. "An early starter. Good deal." He took a casual glance around but otherwise trusted my word.

There was no reason not to. The parking garage was an old building behind a floundering strip mall in Hialeah. The day hadn't started yet and, even when it did, the open parking outside would be the first to get used. The location had been well picked by the cartel. Little road traffic. Not a camera or attendant in sight. Before the sun rose and the shops opened, this place was a barren wasteland.

The predawn hour was important to me as well. Or rather, the darkness was. Exposed to sunlight, my straw mask would disintegrate in a wisp of smoke. Bye-bye disguise.

"Okay, here we go," said Manolo after a phone call and two smokes.

A black Econoline van approached the garage. I'd caught the same sight a month before when I learned of this drop: two men, Honduran as well, and a metric shit-ton of powder in the back. The driver swiped a keycard to raise the gate. Manolo and I stepped up to the van and peeked in the windows.

"*Hola muchacho*," said the passenger, bumping fists with Manolo through the open window. The driver looked me over with annoyance. Maybe Chucho had slept with his girlfriend or something. I just nodded and he drove past with a frown. Drug dealer drama.

Manolo and I wordlessly followed on foot. Like I said, I'd seen this go down before. From a distance and unable to act. This time I was prepared, which is why this was going to be the easiest robbery ever. All I had to do was complete the sale, ditch my buddies, and drive off in a van full of cash. Another contribution to the Cisco Suarez fund, and another damaging setback to my new arch-nemesis, Connor Hatch: primal being and the scariest drug kingpin since Pablo Escobar.

I probably shouldn't underplay the primal being part. Connor's a jinn, sometimes known as a genie. He's a higher being of fire and air, from a world above ours. He's also the guy who single-handedly ruined my life and made me the off-the-grid outlaw I am today.

There are no take-backsies from that. He and I are dead set against each other now. Only with him in hiding and near invulnerable to my spellcraft, I had to settle for hitting his business interests instead. Months of small-time strikes and heists had to be putting a dent in his wallet, and it was only a matter of time before I forced Connor to show his face again.

As far as plans went, it wasn't subtle. That's what I liked about it. But I was getting ahead of myself. Step One was the easiest robbery ever.

An errant honk spun me and Manolo on our heels. His hands grabbed Uzi just as fast as mine. Idling at the curb across the street was a sleek blue Cadillac. The tinted front window slid down and a hunched figure nodded us over.

From my angle, I couldn't see more than that he was white.

I frowned. Not just because Manolo did too. Something was off about this. These weren't our buyers, and they weren't supposed to be here.

"Fucking Nikolai," spat Manolo.

"You know this asshole?"

He nodded. "Russian mobster wannabe. The boss brought him on to help with our security problem."

Security problem. That would be a big fat euphemism for Cisco Suarez. I guess months of small-time strikes and heists taught Connor a thing or two.

My cohort stormed toward the car. I trailed at a distance, stopping at the threshold of the garage and leaning on a pillar. I wanted to get a closer look at Nikolai but needed to make sure he didn't get the same at me. Disguises like mine aren't foolproof, depending on who's doing the looking.

Manolo traded sharp words with the driver, but he didn't antagonize him. Pissed but respectful. After further words were exchanged, the back doors opened and a couple of rowdy-looking fellows stepped out, all broad shoulders and straight foreheads. The bulges in their jackets hinted at serious firepower.

Just what I needed.

Manolo spit on the street in one final show of protest before hiking his shoulders and heading back. The two Russians followed. The Cadillac sped off.

"It's out of our hands," whined Manolo, leaning on a nearby wall and crossing his arms. "We still run support but they take the lead. Boss's orders."

I glared at the approaching men, but their natural scowls put anything I could muster to shame. The first brushed me with his shoulder and pushed me to the side, his cruise ship to my jet ski. The second stared hard as I tightened my fist. I let them pass without incident.

After all, I was running support. Boss's orders.

Chapter 2

I didn't like this.

Extra muscle specifically hired to sniff me out? Not a promising start to the easiest robbery ever. The good news was the two Russian goons appeared to be all mass. Sharp eyes and quick fingers, perhaps, but no signs of magical know-how. An odd choice against me, but I couldn't underestimate them.

The two men traded whispers in a private powwow. Then one headed to the stairwell.

"Hey," called Manolo. "We already secured the building."

He disappeared up the steps without acknowledging the statement. The other treated us to a sneer and some choice words. He spoke in his native language, but his meaning was all too clear.

"Come on, *puto*," replied Manolo. "*Inglés!*"

I didn't point out the irony of Manolo's request for English. Whether the Russian understood it or not, he clearly didn't appreciate the tone. He spread his shoulders and let his jacket fall open, revealing the Kalashnikov underneath. Fucking assault rifles.

"Hey," I barked, stepping between the converging men (and raising Chucho's profile higher than I liked). "We're all professionals. No need for static here."

The Russian stared at me before speaking in a chipped voice that sounded like gravel. "No problem if behave."

I rolled my inner eyes. Way to reinforce a stereotype, buddy. But he seemed cooperative in an overbearing sort of way.

"Watch who you tell to behave," snapped Manolo.

The Russian flashed open his jacket again.

"Let's cut the shit," I said. "We don't like working with you and you don't like working with us, but the boss is shelling out money for us both. This is a simple transaction. Let's just do this and go on our way."

His scowl lessened. I'm a charmer.

"What's your name anyway?" I chanced.

More of a glower now. "You call me Veselovsky."

More inward eye rolling. "Chucho and Manolo. Now we know each other. We good?"

He shrugged. "We good if you listen. You two, Chucky and Mango, stay on perimeter. We have the van."

He turned away and headed for the parked van at the opposite wall.

Manolo hissed. "Whatever you say, pop star."

I gave him the side eye.

He looked at me defensively. "Are you serious? Chucky and Mango? Besides," he said, switching to Spanish, "it's the name of the strip club they work at. Pop Stars."

For some reason the first image that came to my head was Veselovsky spinning upside down on a pole. But I knew what Manolo meant. "How connected are they?"

My friend snorted. "They might be the mob, but they're small-timers. Nikolai owns a restaurant and a nudie bar and now wants a piece of the cocaine business. Don't know why the boss is dealing with them."

I considered Veselovsky as he bullied the Honduran driver of the van. Even back in my youth, the Russians moving into Miami was a thing. They're not huge, but they're vicious, hardened criminals looking for opportunities after the collapse of the Soviet Union. New York was their first stop, but cities like LA and Miami are fertile ground too. If Connor was working with them, they probably weren't as small-time as Manolo thought.

I clenched my jaw. Two wrinkles in my day so far and it wasn't even 5 a.m.

"Trust me, bro," said Manolo, "they're small fish. They just have something the boss wants. Why else do you think he's on his way stateside?"

Everything stopped. "Wait, Connor's coming to Miami?"

Manolo looked at me like I was an idiot. We weren't supposed to use names. It was "the boss" this and "the boss" that. But he forgave the slip in favor of unloading a juicy rumor.

Even though we were twenty yards from the rest of the crew, he spoke low and in Spanish to keep the conversation private. "The boss doesn't trust our expertise. Doesn't even want me to work the meet tonight. He's buying new boats, something to beat the radar, and he doesn't want us anywhere near it."

Tonight. "Asshole," I commiserated. "Like we ever let him down."

"I know, right? Like we're stupid. Between you and me, I'll tell you what's going down."

I raised my eyebrows. "You know?"

He nodded, but before he could say anything, the second Russian emerged from the stairwell and rejoined his companion. They seemed pleased that the garage was, in fact, empty. I took offense at that. I mean, I wasn't really a drug dealing mercenary, but I took pride in my work.

I turned back to Manolo. "Well?"

He leaned in conspiratorially. "I bet he's buying into casino boats."

"Like a cruise ship?"

"Nah, too big. The go-fast boats to Bimini. Gamble a little on the boat, gamble a little in the Bahamas, and back to Miami in time for dinner. The Russians run a couple of those outfits. It would be good cover. They bribe the Coast Guard already."

"They can hide illegal, shady activity with a perfectly legal, shady enterprise." I was impressed. "You know where this is going down?"

"I don't know nothing," he said. "And neither do you. Come on. It's almost time."

Manolo hiked across the lane of the garage, a couple cement pillars down, taking a better flanking position. As perimeter guards, our job was mostly keeping an eye on everything *outside* the perimeter. Our van was parked against a wall and had four guns protecting it, so we were the early warning system and first line of defense.

It would've been optimal for me to move further away in the opposite direction from Manolo, but I wasn't really guarding the perimeter. My interest was purely in the van. The drugs, I didn't care about. Connor would lose them to the street. The cash payment was my target. Connor would lose that, too.

But I now wondered if this robbery even mattered. Money was nice, but the real prize was Connor himself. My strategy was much more complicated than paper and powder.

Jinns are powerful creatures, but they can't directly harm humans they don't enter a deal with. That means, head to head, he was powerless against me. (Ignoring, for a moment, his private army of mercenaries.) But Connor is a being of the Aether, made of fire and air, able to vanish at will. That meant there wasn't a whole lot I could do to him either. I couldn't hurt him directly, but I sure as hell could screw up his plans.

And that's what this robbery was about. But a secretive meeting that his usual mercenaries weren't informed of? *Those* plans sounded much grander, and much more vulnerable to someone with a grudge.

Someone like me.

I had to make that meeting tonight. Some way, somehow.

I considered ditching the Chucho act for a second, but a maroon El Camino with chrome wheels turned down the block. A sharp whistle from my lips alerted the rest of my crew. I rested my hand on my Uzi and resigned myself to seeing this through.

They call this the Magic City. Miami is a city of vice—built on sex, drugs, and crime. I was about to shoot for two out of three.

Chapter 3

The El Camino buzzed into the garage and pulled ahead. I crossed in front of the car and checked the window. A driver and a passenger, both fairly young, and a grizzled fellow in the back. He was portly and balding and could've been someone's grandfather. I could tell he was a strict son of a bitch just by his face.

Columbians. It showed just how much power Connor had assumed that the Columbians were buying from him.

This was the usual help. At least, these were the same characters I'd seen a month before. Unlike the Russians, no surprises here. So far, so good. I stepped aside and waved them on. As they passed, I caught a glimpse of the metal briefcase handcuffed to the old man's wrist.

I followed behind the car. The Columbians slowed when they noticed the extra muscle leaning on the van. The two young guys exchanged a nervous look. I didn't blame them. I didn't like the Russians either.

They parked a couple spaces away from the van. The two vehicles were opposites. The Honduran mercenaries went for unobtrusive black. An old handyman's truck. The maroon El Camino was shiny and blinged up, attracting attention just by existing. The passenger hopped out.

"What the fuck is this?" he asked, talking to our driver but keeping his eyes on the Russians.

Our two guys exited the van, eager to get this over with. The driver shrugged. "Extra security. Don't worry about it."

I stopped twenty feet from the vehicles as they emptied. The old man with the briefcase drew the expected attention. This was no ordinary briefcase. It wasn't skinny and meant to hold paper folders. It was more like a reinforced box, and from the way the man leaned, it had weight. He stood in the vacant parking space between vehicles and a crowd gathered around. Even Manolo inched forward. All eyes were on the briefcase except for those of the Columbian driver. He leaned on his door with his back to the show and lit a cigarette. One of our guys went for the back doors of the van.

"Wait," called Veselovsky, holding his AK at his side. He had good trigger discipline with his finger, which meant he'd done this once or twice. He motioned toward the briefcase. "I want to see money."

Their passenger shook his shotgun back and forth nervously, looking each of us over. He was itching to get out of here already. The old man waved him off and set his briefcase atop the trunk of the Camino. Veselovsky and our driver followed, and Manolo inched forward even more. He was practically part of the group now, leaving me the sole eye on the perimeter. A quick glance to the road showed we were clear, so why the hell was the driver of the El Camino eye-fucking me?

No way my disguise was failing.

The metal briefcase clicked open. The men leaned

forward. I shifted to the right and saw it. Cold, hard cash. It looked good. Brand new stacks of hundreds. A quick calculation put the double-wide box at two million. You could practically see the tension evaporate. Just to be sure, Veselovsky checked a stack of bills and returned it, satisfied. The old man closed the case and smiled.

"You have key?" asked Veselovsky.

"Of course," answered gramps in a decidedly ungrampslike voice. He turned to his man with the shotgun. "Check the van."

The kid nodded and went around back. Our guy opened the door for him. He unzipped a black duffel bag and gave the contents a sideways glance. "Is this the right order, *Papa*?" he asked in Spanish.

"What the fuck you talking about?" asked our guy.

The old Columbian sighed and stepped around Veselovsky to check the van. I wanted to get closer but the Camino driver was still on an island, smoking away from everybody else. He couldn't be left unsupervised.

"There's nothing wrong with the cargo," assured the Honduran at the van.

The Russians watched intently, grips tightening on their rifles. "Problem?" asked Veselovsky. So much for everybody relaxing.

"What are you, stupid?" snapped the old man. "This is what we always get." He rapped the kid on the back of the head and a few of the guys chuckled. The man zipped the bag closed and dropped it in the kid's hands.

If it was the usual order, each bag carried fifty kilos of coke. That was more than a hundred pounds.

The kid hugged the oblong bag and waddled away,

letting his shotgun slacken in his hand. The old man pulled his key chain and popped his automatic trunk a hair. "Load up." The bag carrier moved to the El Camino. The old man looked around for the other Columbian. "Where is that lazy *puto*? Help me out, will you?" He handed another duffel bag to our guy instead.

I stepped toward them. "Put the bag down."

The Columbian kid heaved his bag at Veselovsky. The Russian sensed the same trouble I did. He did his best to bat it down and raise his rifle. Good instinct, but too slow. The kid's shotgun came up and blasted him in the stomach.

My Uzi was firing before Veselovsky buckled to the ground. The kid jerked as if being electrocuted as I riddled him with holes.

Meanwhile, the old man wrapped an arm around the Honduran with the bag and raised a pistol at our driver, stuck in the kill zone between cars. The poor guy didn't even realize anything was going down when his head ruptured like an egg.

The Columbian driver was making his move too. He raised a machine pistol and rolled around the front of the car, simultaneously spraying the other Russian while breaking line of sight with me. The Russian took some lead. There was no opportunity to move around the far side of the van so he dove toward the Camino for quick-and-dirty cover.

Manolo had his gun on the old man, but hesitated. He didn't want to hit our guy who was a body shield. But that hesitation was gonna cost him. The old man raised his large pistol.

"Watch out!" I shouted.

I called on the shadow, feeling the Intrinsics coursing through my arm around the spiked dog collar on my wrist. The spellcraft fetish wasn't necessary, but every bit helped. A slither of shadow materialized from under the van and yanked the old man's feet. He fired the bullet with Manolo's name on it. It went wide and exploded into the concrete ceiling. Both the man and his hostage fell to the floor, but the Honduran rolled away.

Manolo emptied half his magazine into the Columbian boss.

You'd think things were turning our way, but the popped trunk of the Camino swung up. Another Columbian jumped out. Mean-looking guy. Really big. But I was more concerned with the shotgun he pointed at me.

My left hand was up before he could fire. The Norse snowflake tattoo on my palm tingled. Not really a snowflake but a partial glyph of power. With my will, a two-foot semi-sphere of turquoise energy coalesced. I held my shield as the man pulled the trigger. The Columbian's buckshot practically disintegrated on impact.

I spun my Uzi at the new threat but the driver came around to back him up. They both unleashed their weapons on me. I caught the lead against my shield, but the big guy got another shot off. His spread of buckshot hit my pistol and clipped my hand. I dropped the gun and drew my hand back behind my shield, but they weren't done with me yet.

Rather than play hot potato with the oncoming gunfire, I let the shield drop and slid down into the floor. Into the shadow. I became one with the darkness, something not entirely physical. The ensuing hail of bullets and buckshot missed their mark completely. To them, I simply vanished.

"Brujo!" they yelled in a mix of fear and disgust.

Still a part of the shadow, I slid along the ground, just a few yards, toward my van and my crew. The Hondurans were already backing me up. They unloaded automatic fire into the Camino. Both Columbians ducked behind.

I materialized and checked my back. No one else around. We'd been ambushed and hurt pretty bad. Veselovsky was down. Our driver. The other Russian was clutching his stomach. But there were three more of us, and only two of them. The element of surprise was gone. This was a gunfight now, and we had the upper hand.

I scanned the ground for a new weapon while the passenger of the van suppressed the Columbians with gunfire. Windows shattered. Both men ducked. Manolo was skirting the back of the van, moving to the front. Probably had missed the magic show completely. The wounded Russian rolled to his knees and perched his AK on the hood of the Camino. My best move was clear. I'd forfeit cover by running around the backside of the Camino, flanking our Columbian friends while they cowered behind it.

"It's you," yelled Veselovsky through gritted teeth. He leaned against the wheel of the Camino on our side. The lucky bastard had actually lived. Except he'd seen my magic. My straw mask was still on and I still looked like Chucho, but he knew exactly who I was. They'd been sent specifically to look out for me. "You piece of shit."

"Said the drug dealer to the thief." Instead of taking care of the Columbians, I backed around the van.

He raised his Kalashnikov and fired, but I was behind cover. The Honduran passenger reacted to defend me. The other Russian spun around and they sprayed each other.

At the same time, a shotgun fired under the El Camino blasted the Russian's knee apart. The poor guy was braced on the car and all twisted around. No chance to return fire from his position. He fell to the floor and took a second burst in the head. His body wiggled to a stop.

Veselovsky was safely against the wheel, so he continued firing until he gunned down his Honduran target.

"Son of a bitch!" yelled Manolo. He reached the Uzi around the hood of the Econoline and ended Veselovsky. Bullet holes opened across his chest, neck, and face, and he slumped over.

The El Camino's driver peeked out and fired. Manolo ducked behind the van again. The Columbian was a real piece of work, with a glint in his eye every time he let a barrage fly. If he loved this so much, I'd give it to him.

"I could use an assist right about now," I intoned. A skeletal figure wearing conquistador armor materialized beside me.

"As you wish."

The driver of the Camino cackled with crazed laughter and popped up from behind cover. Then my ghostly companion's red eyes flared. The gunman lifted his pistol to his own head and fired.

"It really scares me when you do that," I said. "We got one more."

A buckshot grouping punched a hole in the van, inches from my head. I flinched. The last Columbian standing, the big guy, rolled out from behind the car. I still didn't have a weapon. Suddenly, the man froze, as if the shotgun disagreed with him.

I waited, but the big guy fought against the impulse. He

pumped the action on his weapon and pushed it toward me again. I had to duck before it fired.

"Do something," I yelled.

The wraith did not look pleased. "He is... resisting."

I sighed loudly. "You had one job." Then I pulled out my ceremonial bronze knife and flung it at the Columbian.

I'm not a circus performer or anything, but the man was an immobile target struggling against the wraith's will. I figured it was a fifty-fifty chance the blade of the knife would catch him instead of the handle. Maybe my math was good, but my luck wasn't. The knife hit him sideways and bounced to the floor, clattering loudly.

The man's eyes were wild. He didn't know what was happening, and he'd nearly died. But damn was he a strong-willed fucker. He pivoted the shotgun and fired again. I rolled to the side, under the blast. Scooped up Veselovsky's AK and gunned him down.

It wasn't pretty but it was over.

I hooked the weapon over my shoulder and recovered my blade. I wiped it down, and then did the same with my hand and checked the damage. At least two buckshot pellets had broken through my skin around the knuckles. Others had bounced off my hardened skin. It was an enhanced option leftover from my zombification package.

I flexed my fingers open and closed. Painful, but everything worked.

Manolo came around the backside of the van, Uzi up. It was only me now. The wraith had vanished, and nobody else was alive. He dropped his gun.

"Holy shit, bro! You okay?"

"A scratch."

I stood in the center of the kill zone. Two of my crew leaked on the cement next to the Columbian kid. The two Russians were slumped beside the Camino, with two more Columbians on the far side. Eight dead, including the old man wearing a jumbo briefcase.

My cohort turned to the money. He found car keys on the body but none for the cuffs. I started for their car but Manolo told me not to bother. He went in the back of the van and jumped out with bolt cutters. They cleanly snapped the chain. We threw the case and the bolt cutters in the back. Before I could close the door, Manolo went to Veselovsky.

"What are you doing?"

"The merchandise." He hefted an errant duffel bag and carried it to the van. I helped with the other two. "The boss will be happy. We get to keep the money *and* the drugs."

Four bags of white gold piled beside a small fortune in a box. What did I tell you? The easiest robbery ever. I slammed the back shut and Manolo moved to the driver's door.

"We did pretty good," I said, following him.

"No shit. You saved my life, I think."

I shrugged. "Eh. You probably saved mine too. I'm sorry, by the way."

He turned to me. "Sorry for what?"

"This." I slammed his head into the side of the van, leaving a large dent as he fell to the floor. Manolo moaned on the concrete. He wasn't completely out, but that was good. It would give him plenty of time to book it before the police showed up.

"Pleasure working with you," I said, kicking his gun

away. I jumped in the van, threw it in reverse, and tore across the parking garage. I slowed at the entrance and used the keycard on the dash to buzz out. Then dropped it and my straw mask out the open window. My disguise flickered away. I wasn't Chucho anymore. Cisco Suarez reappeared in full force, bloody white tank top and all.

I drove to the end of the block and was readying a turn to the major street when I saw it. Another maroon El Camino parked up the road. A couple of mean-looking Columbians at the helm sneering. We locked eyes.

I didn't wait to see what they'd do. I stomped the gas and pushed that van as hard as it could go, which meant I was up to the lofty speed of fifty-five in no time. That wasn't gonna be enough to shake them.

Chapter 4

I veered across two lanes of traffic to the highway on-ramp. The good thing about blocky vans is everybody sees them coming. No one wants to be flattened against the things. At the same time, Econolines aren't fabled for their maneuverability. I might have done better in a stagecoach with actual horses galloping ahead of me. Needless to say, any swerve, turn, or hard brake I made, the Columbians could match.

The Columbians. They were their own problem, weren't they? I'd thought this was my robbery, but it was theirs. They were turning on Connor Hatch. Maybe my hits against the *Agua Fuego* cartel were taking their toll. Bringing down Rudi Alvarez, the Passport to Latin America—Connor's power structure was threatening to splinter. And the Columbians wanted their piece of the pie back.

Maybe I could kick my feet up and watch TV while they took out Connor for me. Of course, that didn't keep them from taking me out too.

The Columbians had set their own perimeter control on the deal. Eyeballs watching from a distance, making sure nothing went wrong. And if it did, they were ready to take control of the situation.

I floored the van to max speed, rushing down the Palmetto Expressway like a bat out of hell. Or that was the plan, anyway. A soccer mom in a minivan honked and gave me the finger as she passed. Jeez, I was in a car chase and I wasn't going fast enough for Miami traffic. I'd made a bonehead choice for a getaway vehicle. And now that the sun was coming up I'd stick out like a sore thumb.

Light automatic rounds punched into the back of the van. I jerked my head down and changed lanes, but the Camino in the driver's side mirror stayed with me. Another volley of bullets spiderwebbed the back windows and peppered the interior. The dashboard was mortally wounded. A little too close for comfort.

"Shit," I muttered, nearly curling up in a ball. "You need to take the wheel."

Two orbs of red light appeared behind me. "You wish me to drive?"

"It's the only way. Unless you can get in the driver's head from here."

"That isn't possible under these conditions."

"Great," I agreed. "So I'll deal with it." I hefted Veselovsky's AK.

"You do realize I'm a necromancer from the fourteenth century who—"

I bailed from the driver's seat and moved into the back, pointing to the pedals and wheel one by one. "Stop. Go. Turn. Horses are more complicated."

A lemon-sized hole popped through the back door. I kissed the floor of the van as another one punched through. "Are they firing cannonballs at us now?"

The wraith took over and swerved the van sideways. I wasn't sure if it was an evasive maneuver or learning on the job, but I slipped as I tried to get up. Screw it. I crawled over the duffel bags to the back doors and threw them open.

The Columbian passenger was leaning out the window with some kind of hand cannon. He'd definitely seen too many action movies. Initially aiming at the wheel, he adjusted to target me when I showed myself. I raised the Kalashnikov and the El Camino swerved, sending his own guy's shot wide.

I fired a burst. I started low and hit the blacktop but pulled my aim up to sweep across the car. Unfortunately, the van clipped another vehicle and jerked to the side, sending one of the back doors swinging into my rifle and causing me to miss.

I glanced behind. "What's going on up there?"

"I think this is what you call traffic."

"Well, keep it steady."

As I issued the command, the duffel bag beside me burst from a heavy round. A cloud of smoke exploded outward, sending me into a fit of coughing. I fired wildly at our pursuers to fend them off. A few bullets sprayed the hood and windshield, forcing them to disengage. They slowed down and I was too far ahead to take another shot. We had a small lead but it wouldn't hold forever.

"Brujo," the wraith warned. "I think we have a problem."

I came up behind him and squinted past a crack in the glass. A lane closure. The Palmetto would be at a standstill in less than a mile.

"Take the exit!" I shouted, which would've been a perfectly reasonable request had we not already passed it. I leaned through the apparition and jerked the wheel. The van careened across two lanes, hopped the small curb, and clipped one of those plastic yellow barrels they set up right before concrete walls. Sand peppered the windshield. The Econoline bounced out of control. Somehow we held on and veered sharply down the exit ramp.

I checked our six. Since I'd pushed the El Camino well behind us, they had plenty of space to make the maneuver.

"Keep on the gas," I said.

The van burst onto the street and caught air on the uneven road. We landed hard and something bumped against my red alligator boot. The metal briefcase slid across the bottom of the van. It would've slid right out the back if it hadn't smacked into a duffel bag.

I slid to grab it just as the El Camino screeched behind us. The passenger held a reasonably sized pistol now, staying inside the car while his arm reached out the window. He fired quickly this time. Pop, pop, pop.

I threw up my energy shield and dove to the side as the van opened up like a tin can. A bullet found its way through the back of the driver's seat, but the wraith was ethereal. Had I been driving, it would've been a different story.

The van swerved quickly to the side and scraped a parked car. Its alarm blared, lights blinking. More horns came to life as we crossed a busy intersection. As we sped up, the Columbians slammed on their brakes. The distance between us widened in a instant. In that newfound space, two cars in perpendicular traffic fishtailed into each other.

"Jesus!" I screamed. "What are you doing?"

The wraith turned around with a blank expression. "I'm not sure. The green lights went red and everybody used their emergency horns."

My eyes widened in horror. "That means you're supposed to stop!"

He seemed to ponder that. "You wish me to stop?"

I shrugged in defeat. "Good point. Carry on."

We'd caused a few minor accidents already. Unfortunately, the Columbians had avoided them. The maroon car swerved around the obstacles and gained on us again.

I braced my rifle over the punctured duffel bag, still as a sniper (except for the van mimicking a rollercoaster and the cloud of cocaine in my face). I waited as the drug dealers closed in. The pistol came out the window again. I steadied my aim. A bullet clanged against the metal briefcase, inches away. I kept calm and squeezed the trigger. Gunfire ripped across their windshield. A spray of blood obscured the passenger as the pistol fell to the street. I swept my fire over the driver too but the rifle clicked empty.

Damn. I had a spare Uzi mag in my pocket but hadn't thought to pick up Veselovsky's ammo.

The driver reached over to his associate. Rage overtook him. And then bricks of hundred-dollar bills starting raining out of the van. They bounced off the Camino's hood and hit the street like a plague of frogs.

I rolled over. The briefcase latch had taken a bullet and popped open. Half the neat stacks had spilled to the floor of the van. Many slid toward the open doors. I frantically shoveled the bricks back in.

Meanwhile, the El Camino accelerated. It came at us fast. I braced against the ceiling rack as he rammed the back of the van. I jerked backward but held tight. The metal briefcase wasn't so lucky. It bounced out into the open air.

"No!"

I lunged and caught the handle. The loose lid threatened to fly open, but I caught it with my other hand. I slammed the case shut and managed to keep most of the cash inside.

It was a great save, but it came at a price. Namely, I wasn't in the van anymore. I crashed down hard on the hood of the Camino. My empty AK hurtled to the highway. Still clocking fifty miles per hour, my face was a foot away from the driver's.

He punched the butt of a shotgun through the windshield to clear the broken glass. I grabbed the trigger and pulled, but it clicked empty. He jammed the pipe forward and knocked me in the face. I fell and clawed at the hood to keep from becoming street hamburger. The briefcase slipped from my hands. I scratched for it.

The wraith slammed his brakes. The van nearly stopped, sending the El Camino into it again. The sudden impact plunged me backward. I lost the briefcase and flew into the van, pounding against the back of the wraith's seat. I gasped as my breath left my body. Shook my head to recover my senses.

Both vehicles scraped to a stop. We'd hit something and the car had hit us. I strained to focus on the Camino. It slowly rolled backward to settle several yards behind us. The car no longer had a windshield at all. I turned and saw the Columbian passenger lying next to me in the van. He had a frame of glass attached to him. He wasn't moving.

Beside him was the briefcase of money. I folded it closed and placed it and the remaining cash on the passenger seat.

The Columbian driver was a different story. He'd

buckled up. He now crawled over the air bag onto the hood of his car, his nose broken and bloodied.

"Are you hurt?" asked the wraith.

I stared through the cloud of white smoke, dazed. "I've never felt more fucking awesome," I said. I blew hard and waved the drugs from my face, but there was no helping it. I was like the drug dealer version of Scrooge McDuck, swimming in my riches.

A siren blared in the distance. Police.

"We need to get out of here," I said.

The wraith nodded. "How do we go backward?"

I pushed to my knees. We'd rear-ended a hatchback and caused a four-car pileup. I slipped the van into reverse and the apparition punched it. Fast learner.

The van crashed into the maroon car again, sending the driver forward to join us inside. The wraith switched gears and hit the gas.

"*Come mierda*," said the Columbian, drawing a hunting knife. I picked up the nearest duffel bag as he lunged. His blade flashed and buried deep into the black fabric, spilling more powder. Before he could pull back and try again, I shoved the bag against him, forcing him off balance. With his weapon caught, he had no choice but to hug the bag.

Outside, in the sun, I couldn't have called the shadow into my fist like I did, but one thing about Econolines, they're dark and gloomy on the inside. I wrapped my fist in a glove of darkness and went at the bag like I was training for a heavyweight title.

In one punch, the Columbian found out what it was like to kiss asphalt at thirty miles per hour. The bag tumbled on the street and left a trail of powder in its wake. I considered keeping his friend's corpse for zombie-related purposes, but the damage from the assault rifle and the glass wasn't pretty. I hefted him from the van like so much garbage and slammed the back doors shut. Then I stomped to the front and took over the wheel. I think the Spaniard was disappointed.

We managed to slip the police. They got tied up with the accidents in our wake. The drug dealers wouldn't talk even if they weren't dead, but plenty of witnesses would describe a black van, once nondescript but now riddled with bullet holes and broken glass. It was time to get off the street.

Of course, things were never that simple. My cell phone rang. Normally I would've ignored the call, but it was a burner. No one knew my number except for my good friend Milena, and she wasn't talking to me ever since she'd discovered my dark past. Understandable, really. If this morning proved anything, it's that I was a walking time bomb.

On the other hand, Milena wasn't a woman I could put off. I'd been trying to get her to talk to me for months, always dropping my new number on voicemail whenever I ditched my old phone and picked up a new one. I checked the caller ID. Sure enough, it was her.

I answered and said, "I thought you forgot about me."

"Don't give me crap, Cisco. I need a favor."

"What—now?"

"Yes, now. It's my *abuelo*. Someone beat him up last night and I'm at the hospital with him."

I skidded the van to a stop. "Which hospital?"

"Jackson Memorial."

I surveyed the cartel van and rubbed my face. It was stupid to take a detour, but maybe she was opening up to me again. I didn't want to miss the chance to reconnect.

I flipped a U-ey and sped toward my friend and her grandfather. "Don't worry, Milena. I'm on my way."

Chapter 5

I strode down the bustling maze of hospital halls until I found the room. Milena sat at her grandfather's bedside. The old man's face was black and blue, his arm was bandaged, and he was hooked up to an oxygen mask.

"Hernan?" I said, leaning over him.

"He's sleeping," whispered Milena.

I froze when I saw her up close. She'd been crying, but wasn't anymore. Now she just looked worn out. At the same time, there was something in her face. Relief, I thought. She was happy to see me. I was happy to see her, but I didn't know how to say it.

"Milena, I'm—"

"Shut up, stupid." She clamped her arms around me and buried her face in my chest.

I wasn't sure what I was about to apologize for. Being a mindless slave of a vampire for ten years meant I'd done bad things, but Milena had known me before things went bad. She had to know who I truly was. I wanted to explain anyway. But she was right. It was stupid. Maybe shutting my mouth for once wasn't the wrong way to go. But I couldn't leave it at that.

"I've missed you," I told her. She drew her head away

and looked into my eyes. She didn't say anything, but she smiled. That was good enough for me.

Milena's grandfather cleared his throat. "Did you bring me some *café*?" he asked in Spanish. He didn't speak very much English, so we all switched.

"What happened, Hernan?"

He frowned and looked away, so Milena answered for him. "Someone came to his house last night. They beat him up and left him on the kitchen floor. He was there all night. Can you believe that? Good thing I passed by extra early this morning or he would've been there longer."

The muscles on my forehead tightened. The old man had to be in his seventies. With the bruising and cold light, he looked more fragile than ever. "Who did this?" I asked.

Milena opened her mouth but Hernan waved her off.

"I don't want to be a bother," he said, his voice muffled by the mask. "Forget it."

"No way," I said. "This isn't on you at all. Just tell me what happened."

His face hardened for a moment. A little bit of the stubborn old man came out. But that persona shriveled under the glare of his granddaughter. I almost shriveled too. She was good at it. Hernan worked the oxygen mask away from his face with a sigh. "I don't want you to get hurt, Francisco."

"I'm not the one who's gonna get hurt."

He stiffened when he recognized my intent. I didn't think he was opposed to justice, per se, but maybe a tiny bit of my true nature leaked out. The black stain on my soul, forever a part of me. The part I couldn't show other people. I straightened up and tried to look like a man who didn't want anybody dead.

"I need to know," I insisted.

Hernan nodded. "A man came by the neighborhood last night. He visited your old house down the street."

My face darkened. This was about me. That's why Milena had called. Not for support. Not for friendship. But to fix something I broke. I let the old man tell his story.

"He was talking to the neighbors, trying to track you down, Francisco. I guess he heard my Milena was childhood friends with your sister and ended up at my door. He wanted to know if I'd seen you. I said no. He didn't believe me."

Milena squeezed his hand. "You always were an awful liar, *abuelo*."

"This is true," he said proudly. "They'll put it on my gravestone."

"Don't talk like that," she chided.

Hernan turned back to me. "This man knew I'd seen you and knocked me on the floor."

I clenched my jaw. No doubt this was about Connor Hatch. I'd been taking potshots at him for months without retaliation. I wasn't surprised he'd finally come at me. Except he was doing it through my friends. Just like I was hitting his drugs, he'd hit Hernan.

I'd been certain they were insulated. Milena was out of this. The one good thing about our fractured relationship was that she was safe away from me.

So much for that silver lining.

"He worked me pretty good," continued the old man. "I tried to hold out, but I couldn't do it. He was going to kill me."

Some punk beating up an old man didn't sit right with me. Connor was a gutless piece of shit who would do anything to preserve his power. "It's okay, Hernan. You shouldn't have lied to him."

He shrugged. "I admitted that I'd seen you. I said you came by looking for your parents, and I told you they were dead, and you left. That was it. I left out Milena. I said it was just me at the house and I saw you that one time and you left. He believed me."

"How do you know he believed you?"

The old man smiled. "He stopped punching."

I tried to return the smile. That's what he wanted. Hernan was a character for sure. A real sense of humor. For a man his age, he was taking this like a champ. But I couldn't. My stomach turned. I was the cause of this.

"It's close enough to the truth," added Milena. "What you told him. It's probably why he believed you. It's not like you knew where Cisco was, anyway."

I nodded. "You did good, Hernan. But I need you to tell me everything you remember. Did he say who sent him?"

He shook his head. "He didn't tell me anything. Not a thing."

"So tell me what you saw. Was he with anyone? Did you see a car? Was he wearing a uniform? What did he look like—South American?"

"No. A *gringo*."

Milena slapped his shoulder gently. "*Abuelo*. That's not a nice word."

"I'm sorry, darling. A white guy. Bald with a black beard. Very big. Not tall but wide. Like nothing could knock him over."

"We'll see about that," I said.

Hernan clutched my wrist. "He looked like a maniac, Francisco. He had green markings on his face."

"Paint?" I asked.

"No. A tattoo. Some kind of symbol. Like on the card."

I thought for a second. "What card?"

The old man pointed to Milena's purse. She pulled out a card and handed it to him. He thought over it before holding it out to me. "The bastard told me, if I ever saw you again, to give this to you."

I snatched it. The backside was colored with a plaid pattern like something you'd see on a playing card. The paper stock was thick and textured to stand up to wear, with just a bit of shine. I flipped it over and saw what could only be a magical rune inscribed on the plain white surface.

Hernan reached for his oxygen mask and Milena helped fit it around his mouth. After a long breath, he said, "I thought he was going to kill me."

I turned away. I didn't want either of them to see that dark side of me boiling out again. I walked to the window and took a few breaths myself.

Milena came up behind me and switched back to English. "Can you find him? Can you get the guy who did this?"

I waited a moment and said, "I need to. It's the only way to make sure he doesn't come back." I glanced at the strange rune on the card again.

"What does it mean?" she asked, half afraid of the answer.

I traced the symbol with my finger. "I have no idea."

Chapter 6

I didn't stay long. Not very neighborly, perhaps, but I was still technically mid heist. I had to stash the money, figure out what to do with the drugs, and dump the van, all without drawing the attention of the police or any number of underworld scumbags.

In the elevator, I pushed the button for the ground floor. Before the doors could slide shut, Milena jumped between them. When the door nipped her, she yelped a little the way ladies do. Then she turned around and kicked it to pay it back for embarrassing her. The whole thing was cute. When she finally allowed the doors to close, we were alone.

She had trouble meeting my eyes. Trouble speaking, too. "Sorry for being... you know... about... you know."

I smiled. "You have a way with words. It's like you conjured a painting in my head."

She smacked my shoulder. "You're *really* gonna be like that now?"

Now it was my turn to look down. "No. I'm sorry too, okay? A lot of really bad stuff happened. It's *still* happening. And it's all my fault."

"Don't say that, Cisco. You're trying to help. You're here now."

"Maybe I wouldn't need to be if I'd stayed dead."

She shook her head sullenly but didn't say anything. The elevator ding spared both of us. We weaved through the group waiting to ride up and stood listlessly.

"I'm supposed to be out of town," she said. "You know that? I don't work for a few days and was meeting friends in Key West. That's why I went to his house so early. The plan was to beat the traffic. I was just making sure he was stocked up before I left."

I nodded. I couldn't tell if she was trying to change the subject. I just wanted to get out of there.

"God," she said. "Could you imagine if this had happened after I left?"

I winced. There wasn't any need to imagine. The world was bad enough as it was. There wasn't any need for the guilt I was feeling either. But there it was. That's life sometimes.

"I'll get him," I said forcefully. It was meant to be reassuring but came out wrong. She nodded. I smiled weakly and broke away a little too fast, rushing down the hall toward the hospital entrance. Her sandals clacked against the floor as she raced to catch me.

"Hold up," she said. I paused. She rounded to face me. "I've been thinking about this lately. A lot. And I thought it was so dumb to blame you for things you did while you were dead. All this other trouble going on, all these other shady deals, most of it started far away from you, Cisco. Despite the way you carry on, you're not the center of the world."

"You sure about that?" I asked with a smirk. Milena had a way of taking you down a peg but making you feel good about it.

Honestly, hearing her say that took a load off my soul. It was still black, mind you, but having Milena be able to look at me again made the world keep turning.

"Thanks," I said. "I mean that. I'll find out who did this to Hernan, and not just because he did it to get to me."

She nodded with her hands clasped behind her back. "I know."

I took one last look at her, soaking it up, hoping she would always look at me with those eyes. Then I went out the automatic double doors.

I was halfway across the parking lot when I noticed her sandals still clacking away. I turned to see what she wanted but she just matched my gait. I'm a little slow so I nearly made it to the van before realizing what was going on.

"What do you think you're doing?" I asked, not passive-aggressive at all.

"I'm going with you."

I stopped. "No, no, no. You heard the old man. This guy doesn't know about you. You're staying out of this."

She snickered right in my face like I was bombing a stand-up routine. "Not a chance, Cisco. I told you I have some time off. I can't go to the Keys anymore. You think I'm capable of doing anything else except worry about this?"

"But—" I wasn't sure what to say without sounding like a broken record. We both knew I'd do the same thing in her position.

"Don't think too hard," she said. "Just go with it. Remember how I handled myself during that ghost attack?"

"Right. The poltergeist. Not too shabby."

She arched her eyebrow and shifted her head to the side.

"Not too shabby? You couldn't have boosted that garbage truck without me. Besides, how many times have I helped you out with car trouble? I rode with my *abuelo* in the ambulance here. My car's at his house where I found him. Now it's my turn to ask for a ride."

A siren faded in from the distance, approaching fast. I turned my back to it and lowered my head. An ambulance pulled into the emergency entrance. I sighed. Every second I delayed increased my risk. I knew talking Milena off this would be time consuming, if it was possible at all.

"Fine," I said, leading her to the beat-up van. I unlocked the passenger door first and the wraith materialized in the seat.

"Is this wise?" asked the Spaniard.

"Shotgun," called Milena as I walked around to my door. We both climbed in and she shooed the apparition away with her hand. "Sorry, *señor*, but you have to sit in the back with all the—Cisco, why is the back of this van covered in cocaine?"

I checked and she was right. A veneer of fine white powder dusted the bags, floor, and shelves of the Econoline.

"Remember how you said all the bad things I did when I was dead didn't count?"

She nodded.

"Well, I'm still doing bad things. Besides, why didn't you assume I was selling churros out of the van and that was powdered sugar?"

"I work in a strip club, remember? Believe it or not, I've seen the stuff once or twice."

"Shocking." I started the engine and the Spaniard chose to vanish rather than sulk in the back. I made it two blocks before she asked a follow-up question, which must've been some kind of record considering the circumstances.

"You're a drug dealer now?"

"Why? Do you know someone looking to pick up two-hundred keys of coke?" I remembered the bag I'd lost. "Make that one-fifty."

I'll spare you from describing her glare.

"No," I relented. "I'm not a drug dealer. It's the guy I'm going after. The one mixed up in dirty Miami politics and a secret wizard cartel and the leader of the now-defunct Covey. Not to mention being responsible for, oh, I don't know, the death of a certain Cisco Suarez."

She took the news in stride. "You still talk about yourself in the third person?"

"Occasionally. For effect."

"Well, stop it."

"Cisco will take it under advisement."

I stopped at a green light and waved an old man with a cart to my window. She frowned. "What are you doing?"

"All this talk of churros is making me hungry."

She laughed. "No one's talking about churros except you."

The man poured at least a cup of sugar into a small paper bag filled with freshly fried curls of dough, shook it up, and held it to me.

"One dollar," he said.

I felt at my pockets. Then leaned over and peeled a fresh hundred from a nearby brick. I traded the bill for the bag and drove on.

We munched deep-fried chunks of heaven, crispy on the outside and chewy on the inside, steaming just short of burning my mouth. Eventually, Milena realized I wasn't driving her home.

"Wait a minute. We're going the wrong way."

"No, we're not. This van is hot and full of drugs. I need to get it out of sight as soon as possible. I can give you a ride home in my pickup."

"Oh, sure, but we can make a pit stop for churros."

I shrugged. "Priorities."

Chapter 7

Getting into the Everglades on Tamiami Trail, I thought I noticed a car following us. I pulled over to a patch of long grass and waited. A black car with dark tints raced past without incident. I waited a bit longer but decided my mind was playing tricks on me and kept going. The road was now clear, at any rate.

I live in an abandoned boathouse off a dirt road occasionally used for swamp access. The path is overgrown and mostly forgotten—great qualities in a hideaway. Unfortunately, the amenities leave a lot to be desired. The building is large but otherwise spartan, basically just a boarded-up shack of corrugated metal on a concrete foundation.

The platform on the side facing the swamp is large enough that boats can be towed right up to the doors and rolled into the garage. The actual water access is closer to the road. I drove the drug van past that ramp, through the overgrowth, and up to the abandoned boathouse. I hopped out and opened the roll-up loading door, then pulled in. And just like that, we were safe.

First things first. I grabbed the briefcase of money and checked to make sure all the stacks were legit. Seven-fifty large. I'd lost more than half of it on the road, but not a bad score overall. I pocketed a wad and stuffed some in my old pickup truck. The rest I left in the briefcase, which I shoved into the small lead safe nestled in the corner.

The safe had been hardy at one point, but it wasn't exactly what you'd call secure anymore. A few months ago I'd lost the key and needed to get it open. It took three crowbars, some metallurgical cantrips, and a whole assload of shadow magic to break into it. *Ocean's Eleven* it wasn't, but it got the job done. Except the door couldn't fully close anymore, much less lock. That meant it had more in common with an unplugged refrigerator than a safe, but there you go.

I unhooked the Horn of Subjugation from my belt. As far as colonial-era necromantic artifacts went, this one was a doozy. It was the cause of much of my current mess, as well as the source of the ghostly Spaniard who served me. I was so careful around the Horn I usually left it behind, but some of the bigger brawls I'd been in lately warranted the extra firepower.

It was a bull's horn, mostly white but with a flare of brown at the tip. Both sides were capped with metal to function as storage for conquistador gunpowder. Only the rebellious natives had gotten the better of the Spaniard and used the Horn in a ritual, wrapping it in Taíno gold and sealing it with spellcraft. A number of indigenous pictographs lined the soft metal.

Which reminded me. I had an expert in a museum who'd been taking a look at it. She was ignorant of the occult implications but fascinated by the cultural ones. That fascination hadn't yet translated into progress, though. Dr.

Trinidad was attempting to decipher the Taíno glyphs for me, which was a tall order because it was a dead language.

"Oh, no." I slapped my forehead and withdrew my phone, holding a finger up to Milena to let her know I'd be a minute. I put the Horn in the safe and the wraith appeared, ready to protest. I gave him the finger too.

"Dr. Trinidad," came her voice over the line.

"Hi, Doctor. It's... Mr. Rose..." I said, trailing off. I wasn't happy with my alias but there was nothing to do about it now. "With the Taíno artifact," I added.

"Ah, yes. How's the music business going, Mr. Rose?"

"Please, call me Axl." I grimaced. This is what happens when you have no imagination. I plowed ahead with my cover story anyway, trying to preserve what little dignity I had left. I assumed the doctor knew it was a pseudonym anyway. "And I already mentioned, I'm not *that* Axl Rose."

"Of course," she said flatly. She coughed and I thought I heard something in the background. "I'm sorry," she said, "I'm a little under the weather."

"Good timing then. Something came up and I need to cancel our appointment."

"Not coming in today?" she said. There were muffled sounds that I couldn't make out, like she was in the middle of working on something. Beats me what museum curators did all day. "That's—um—I hope that's not on my account. I just have a cough, but I can still take a look at the powder horn if you bring it by."

I paused. Something didn't sound right in the doctor's voice. "Have you made progress with the pictographs?"

She cleared her throat. "Nothing concrete, Axl. I wish you would allow me to examine the actual Horn instead of poorly printed photographs. If you bring it, I believe I can make some sense of it. Or take some professional photographs, at least."

Both the wraith and Milena watched me intently. They knew I smelled something.

"I will, Doctor," I answered plainly. "Just not today. I really can't. I'm sorry." I ended the call before she could protest again. Then frowned and patted the phone on my hand a few times, mulling over the conversation. Going over each word. Eventually I pulled the battery.

"It is not wise to ignore the expert," warned the wraith. "We must unravel the Taíno seal."

"Not now," I said.

"Is there a problem?" asked Milena.

"I'm not sure."

I'd been meeting curators for weeks now. First came the cover story of working for a collector. Then I put out feelers for their Arawak knowledge. Dr. Trinidad had been the candidate with the most applicable experience and the willingness to skirt proper channels in the interest of intellectual curiosity. I'd met with her twice and she came off as extremely capable. She wanted hands on the Horn, obviously, and I wanted to limit her exposure.

So her pressing to see the artifact wasn't strange by itself. But there was something about her voice. I couldn't be sure, but I didn't stay hidden all this time by taking chances. I strolled outside and chucked the burner into the swamp. A stray alligator saw the splash and headed toward it.

Milena chuckled as I returned. "You really do go through those things like candy. Which reminds me. I have another stack for you in my car. I'll hand them over when you drop me off."

The Spaniard floated forward. "I am sorry to see you leaving so soon, *señorita.*"

"I'm not leaving yet. Cisco and I have work to do."

The skull swiveled indignantly towards me.

"It's true," I told him. "Her grandfather was attacked last night. I need to find the lowlife who did it."

The wraith's breath scraped through his desiccated throat. "No time for that, brujo. You heard the cartel this morning. The jinn is preparing a meet tonight. We must prepare."

Milena started to speak, but I held up my hands and shook them both off. "We will," I said firmly. "But I can't let what happened to Hernan slide."

The wraith's eyes flared. "Our bargain struck calls for vengeance against Connor Hatch. In return you've agreed to free me from my bindings. This adjacent quest does not fulfill either purpose."

What, you didn't think the Spaniard was helping me out of the goodness of his heart, did you? Yes, promises were made. I had an obligation. But we never set a timetable.

"This is Connor too," I reasoned. "They attacked the old man to get to me. That means if we catch this scumbag with the face tattoo, he could lead us to Connor."

"Given many assumptions," returned the Spaniard angrily. With full conquistador helmet and breastplate, he was a frightening sight. "This displeases me," he said, and vanished.

"It's not like we have a better lead," I called out. No answer. I hissed loudly. Sometimes my life felt like a well-rehearsed reality show.

"Forget him," said Milena.

"Already did."

She smiled halfheartedly. "I don't want you to lose your chance, you know. If you need to deal with this creep another way, you can."

I could be a stubborn son of a bitch. I wasn't changing my mind now, even if they both ganged up on me. "I know," was all I said, but the intent was in my face.

Milena gave me a full smile now, pinched eyes and a set of teeth. "So where do we start?"

"Well, I hate to say it, but 'a white guy with a face tattoo' isn't enough to ID this dude. It's a solid identifying trait—maybe someone in the biker community—but we still need to ask around. The card he left behind is the only substantial lead. But it might be dangerous."

"Dangerous how?"

"I'm still working that out."

I walked to a dark corner of the room and induced the Intrinsics into my pupils, widening them till they overtook my irises completely. The charm allowed me to see in pitch black, but that wasn't all. It also allowed me to see the trace energies of spellcraft, if they were strong enough.

In this case, I confirmed the symbol was somehow enchanted, a script carefully applied to a blank playing card, but I could discern nothing else.

I cut off my examination the second I sensed it. Something in the shadows, reaching out for me. I grabbed the silver dog whistle that hung on a strand of black twine around my neck, closed my eyes, and listened.

Except there was nothing to hear.

One of my thralls, a Cuban tree frog that I'd reanimated,

was suddenly snuffed out. That happens sometimes. My spellcraft obscures their rotten flesh, and predators in the Everglades aren't too picky when hungry. Zombies in general aren't very smart. Their job is to sit still and watch. They often do that right up until they're eaten. I'd lost so many frogs by now that I stopped naming them.

But then another twitch. Another frog. What was going on? I took over the eyes of the nearest sentry, a stealthy Mangrove Cuckoo perching overhead in a tree.

The path is clear. The night is quiet, but a strange fog obscures my vision. I cannot see through the mist. It—

Just like that, the bird dropped dead. Deader than dead. The permanent sleep. Like the other animals, it was just a hunk of putrefaction now.

I'd been lax lately. Only had a few more thralls around. I rubbed the silver whistle and jumped into my most powerful.

I glide on dark water, my reptilian body fully submerged save for my head that breaks the surface. It is safe here. None see me, and those in the water that do stay away. I paddle closer to the river's edge. The thicket of trees is too thick to make out any intruders on the main path.

I speed to the shore and climb out halfway, getting a better vantage on the point of approach. To my left is the boathouse with my master, to the right the road, but in the middle a chokepoint where the intruder must cross.

I see movement, but the figure stays behind the trees. A thickening mist rolls along the ground and into the air above. It obscures the sun. The smoke gathers around me.

"No," I said aloud, opening my eyes. I checked the boathouse, but we were alone. I closed my eyes again and regained my connection.

Spellcraft is afoot. An attack. As the fog tumbles toward me, I back into the water. The mist cares not. It falls on me, clouds my eyes. My being. I sink.

My eyes jerked open. I was breathing heavily now. Scaring Milena too.

"What... What is it?" she whispered.

I drew the shadow to my hand. "We have company."

Chapter 8

I slammed down the garage door. Couldn't lock it from the inside. Under my command, I recalled my final minion. A white pigeon flew into the boathouse through an opening under the awning. It settled in the rafters, a single wafting feather the only evidence of its passage.

Moving to my shelf of meager possessions, I grabbed the thick cloth mask. Unlike my silver whistle or dog-collar bracelet, the burlap isn't a spell fetish. It has a charm woven into its threads, meant for protecting its wearer from the noxious fumes of various voodoo rituals. I wrapped the cloth around my nose and mouth like a bandit and told Milena to stay put.

The intruder was likely at the front door, but that was permanently sealed after respective incidents with a zombie high priest and the SWAT team. The metal was welded shut now. It would be easier to go through the wall.

The next best way in was the opposite door on the back wall, unless you wanted to wake up the devil rolling up the garage doors. I figured our visitor would opt not to do that but still use the concrete walkway to pass silently.

Me? I didn't need to raise the door. It closed loosely, sitting an inch above the foundation. A poor barrier at night when rats and snakes seek shelter, but during the day the little breeze it allows through is welcome. Since the outside platform has an overhang, the entrance remains in just enough shadow to allow me to slip in and out silently through the small opening.

I waited and listened for the steps to pass. The intruder was good. I didn't hear any sounds but I knew they had to be out there. I fell into the floor, becoming one with the darkness. I softened to a blur and glided underneath the door, then solidified.

I stood in a thick haze of olive green. Bathed within was a figure making his way to the back of the building. He had already passed me. The mist made him indiscernible, but I had a feeling who it was.

"Jean-Louis Chevalier," I announced boldly.

The man jumped and spun around at the ready. When I didn't attack, his posture noticeably relaxed. After a moment of hesitation, he waved at the fog and it cleared away.

Chevalier was a bokor, a voodoo animist. A member of the Little Haiti Bone Saints. His face was all done up with white makeup to look like a skull. Boy, I should drag out the Spaniard and really show him a skull. But that was still my secret.

The bokor and I had crossed paths a couple times, mostly trying to kill each other. We'd found common ground in the end, but there was still a bit of unfinished business between us. As in, we agreed to put off our blood feud and fight to the death at a later time.

Apparently, right now was that time.

"How did you know it was me, Suarez?" he asked. He spoke in dulcet cadence, his accent thick but his words crisp.

I shrugged. "You're the only other person that knows I come here. The real question is, what're you doing sneaking around and taking out my pets?"

He was a necromancer, like me, only he was a full specialist. His patron was the Baron of Pestilence. The Bone Saints are a flashy gang in general, but Jean-Louis Chevalier took the cake. He wore decorative plates of silver over his fingers that ended in sharp points, had matching nose studs and earrings. Silver's important to our spellcraft.

The bokor waved off my concern. "Bah. You killed a pet of mine once, did you not?"

"That dog was busy chewing on me at the time."

He smiled somberly. "Then we are even."

"Is that so? Or have you come to finish what we left undone?"

Again, silver fingers waved dismissively. "I have forgotten about that, Suarez. We are no longer enemies."

I studied him for a moment and decided he was sincere. "Good. Then I don't need to tell Leatherhead to bite your leg off and drown you in my swamp."

The bokor turned slowly and saw my gator inches behind him. "That would be appreciated," he said nervously.

That wouldn't be a good way to go. No doubt he'd felt the same and had used the mist as a precaution. Great spell, too. Knocked the unlife out of all my thralls within seconds. Almost got Leatherhead, even. But any necromancer paying attention's gonna be alerted when his pets start dropping like flies. Chevalier might as well have marched down the Everglades path yelling through a loudspeaker. Which is why his coming in peace was plausible.

I heaved the roll-up door open and waved him in, pulling my voodoo mask so it hung around my neck.

"It's not much," I said to our visitor, and I wasn't being modest. A metal shelf, a lead safe, a bedroll, a truck, and a van. He took it in, unimpressed. I didn't care. My mission of revenge didn't require much.

"Milena," I called out, looking around but not seeing her. "You remember that voodoo street gang that chased me around the city trying to kill me?"

Her voice echoed off the walls. "That's a hard thing to forget, Cisco."

I cocked my head. "This is one of their top casters."

Chevalier cleared his throat. "Leader, actually." I couldn't hide my surprise but he didn't make a big deal about it. "There have been many deaths in Little Haiti, recently. Quick turnover lends itself to quick promotions."

He was referring to the gang war that broke out. One of Connor Hatch's longest cons: to depress property values, buy up a bunch of Miami, and get politicians in his pocket to boot. That was a fun conspiracy to unravel. Destroyed careers and froze assets. But it hadn't cleaned up neatly. The spark of violence in the streets didn't extinguish. The blood didn't wash away. And now the man beside me with skull face paint headed up the most notorious of the voodoo gangs.

Milena spun around the back of the drug van and pointed a pistol at the bokor. "Nice to meet you, asshole."

Chevalier looked like a cat trying to hide in an open field. You know, they kinda lower their profile and freeze but anyone with two working eyes can see them clear as day. I let him sweat for a minute until the laughter bubbled out.

"Where did you get that?" I asked her.

"It's not yours? It was in the van."

Huh. I'd never actually searched it. Milena was right. She was resourceful in the clutch. Plus she looked hot with a gun.

The bokor waited until Milena dropped her arm. Then he eyed me suspiciously. "I thought you would've left town by now."

"What, and leave all this?"

He frowned. The Haitian didn't really have a sense of humor. Everything was serious. He was like an existential goth kid. "Staying alive is the smart thing to do." See what I mean?

I decided to get serious too. "A lot of people thought they had the upper hand on me. Thought they were smart. I put them in the ground. I'm not done yet."

"I know this," replied Chevalier, strolling toward the van. Milena backed away as he glanced between the open back doors. "You've been choking the supply."

"The supply?" I asked. Then I got it. "That's what this is about? Cisco Suarez making things difficult for your street business?"

He nodded without a trace of mirth.

"I don't buy it. One guy, affecting the cocaine flow through Miami?"

"Joke all you want, Suarez. The market reacts to outside forces. And you've been quite the force lately. We were expecting delivery of one of these bags an hour ago."

Jeez. The Columbians had lined up buyers before they had the product. "And you're here now. That was fast."

"Urgent business requires swift action."

The bokor scanned the contents of the van carefully, without touching anything.

"I assume you were prepared to pay for that bag," I said.

"Of course. I have eight-hundred thousand dollars ready for the transaction. What are you doing with the rest of it?"

"There's gotta be three times what you were expecting in there. Why not triple the price?"

Chevalier turned away and took a thoughtful lap around the boathouse. I got the feeling he was doing more than just considering my offer. "I don't have that kind of capital," he concluded. "But it would be a favor to take it off your hands. Without the resources to distribute it, the stash would only bring trouble."

He was probably right about that. I didn't mind taking money from drug dealers, but I wasn't one myself. Chevalier's money would double what I already had. I might be homeless but I wasn't poor. Truthfully, money kinda just sits around when you don't have a power outlet to stick expensive electronics into. And a Maserati probably wouldn't handle well in the Everglades. But those creature comforts were for later. For a time after I'd exacted revenge. For a time when, maybe, I could actually have something resembling a real life. Now wasn't that time.

The new leader of the Bone Saints examined the trinkets on the metal shelf. Again, he was respectful not to touch anything. Best way to piss off an animist is to touch their spell tokens.

"You have the Horn," he said nonchalantly. "Do you not?"

And there it was. The real reason for the bokor's visit.

You see, the Covey had architected my quest to find the

Horn of Subjugation. Sure, they'd used me to start a gang war and hit minor rivals, but my shadow magic was the Taíno link they needed. The way to find the Spaniard. And it had worked.

The wraith was more powerful than even I cared to find out. You think making someone blow their head off comes easily? Truth was, I hadn't fully realized what the "subjugation" part of the artifact's name referred to. I presumed the Spaniard had controlled the natives as his minions, had performed unspeakable acts in the pursuit of power. Their ire had been well earned.

And this is my ally we're talking about.

Naturally, the Miami necromancer community was a bit skittish to hear of the Horn. Their power, they thought, was absolute. Life and death. The last thing they wanted unleashed in their city was an object that could bring the spellcraft of death under its thumb.

The Horn was the real reason Chevalier had come. The drugs were just a pretense.

"I never found it," I said flatly. "That was the vampire and the others. You know that."

He nodded, humoring me but not worried about selling it. I approached him as his eyes passed over the lead safe.

It was unlocked, but it wasn't undefended. I kept it blanketed in shadow. Nothing overt, but enough that the eyes should pass over it. A simple trick, for sure, but an effective one. Problem was, most of the simple tricks don't work on other animists. It's not that we're immune to illusion, but we tend to be familiar with the trade. Our eyes look for the card up the sleeve or the spare that was palmed.

I got lucky. The bokor continued past and finished his

survey of my home, coming to a stop before me. "You will alert me then, if you find it?"

I clenched my jaw. "I'm not looking. Like you said about the drugs, it would only bring trouble."

He appeared satisfied. "So you agree to let me take the van?"

"Actually," I countered, "I'll agree if you can supplement your original payment."

His voice was impatient. "I already told you, Suarez—"

"Not money," I interrupted. "Information. You're the head of a big bad gang now. Your finger's on the pulse of the magical community."

"Ah. You want information."

"You're damn right I do. There's a thing going down tonight. Don't know where but it might involve go-fast boats. Word is Connor Hatch is coming into town to personally make the deal."

He repeated the name with a grim expression. "Connor Hatch."

"Head of the *Agua Fuego* cartel. These are his drugs you're buying. You know him?"

"Just what the street knows."

"And what does the street say about the meet tonight?"

He shook his head. "The street has been unusually silent on that subject."

Milena jumped in. "But you can find out, right?"

"I do not have cartel connections," he insisted.

She rolled her eyes. "But you can make them, right?"

He scowled at her.

"It's important," I added before they butted heads some more. "I know going against *Agua Fuego* is bad business, but

I just want information. Keep in mind this is the guy who started your gang war. Who wants the Horn of Subjugation."

He smiled slyly. "This is also the man who killed you, yes?"

"It is. In a roundabout sorta way."

The bokor nodded. "So you give me the drugs and I give you your vengeance."

"Don't forget that bag of money," I added.

His smile stiffened, but he agreed to terms. "I knew I liked you, Suarez."

I shook his hand on the way out. "As long as you don't knock my zombies out of commission anymore, the feeling's mutual." I watched him leave just to make sure, and I sent out the pigeon to keep eyes on him further down the path.

Milena finally relaxed. "Can you trust that guy? He looks kinda scary."

That guy had helped me take down the murderous vampire who started this whole ride. I knew Chevalier could be dependable, if he wanted to be. "Right now," I answered, "I need someone scary."

I pulled the stiff card with a magical rune from my pocket and glowered at it. Researching the Horn was on hold, but researching this thing needed to happen stat. Chevalier was working the gang angle. That gave me time to check in on an old friend.

Chapter 9

I parked my beat-up pickup outside the tattoo shop. Loose gravel crunched under my boots on the way to the sidewalk. Milena hopped beside me with a spring in her step.

"Is this where you got your ink?" she asked.

I rubbed the protective Nordic runes on my left palm and forearm. "If the stories are true." They were done back when I was a thrall, so I had no memory of the experience.

She gave me the side eye but moved on. "So what are we doing here?"

I pulled on the parlor door and was surprised to find it unlocked. Not many people looking to get work done at nine in the morning. Especially not the crowd that came to this joint. "We're looking for a guy with a tattoo, right?"

Milena brushed past me and went inside. I probably should've warned her about the business owner, but she was intent on handling herself. Showing me she was capable. I saw a little of me in that. She had a problem and was tackling it head on, whether or not smart came into play.

I held the door as she went ahead. A scrawny old guy with a long biker beard greeted her. His bare chest was covered in tattoos of all stripes. Flags, Lovecraftian creatures, and girls showing their naughty bits. He wore red-tinted glasses and looked like a cross between a homeless vet and a rock star, though the illusion was shattered by his round pot belly. That was from the beer.

"A new customer," he said in a voice only a smoker could have. "Got any tattoos, little lady?"

Milena chuckled. "Wouldn't you like to know?"

He snorted. "That's a no. A virgin, then."

She turned away and rolled her eyes. I closed the door gently but remained in the entrance nook and watched.

"Let me guess, honey," said the man, sizing her up. His finger ran in the air, pointing at her up and down before pausing on her generous behind. "Butt cheek?"

Milena scowled. "In your dreams, creep." This was going well. "You could have a daughter my age."

"Could but don't." He straightened up and his voice took a hard edge. "Listen, lady. You're the one strolled in my shop."

That was Kasper. This was his place and he was taking zero shit, even if he liberally applied some himself. He was in his sixties. I figured that kind of stubbornness just came with the territory.

"She's with me," I announced as I stepped into the room.

He jumped when he saw me. Maybe I'd subconsciously wrapped myself in shadow to let their conversation play out. We were friends on paper but he'd probably expected to never see me again. It was fun to give him a little jolt.

"Cisco," he said carefully. "Damn, broham, you look pretty good for a dead man." He pulled me away from the door and checked outside to make sure we were alone. Then he locked us in and flipped the sign from "open" to "closed."

The shop was a mess, but then it always was. Papers and signs with symbols on them tacked to every surface. Writing directly on the walls underneath and between. Medieval weapons like polearms and axes hung on display. And junk of just about every imaginable kind was piled on the counters and chairs. I started to clear some away so we could sit, but I wasn't sure where to set the stuff down.

"Hey," he started awkwardly. "I want you to know it was wrong of me to kick you out before."

"Wrong?" I exclaimed. "You damn near saved my life."

"I'm sorry anyhow. I was a little quick to rush you out. You know you're always welcome in my shop." He held out his hand. I dropped the junk I held and welcomed his grip.

"Plus," I added, "the heat on the street died down, the cops aren't chasing me anymore, and the Covey's been decimated."

Kasper shrugged. "That too." He snatched a pack of smokes from a wooden picnic bench along the wall, swept his boot across it to clear the tools on top, and sat down. "I'll tell you what. I'll be glad never to lay eyes on that vampire again." After lighting up reverently, he cut to the chase. "So, what can I do you for?"

I gave up on trying to sit anywhere. Milena managed to clear enough space from the work chair. It was a vintage cast-iron number with leather padding and foldable back and leg rests. She tested the backward lean as she sat. Milena has an ample chest and the position really complimented her profile. I turned back to Kasper. His eyebrows reached for the sky. I cleared my throat.

"I'm looking for someone," I said. "White guy. Bald with a black beard. Some kind of script symbol painted on his face."

Kasper laughed. "Believe it or not, broham, I'm not privy to every ink job in Miami. And that's assuming the work was done here."

"Maybe there's a biker connection?"

"The surly sort, huh?" Kasper chewed his lip. "Still. Bald, beard, symbol—it's not ringing any bells."

A jarring clang of metal spun me around. Milena had pulled an unexpected lever and reclined the seat to a flat bed. Her legs flailed in the air for a second before she rolled forward to the floor.

"*Hijo de puta!*" she spat. She kicked the chair.

Kasper and I shook our heads and returned to business.

"It's not the ink, is it?" he asked. "It's the symbol. That's why you came to me."

I walked over silently and snapped the mystery card on the wood surface beside him.

Kasper's what some call a scribe. An animist gifted with written language. Not only is he familiar with a number of scripts, he's able to infuse natural power into the symbols. He's why my tattoos do what they do. I don't directly channel the power of the Norse gods. The enchantment in the sigils do. A number of similar armor runes run along his body.

Kasper frowned at the card for a minute before picking it up and turning it over in his hands. Milena and I waited silently.

"Blood," he eventually said.

"What's that?"

"Blood." He flipped the card to face me and pointed at the symbol with his cigarette. "That's what this rune means.

Where'd you get it?"

I grunted. The meaning of the word put a bleaker spin on someone visiting people from my past. "Some asshole's looking for me. Roughed up her grandfather and left it with him as a message."

"Looking for you?"

"Apparently. Crap, he can't track me with this, can he?"

Kasper waited a moment before replying. I wasn't sure if he was thinking or enjoying his nicotine.

"No," he answered. "That kind of scrying takes more than a symbol. And it gives off loads of power. Someone with your skill would sense it."

Milena crossed her arms over her chest. "A better question would be: Can we find *him* with it?"

Kasper pushed his lips out, which made his mustache look all poufy. "That might just be exactly what this is, little lady."

We all traded glances. I felt like the dumbest person in the room. "What are you trying to say, Kasper? What is that thing?"

He handed it back to me. "A summons of some sort. Presumably for him."

"A literal calling card?"

"Pretty much. I think it's a challenge."

Milena arched an eyebrow. "What, like, he's gonna stomp people until he finds Cisco? Is this guy stupid? I've seen Cisco fight."

I tilted my head. "There are scarier things out there than me, you know."

She snickered. "I never thought you'd admit that."

I shrugged with a smile. "Just haven't met any yet."

She rolled her eyes and turned to the shop owner. "Can you see where this *come mierda* is right now?"

He released all his smoky breath in a loud sigh. "I'm afraid it doesn't work like that."

"So what do we do?"

"That part, I'm not so sure of." Kasper extinguished the cigarette directly on the bench and left the butt there. "Look, we assume this guy's an animist, like us. Excluding you, little lady. Somehow, this symbol is attuned to the man who left it. It might depend on his magic. You two know anything about this guy?"

I scratched the back of my head. "White guy. Bald. Face tattoo."

"I got that much. Doesn't tell us a lot. You can always track him down old school, but that might take a while."

"Uh-uh," said Milena. "We're setting this guy straight today. If you're telling us this card can send some kind of magical text message, it can't be that hard to figure out."

Kasper nodded, coughed out a loogie, and then straightened his beard. "You could always try the basics. A circle, a candle—standard séance stuff. But that's your specialty, broham, not mine. You might try to work in the Slavic pronunciation of the rune: *Kree*."

I traced the symbol lightly and repeated, "*Kree*."

"Whoa!" said Kasper, jumping to his feet. "Not here. Not here."

I smirked and twirled the calling card in my fingers. "What happened to 'You're always welcome?'"

"Very funny. You do what you gotta do, Cisco, but I'm retired from field work. I mean, it goes without saying, but meeting this guy on his own terms has obvious disadvantages."

I stared at the rune and grunted. It was theoretically so easy. "Yeah," I agreed.

"What?" asked Milena. "What does he mean?"

I tried to let her down quickly, before her hopes were too high. "He means this is a trap. It might not call our guy at all. Or it might call him and twenty of his friends and a Nether fiend. It's too risky to use."

Milena looked to Kasper for a counterpoint but he just nodded. She deflated. I felt like using the card just to lift her spirits.

"I'm sorry, little lady. I hope the old man will be all right, but I can't glean anything else from the rune. I'm gonna get a beer."

She pouted and Kasper made for the back, but I stopped him. "One last thing," I said, flashing the card at him one last time. "Disregard the enchantment aspect of this symbol. Forget the magic. You said it has a Slavic pronunciation?"

He furrowed his brow. "Yeah, some kind of bastardized Cyrillic script. Proto-Slavic, maybe. Why?"

I hazarded a guess. "Is that kinda like Russian?"

"It's the root language, broham. It existed before there was such a thing as Russian. It's that old. And I'd watch it if I were you because old things signify power." Kasper paused then grinned, seeing the connection. "Wait a minute, here. You telling me that after all this, you're mixed up with the Russian mob too?"

I pocketed the card and stomped to the exit. "Actually, it looks like they're mixed up with me."

Chapter 10

Screw the Russian's fancy calling card. Doing things his way was a last resort. If I was at a complete loss I'd still consider it the stupidest of alternatives. But I wasn't there yet. My tank wasn't empty. I had a line on Russian organized crime in Miami. Just picked up a new lead this morning, courtesy of the nickname Manolo gave Veselovsky. Pop Stars strip club.

True, some might call it dumb to walk right into the heart of operations of the same criminals who'd been hired to dispatch me. Veselovsky hadn't known about the Columbian betrayal. He'd been there for *me*. And the rest of the Russians likely wanted me dead as well.

That meant I had to go incognito. I didn't have another straw mask handy—those required days of prep work and time I didn't have—but it's not like the Russians knew what I looked like. Not the living ones, anyway. To them I'd be just another schmuck. The important thing was to curb my spellcraft. Visible magic would make them put two and two together in no time.

Our drive took us to Sunny Isles, north of North Miami Beach, in a ratty, sun-baked business district. The strip club recon started uneventfully. The nondescript building sat in an empty parking lot under a sign of flashing pink and purple. The O in Pop Stars was ornamented like an explosion, and the whole thing was framed in giant lips. These places aren't known for their subtlety.

The door at the front was locked up tight.

"I guess they don't serve brunch," I said.

Milena shrugged. "I bet someone's in there." She led me around the building. You couldn't see it from the street, but a brick wedged the back door open. She moved to go inside.

"Hold up," I said. "I'm not comfortable with this."

She puckered her lips. "Never seen naked ladies before?"

"Not that. You. There's real serious business going down inside. I think it's a mistake for you to come with me."

"Please, Cisco. This is my element. I know how to handle these guys."

"No," I told her. "You don't. At least let me check out the place first. You can wait by the truck."

She made a noise like the air had been knocked out of her. "You serious?"

"Let me check it out, Milena."

She turned away and crossed her arms. "Whatever."

I stepped inside and set the door quietly against the brick behind me. A hallway led to closed black curtains. Doors on either side of me. I tried both knobs as stealthily as I could—they were locked—and then I crept to the end and peeked past the black velvet.

The curtains framed the main room, but it wasn't much to look at. A small stage along the right wall, booths along the left, and freestanding tables and chairs in between. The entrance was on the far wall next to a raised DJ booth. On my side, a long bar ran along the wall. In fact, the curtains emerged directly behind the bar, but there was a lift-open section of table that granted access back and forth, currently up.

"Classy joint," commented Milena over my shoulder. I jumped.

I turned to Milena with a scowl, but she stood her ground with a triumphant smile. "Makes where I work look like the Grand Hyatt."

I shook my head to double down on my displeasure and checked the room again. It was weird seeing a place like this devoid of all the flashy glitz and music. All the energizing visuals were shut off. In their place, white overhead lights sharpened the room with a worn veneer. It looked empty, but I couldn't be sure from here.

"Once again," I whispered to Milena, "stay here."

I brushed past the curtains. No one working the bar. A couple other hallways at each corner flanked me. I checked them to be sure. The left contained bathrooms. The right had private dance rooms, which were essentially booths with low love seats. Some changing rooms backstage led me to the elevated stage back in the main room. Only it wasn't empty now. A man walked from the bathroom and zipped up his fly.

We both froze.

"What are you doing here?" he demanded. He spoke quickly, unsure what to make of the situation.

I smiled casually as my mind scrambled to come up with a lie. I maneuvered around the stripper pole, careful not to touch it, and hopped off the stage. After all that I still hadn't thought of anything. Maybe I could try the Axl Rose shtick again.

"Who are you?" he asked, his voice gaining steam.

"Who are *you*?" I shot back. I'm sharp like that.

"I'm the bouncer."

Good answer.

He stepped toward me confidently, which was weird because he wasn't especially large. I had him on height and mass. He was just a dude with a crew cut, a strong brow, and a burgeoning goatee. I wondered what qualified him to be a bouncer at a place like this. But as he neared I saw the tattoos on his scarred knuckles, his cauliflower ears, and his bent nose. The dude may have been a welterweight, but he looked like an MMA brawler.

"One last time," he warned. "What are you doing here?"

"I'm sorry," called Milena from behind him.

He flinched and spun around. A bit jumpy, this guy.

Milena sauntered up like a sidewinder, commanding all our attention with the sway of her hips. "I didn't see anybody and asked my boyfriend to help me look."

He examined her with a sulky face. She stood with her chest out, back arched, and put on her best entertainer's smile. She was good at it, and that's all he cared about.

"You here to see Nikolai?" asked the bouncer.

Milena's eyes swiveled to me. She hesitated only a moment. "I sure am. I'm not too early, am I?"

"That depends on Nikolai." He pointed to the hallway we came from. "Okay. Head on back. The office is the door on the left. Just knock." He turned to me. "But your boyfriend stays here."

She locked eyes with me in momentary panic. It was fleeting. She had to go in there alone to see what this Nikolai guy looked like. She was determined to do it even if she didn't like it. Hell, I liked it less than she did.

"Fine," she said, lilting her head like it was no biggie. She headed to the office.

"Wait," said the bouncer. He walked over to her and said, "Hands out."

"What do you think you're doing?" I warned.

She glared at me, her voice going low to convey she meant business. "It's fine, baby. I really need this job."

I gritted my teeth as the man patted down her arms, legs, and body. His search was a bit liberal when it came to her ass, but he saw me seething and decided not to push too far.

"Fine. Go," he said, smirking like a guy begging to be decked. She quickly got out of there. The bouncer waited till she was gone and chuckled. "She really your girlfriend?"

"That's right, buddy."

"Don't take it so personal. Just doing my job."

"No one's supposed to enjoy their job that much."

He shrugged melodramatically, like he was enjoying this too. "Perks of the biz. You know, if she does get the job, Mr. Boyfriend, you won't be allowed in when she's dancing."

"I know the rules," I snapped. His smugness aggravated me. It also made me want to pile drive his face into the sticky carpet.

But maybe I could use his cockiness. Braggarts often speak too much when they think they have the upper hand. And our little friend here definitely thought he was the big dog in the room.

"Why don't you sit down," he suggested flatly. "Relax. She'll be in there awhile."

I nodded and pretended I was unsure. "A drink?"

"Sure." The man moved behind the bar and closed the flip-up table to lock me on the outside. He grabbed two glasses. "Any requests?"

I didn't sit. I planted my foot on the metal footrest and leaned into the padded table. "I'll have what you're having."

He shrugged and proceeded to mix milk and weight-gain powder in a blender. When he poured the two glasses, I stared at him blankly.

"Creatine activates muscle growth," he explained, taking a swig. "Strength, not size," he added with a sneer. "Remember that." Was this guy overcompensating or what?

I wasn't interested in my shake. "I was kind of assuming you'd be drinking something a little harder."

"It's ten in the morning."

I shrugged.

He wiped his milk mustache and reached for a bottle of vodka behind him. "What, this?" He slammed a shot glass on the bar and poured a couple fingers of swill for me. I probably should've stuck to the shake. "People always assume I drink vodka because I'm Russian. Well, guess what? I'm not Russian. I just work for the Russians."

I eyed the bouncer. "You're not Russian?"

"No, I'm Ukrainian. Big difference."

"Big?"

"Very big. The Russians are the ones with the money up here. Me? I'm just the muscle."

"Hence the creatine." Ukrainians versus Russians. I could use that.

I downed the vodka in one gulp and bit back the burn. My throat was on fire. The only way I could play it off casually was by chasing it with the protein shake. His eyes widened.

"Good, huh?"

I nodded. "I can feel my muscles activating as we speak."

He didn't say anything so I took the opportunity to examine the pictures on the wall behind him. Lots of group shots, usually a few girls surrounding one guy. The same guy was in a lot of the pictures, getting a lot of female attention. He was an older guy with a wrinkled face and a sharp nose.

I nodded toward the wall. "Who's the hotshot?" I asked.

The bouncer smiled. "Your girlfriend's finding out for herself right now. That's Nikolai. You better watch out 'cause he has a way with women."

He giggled like a dumbass when he saw the look on my face. An old, skinny guy like that? I wasn't worried about Milena anymore. But it was immediately clear that Nikolai wasn't the guy we were after. What was she still doing in there then?

We stood there without conversation for another minute or two. Turns out, waiting with a bouncer while your stripper girlfriend auditions for the boss is an awkward social situation. I knew Milena wouldn't really do anything compromising and it was still off-putting. A new plan was forming in my head, one where I would pump this lackey for information and grab Milena and get out of Dodge.

I couldn't ask him about Connor or the boat deal. Anything tying to the meeting tonight would spook them, force them to call the whole thing off before I had a chance to infiltrate it. But the guy who'd gone after Hernan was actually looking for attention. He wanted to get called out. He was fair play, so I took the shot I had.

"I know I won't be allowed here," I started, "but sometimes I come by on business."

The bouncer pulled his glass from his mouth. "I've never seen you."

"You might've seen my friend. He comes around a lot more. Bald dude with a black beard. Tattoo right here on his face."

The bouncer paused and narrowed his eyes. It was a reflexive movement that betrayed his words. "Never seen him either," he lied.

I shrugged and looked away casually. "That makes sense. I guess he'd only associate with the top guys. You know, the Russians."

His dour face studied me before exploding into laughter. "It doesn't matter who you know. It won't help you here."

I acted unconcerned but the bouncer grew suspicious. I slid along the bar and positioned myself so I could peek down the hall through the half-open black curtains. Still no sign of Milena.

The Ukrainian killed his glass and tossed it into the sink. He dumped out the remainder of mine and shook his head like it was a waste. He ran the faucet but studied me the entire time. Finally he broke the silence. "This man with the face tattoo," he asked like it was just small talk, "how do you know him?" Oh yeah, interested in a guy he doesn't even know. I like how that works.

"I forget," I said.

He chuckled and shut off the sink. Then pulled a revolver from underneath. "Maybe this will jog your memory, no?"

Chapter 11

With the gun pointed at me, I fought every urge I had not to throw up my shield.

Spellcraft, remember, wasn't something I could readily use without giving away who I was. One pull of the Intrinsics and they'd know I was Cisco Suarez, the shadow charmer taking out Connor's shipments. The very man they'd been hired to stop.

Then again, maybe me asking about the tattooed man had already blown my cover. If they knew him and he knew me, wouldn't they connect the dots? This is what happens when I wing things. Maybe I'd just spooked them. The whole operation would be shut down. No more secret meeting. If I knew Connor, he wouldn't even make landfall in Miami if he thought I was on to him. But that was making quite a few leaps in logic. I had to believe everything wasn't wrecked yet.

So I stared down the barrel of the revolver, hoping my Ukrainian friend slash protein-shake junkie wasn't willing to commit homicide in his place of business in the middle of the morning.

"Relax," he said in a notably unrelaxing tone. "Sit down."

I took the barstool beside the flip-up table so I could keep an eye on Milena's progress (or lack thereof).

"This is not what you think," he said.

I arched an eyebrow. "That's not a loaded gun you're pointing at me?"

He cocked his head. "I guess it *is* what you think. But it's more than that." He flipped the revolver open and dropped all six rounds into his palm. He placed five below the counter out of sight and squeezed the last back into the chamber, then spun it closed. "You like Russians so much," he said, "I figure you like their games too."

I swallowed slowly. "You don't have a set of those stacking dolls in the freezer, do you?"

He pointed the gun at my head. Maybe blowing my cover was worth it. A quick survey of the area was disheartening. The white overhead lights killed much of the useful shadow in the room. That meant I couldn't phase out where I was.

My shield was the next most reliable option, but at arm's length things get hairy. It's not hard to twist an arm around an obstacle in close quarters.

That left my magically enhanced skin. My stint as a zombie had left me with hardened flesh and healing abilities. Bullets have bounced off me before. But again, at this range and pointed right at my head, those were bad odds, even with only one in six bullets chambered.

The bouncer reveled in commanding my attention, and he finally got to the point. "You like asking questions," he mused, "so let's make it a game. We both ask questions. You first, then me, and we need to answer truthfully or—" He nodded at the gun.

I swallowed nervously. I still couldn't get the flavor from the damn protein shake out of my mouth. "Can't we just play chess or something?"

His expression didn't lighten. "Is that your question?"

"No," I said quickly.

"Then ask."

What was this asshole getting at? He wanted to know who I was, but why the pretense of Russian Roulette? Why the concession to answer questions of my own?

"Okay," I said as slowly as I could. (I should've picked a longer word to stall with.) "I have a question. I ask you, and you have to answer truthfully or pull the trigger?"

He nodded.

"Fine then. Do you know the Russian with the face tattoo?"

He lowered his weapon and chuckled. "No. Not a *Russian*."

Damn it. Did I mention I was awful at Twenty Questions? Somehow I doubted my luck would hold up for half that many right now.

"My turn," he said, jutting out his chin as he thought how best to phrase his question. "How do you know this man you ask about?" He pointed the revolver to remind me I was on the spot.

"I don't. He's looking for me, so I'm looking for him."

The bouncer stroked his goatee, the stuff behind his broad forehead working overtime to decide if that was a fair and truthful answer. He fingered the trigger. He wouldn't actually kill me in the middle of the strip club, would he? Then again, maybe Russian Roulette was why the carpet was sticky.

"Wait," I said, reaching into the back of my jeans with two fingers and withdrawing the calling card. "He left this. See?"

The Ukrainian backed away as if he was scared to touch it. He nodded quickly and lowered the pistol. "Put that away."

I did. The prop worked. He clearly believed me. Now it was my turn. "Do you know a *Ukrainian* who has— No, wait." The bouncer smiled and I rethought my phrasing. "Who's the man with the face tattoo who left me this?"

"You learn quick," said the Ukrainian, waving the revolver. "Pressure stimulates us. It's like creatine for our brain, no?" I waited silently for his answer. He crossed his arms over his chest and made sure the back hallway was clear. Then he lowered his voice. "This man you look for is Vukasin Petrovic." He spit a loogie on the rubber mat behind the bar after voicing the name. Maybe the Department of Health would break down the door and save me.

"Petrovic," I mused. "Sounds Russian to me."

"He is not Russian *or* Ukrainian. He is Serbian. And he does not work here, so you are looking in the wrong place."

Wrong place, but a name at least. "How do I know you're not lying?" I asked.

He shrugged. "Because I do not pull the trigger with the gun to my head."

I suddenly realized how unfair this game was. The bouncer wouldn't likely catch himself in a lie and shoot himself. I wondered if there was such a thing as a fair game of Russian Roulette.

The bouncer watched me squirm. His smile broke out

into a laugh and he volunteered more information. "This man, Petrovic, he is an animal. The bosses don't like the Serbians, but they work with them sometimes. Animals can be useful." He sized me up. "They can also be dangerous. If Vukasin Petrovic is looking for you, you should run."

I narrowed my eyes. "Why is that?"

His overconfident grin didn't waver in the slightest. "Your question is over," he said. "It is my turn now. And I want to know about you." He leaned toward me. "Who do you work for?"

I thought for a moment. It was an easy answer but the gun complicated things.

The bouncer had messed up. He should've asked who I was. But he probably assumed I was like him, a hired gun with a job. He didn't give a shit about a random tough guy asking around. Everything with these guys was politics. He wanted to know who'd sent me and why. He had the why, so he wanted to see which outfit he was dealing with. He wouldn't be expecting my next answer either.

"I don't work for anybody," I told him.

His face tightened and he squeezed the trigger. The hammer struck and the gun clicked before I'd fully fallen backward off the stool. I landed with my left palm out ahead of me. The gun hadn't gone off. I cut off power to the Norse tattoo. I closed my hand to cover up its fading glow.

The Ukrainian peered over the bar and laughed again, trading tension for levity. "You're lucky. You got a free lie."

I stood indignantly. "It wasn't a lie."

"I can tell."

"My ass you can."

He laughed it off. "It's okay. You're still alive." He spun

the wheel of the revolver to reset the odds.

I stood against the bar. "My turn, asshole. Where can I find this Vukasin Petrovic?"

"No," he said. "That's not how the game works. You lied, so it's still my turn."

"But you pulled the trigger."

"And you lived. But it's still my turn. I get another question."

He pointed the gun at me. I clenched my fists. The bouncer cocked his head from side to side. Made it seem like his decision was as casual as wondering how many scoops of ice cream to get on his cone.

"I want to know... who you are working for."

I scowled at him. "That's the same question."

"I want a different answer."

My heart pounded in my chest. The last one I hadn't seen coming. Hadn't thought he had the balls to shoot. This time I knew he'd fire.

The Ukrainian clicked his teeth. "Come on now. No answer is the same as a lie."

I clenched my teeth. I could either blow my cover or give him false info. The truth he wanted. But maybe he'd pull the trigger anyway. Maybe he was just playing with me.

Somehow, this game of Russian Roulette turned into a staring contest. Our eyes burned, each seeming to become more dangerous than the revolver. I noticed a slight chink in his tough guy facade, like maybe I'd force him to kill me right here and now, and maybe he didn't really want to do that. Then again, the bouncer didn't look like a man who made well-thought-out, long-term decisions.

He pulled the trigger back a hair.

"I work for Vukasin Petrovic," I chanced. "And I'm pretty pissed off you just gave out his name."

The bouncer's eyes bulged. He lowered the revolver quickly, like if he did it fast enough I'd forget the whole thing. But then he hesitated. I could see it on his face. Maybe I worked for Vukasin, maybe I didn't. But probably, I didn't.

The door to the back office twisted open. Milena stormed out. "Hands off means your face too, perv!" she shouted back inside.

The bouncer turned slightly but raised his gun to me at the same time, watching me from the corner of his eye. "Get back in there!" he yelled.

"I'm a businesswoman," she snapped. "I don't work for pigs!"

I slid a hand under the lift-up tabletop and jerked it open. The bar top forced the bouncer's arm up and struck him in the head. A sharp report loosed from the revolver. The overhead light exploded into sparks behind me. Crazy motherfucker actually had a loaded gun.

The Ukrainian wobbled on his feet, slightly dazed. I slammed the swinging table into his head two more times until his legs gave way.

"Where's your creatine now?" I taunted.

I stomped down the hallway. Milena watched from the exit, eyes wide with alarm. The shriveled up old guy from the photos on the wall emerged from the office. Nikolai. He looked smaller and skinnier in person. He held up his finger in protest but thought better about saying anything. I put my shoulder into him as I passed.

"Don't follow us," I warned.

Milena was still jumpy from the gunshot. "Was that what I thought it was?"

I grabbed her arm and pushed her into the sunlight.

Chapter 12

I forced the pickup over the curb on the drive out and kept an eye on the rearview mirror. No takers, apparently.

"Live and learn," I said in a deflated breath. "Turns out it's *not* a good idea to walk into mob central and ask what they're up to. You okay?"

"I'm better than okay," Milena cackled. "How often do you get to go on a job interview and slap the boss in the face?"

I conceded the idea had appeal. I just didn't like whatever spurred the slap. "I'm sorry you had to be exposed to that."

She snorted. "I get a lot worse all the time. I know how to deal with jerks like that. I can handle myself. Besides," she said, reaching into her back pocket, "I needed to get close enough to swipe this." She presented a scratched up cell phone.

"That his?" I exclaimed. "Nicely done."

She half shrugged. "I've picked a pocket or two in my day."

I didn't know what to say. I was impressed. It only took a few seconds for her to grunt in frustration.

"It's password protected."

"Try 1234," I suggested.

"Already did."

I drove in silence for a bit, puzzling it out. "The address to the club is 2230. Try that."

She laughed. "I have a better idea." She typed in a code and clicked her tongue in satisfaction. "Unlocked!" She sat quietly with a devilish grin, torturing me.

"You're gonna make me ask?" I asked.

She arched an eyebrow. "He's a pig who owns a strip club. I'm just surprised 6969 wasn't the first thing I tried."

I chuckled. She examined the phone while I pulled onto the highway.

"I got a name," I told her. "Vukasin Petrovic."

"Vuka who?"

"It's Serbian, apparently. He's the guy who knocked Hernan around. The bouncer inside recognized the description. He was scared of the card. Sounds like the guy we're looking for is not actually part of the Russian mob, but tied to them somehow."

She listened as she scrolled through the contacts. "No Petrovic. A couple Petras and a Peter though." She frowned. "No Vukasin either. Closest we get is a Vucari."

I grunted. None of those sounded promising.

"Location data's off," she reported. "I don't see any location history, either."

"So we didn't get much of anything," I whined.

"I'll find something," she said. "You just need some patience."

"What, me? Patient? No problem."

As if to compound the statement, my windshield wipers flicked on. The blades rubbed over the windshield with the high-pitched squeals of a dry squeegee. It set my teeth on edge. After the third time, Milena turned to me.

"You gonna stop being a prick?"

"It's not me," I said. "It's the poltergeist. I swear. Look, the switch is in the off position."

Milena froze up. "There's a ghost in here?"

I twisted my wrist back and forth, my hand a balancing scale. "Eh, at this point the truck's *barely* haunted."

"That's not funny, all right? What if it wants to kill you?"

"Been there, done that."

"What if it's a spirit that needs help?"

"What, like 'I can see dead people?' It doesn't really work like that."

"You know that for sure?"

I chewed my lip. "I'm the expert, right?"

She didn't look convinced. "What if this is like a four-out-of-five dentists thing? There has to be disagreement among the experts, right?"

I gave her the side eye. "Am I the fifth dentist or one of the four?"

"Ugh. You're hopeless."

She shook her head and went back to studying the phone. When the wipers rubbed the glass again, I slammed my fist into the dashboard. Message received, the wipers stopped. It wasn't exactly an exorcism but it would do for the drive.

The ghost in the truck may have gone incognito but my sour mood stuck around. I wasn't sure why. The more I figured it, something about locating Petrovic was getting under my skin way more than cracked wiper blades ever could.

This was a game to him.

I mean, I couldn't find the guy and I had his calling card. How sad was that? But that was how he'd designed the game. For all I knew, he'd expected me to ask around for him. Maybe the MMA-wannabe in the strip club was supposed to tell me his name.

Or maybe I was getting paranoid. One thing was sure, Petrovic wanted to meet me, but on his own terms. If I could find him on mine, surprise him, then the whole power balance of our relationship would flip dramatically.

But the bout couldn't start until we crossed paths. I was restless. I was a boxer without a punching bag.

That wasn't all of it, either. No, sir. I was tense. Granted, Russian Roulette's pretty much the opposite of a relaxing massage, but I was antsy in general. After months of avoiding me, Connor Hatch was coming to town. One misstep—if I overplayed my hand—he'd fold and walk away. I'd keep the table scraps, but I wouldn't get him.

While I drove, Milena went through the pictures on the stolen phone. Friends at the club. None matching our punk-rock suspect. Close-ups of women. Lots of those. Some other shots of empty bars, local restaurants, foreclosed properties by the River—stuff like that. I could only guess they had to do with Russian business interests.

When she showed me pictures of the casinos, I perked up. Most people don't think of Miami as a casino town, but times have changed. Sure, we always had the casino in the Miccosukee Indian Reservation, and the large casino cruise ships would sail to international waters and open their tables, but recent legislation allowed larger establishments to set up shop.

As far as I knew, the Russian crews conducted business at the Hard Rock and Magic City casinos. That in itself wasn't surprising for a bunch of gangsters, but I recalled the casino angle Manolo had mentioned in the morning. It was a two-bit theory from an underpaid mercenary, but it was a start. Unfortunately, the phone pictures didn't have anything of note besides some party shots on the outskirts of the casinos. After she had been through every picture twice, Milena hadn't seen a single tattooed face.

So my tension increased. The nagging doubts. I tried to step away from the micro-problem and envision the big picture. Trace over my footsteps and make sure I didn't miss anything. Passing Downtown, I thought of the Historical Museum and the phone call with Dr. Trinidad. There was something that went unsaid in that conversation. Some kind of link to what was going on.

"Slight detour," I announced. I exited the highway into the lunchtime traffic of Downtown Miami. We cruised between the high-rises in the heart of the city. "I've been meaning to run something down. It might be a waste of time, but it should make the Spaniard happy, at least."

I pulled along a large plaza and found an open parking spot on the street. Milena took her eyes off her task for a moment. "What's Downtown?"

"Dr. Trinidad at the Historical Museum."

"You mean HistoryMiami?"

"Yeah, they changed the name while I was dead. Apparently everything has to be a brand these days."

She shrugged halfheartedly. "Zoo Miami did the same thing."

"Zoo Mi— Wait, it's not called MetroZoo anymore?"

"Nope. They changed names around the same time."

I hissed. "I was only gone ten years and I feel like an old man pining for the good old days."

"Anyone ever tell you you're dramatic?" Milena crossed her arms. "You expect this doctor to tell you something about the Horn that will help?"

The straightforward answer was no. "That's just it. This isn't about the Horn. There's something else. The Horn's a hot commodity. At this point I wouldn't dare walk it in there. It's almost as if Dr. Trinidad somehow realized how important the artifact is."

Milena grunted. "Ancient antiquities are so boring. I'll wait in the car and keep trying to find a lead on the asshole who hit my *abuelo*. Leave the keys so I don't melt."

Worked for me.

Chapter 13

I made my way from the blaring sun into the temperature-controlled museum interior. The Historical Museum is one of the oldest in the city, the largest in the state, boasting an impressive catalog of native artifacts. Of course, their usage of the word "artifact" is purely academic. They don't know anything about animists or Intrinsics or conquistador wraiths. We'll keep that our little secret.

All recovered artifacts from the tri-county area are sent here for initial impressions. The Horn hadn't been recovered in South Florida, of course, and I'd never submit something so dangerous to unwitting hands, but the experts could provide me with invaluable assistance. That went without saying.

Now was a good time to drop by, too. It was close enough to our originally scheduled appointment. I'd canceled, but Dr. Trinidad should still have the opening. With any luck, I would catch her with a few moments to chat.

I made my way down a bustling hallway, holding my head down in a meager attempt to keep a low profile. The place looked like an old school, replete with appropriate stragglers and staff, all wandering with their own agendas.

Some sort of training seminar huddled in the distance. I'd been here before and everything was business as usual. When I was almost at the door to Dr. Trinidad's office, it opened. I spun and faced the wall. Put my cell phone to my ear and acted like I was mid conversation.

A tiny woman with jet-black hair stepped out. She had to be a foot shorter than me, with shoulder-length hair as sharp as icicles. She wore a black leather jacket and tight pants. Stylish and pretty. Her stoic face stood in stark contrast to her softer qualities, as if every part of her being was trying (and failing) to fight off the overwhelming impression of cuteness. My type in some ways. Not as elegant as Emily or a bombshell like Milena, but striking. That was the best look I was willing to get without announcing my presence.

The woman stormed out of Dr. Trinidad's office with hard eyes, clearly upset at some development. My back to her as she passed, she muttered angry words under her breath. I couldn't catch them. On the plus side, she seemed too upset to notice anything, including me. To play it safe, I faked my phone call until she swayed her little hips right out of sight.

Yup. To play it safe. It had absolutely nothing to do with how attractive she was.

After it was clear she wasn't gonna come back and ask for my number, I headed in to Dr. Trinidad's office. It was a large area lined with tables for cataloguing things. The doctor rested against a countertop with her eyes closed, looking worn down. She stiffened suddenly when I closed the door.

"Problem, Doctor?"

The question came out a bit more accusatory than I'd intended, but I left it in the air. Instead of relaxing her posture when she saw me, she remained frozen, like I was a T. rex waiting for her to move so I could snap her into my jaws. Her eyes flicked to the door.

"It's business..." she answered, and shook it off.

I strolled forward slowly. Naturally. Nonchalant-like.

"Who was that?"

See? Just making small talk.

"A colleague," she said. "From the Chicago office. It doesn't relate to our business, if that's your concern."

"You sure about that?"

The doctor returned a deadpan stare, offended. "I have been truthful with you, which is more than I can say about you, Mr. *Rose*."

She was gonna keep stabbing that wound till I bled out. She wasn't wrong in her reproach, either. I was asking a lot of her, off the books and with a fake name. Now I felt like a dick.

"You indicated you weren't coming in today," she said.

"I wasn't going to bother you while you were sick," I lied.

She cleared her throat. "I'm under the weather, but I can still work. I can examine the Horn now, if you've changed your mind."

"I didn't bring it. You sounded strange over the phone, though. Have you learned anything since last week? Anything you're not telling me?"

She sighed, pulled herself off the counter, and opened a drawer on the opposite wall. She withdrew the three color photographs I'd supplied her.

"Based on the meager evidence in my possession, I was able to make a few preliminary conclusions."

She waved me to a desk against the far wall and sat. As I came up beside her, she arrayed the photos before us. The Horn of Subjugation must've been an impressive piece from her perspective. A large horn of a bull, slightly yellowed, brown at the tip. The white background had been used as a canvas for colonial etchings. A ship, a conquistador mounted on a horse, and other Spanish-inspired artwork. Both ends of the Horn were capped with dull metal, but the real treasure was the gold wrapping. Taíno symbols adorned those. The natives had no written language but they did love them some pictographs. The symbols scrawled into the gold lining were rudimentary and open to interpretation.

"My first observation," started the doctor, "is that this gold is probably not pure. It's most likely tumbaga, an alloy of gold and copper. The outside sheen is washed down to gold, but these scratches show traces of copper beneath the surface."

I watched Dr. Trinidad blankly. "There goes my resale value."

She smiled primly. "It is a small matter but it does strengthen the wrapping considerably while keeping it malleable for etching." The woman admired the photographs for a moment. "It's interesting to see the clash of Taíno and Spanish designs. And the obvious metaphorical victory."

"Victory?" I prodded.

She eyed me like I was an idiot.

"I... Uh... I'm not good at metaphors," I explained weakly. "Like a donkey."

She waited.

"That's it," I said. "Like a donkey. See what I mean?"

The corner of her mouth curled. "Ah, a language joke. How *do* you keep the ladies at bay?"

"It's really hard sometimes," I said under my breath. I didn't want to tell her it was actually pretty easy when my mere presence was enough to give people panic attacks. I scratched my head and did what I probably should've done beforehand: kept my mouth shut.

Dr. Trinidad appreciated the gesture. "The metaphor is the victory of the natives over the conquering powers. Here you have a symbol of Spanish oppression, a powder horn, representing superior technology. Destruction. The bane of life. Then you have the Taíno influence on the piece. The tumbaga wrapping, overtaking it, sealing it shut."

I nodded. I was an idiot but I wasn't a moron. I could keep up with that much.

"The pictographs are a trouble point, as we knew they would be. Besides the limitation of these poorly lit photographs"—she shot me a glare—"it is almost impossible to assume we know what most of these symbols represent." Before I cursed aloud she caught me with a "But."

She pulled the farthest photograph over. A close-up of the etchings. "These three symbols strike me as peculiar. The first, a circle, could represent the sun. Or life. The middle is quite obviously a man. This third symbol I believe is a bat. We've seen it before on funerary dressings. Now," she said, taking a moment to turn to me and figuring out how to explain herself to a layman, "this is a leap of logic, but in Taíno culture, bats represent—"

"Death," I cut in.

Her eyes widened in surprise. No, I wasn't big on history, but Taíno bats were old news to me. The deep death spell I'd cast on myself a decade ago was called the Wings of Night. It was a reference to the bats of the Caribbean islands. The natives believed them to be spirits from their underworld, Coaybay, visiting them during the day. The only way to and from their promised island was on leathery wings. Aside from death, of course.

"That's right." The doctor nodded approvingly and returned her attention to the picture. "Now, the interpretation of these symbols is open for debate, but to me it looks like the three are grouped, offset from the others. It shows some kind of relationship. My guess is that this references a deity of some sort. A man between life and death."

I chewed my lip. "Always with one foot in the Murk."

"What's that?" she asked casually.

"Nothing, Doctor."

She turned to me again. "Is the piece empty?"

I shrugged. "I haven't opened it, if that's what you mean."

"But have you considered what's inside?"

I nodded. "Sure. Spanish gunpowder for a matchlock. That's what the horns were for. It's like you said, a metaphorical victory. I can't tell for sure, but it feels close enough to that from its heft."

She watched me carefully and cocked her head inquisitively. "What if it contains another kind of powder?"

Her gaze made me feel like a student who'd been caught sleeping in class. I had to admit she stumped me on that.

"What kind of—"

"Ashes, I would guess. Inside the Spanish powder horn are the burnt ashes of an important man or woman. The funerary markings support that theory."

I took a step backward. The Spaniard wasn't just bound to the Horn in spirit but in body as well. The powder horn was no longer a storage for black powder, but an urn.

"Eew," I maturely noted.

Dr. Trinidad crossed her hands in her lap and studied me. "Indeed," she said. "And I have to ask you, Mr. Rose, why you feel you need to personally hold onto this piece instead of turning it over to qualified authorities?"

I clenched my jaw. We'd been over this before. "Your museum has no right to it. It wasn't recovered in South Florida."

"I'm not speaking about legality, but ethics. The piece belongs to a larger collection. It deserves to be studied and treated with respect."

Her argument was sound, but it ignored the homicidal necromancer that came as a package deal. I tightened my voice and said, "Let's move on."

The curator sighed. "Move on?"

"With what else you've learned."

"I'm afraid that's the extent I can discern from the photographs. As I've stressed, my research is limited without being able to study the artifact itself."

"That won't be possible."

She crossed her arms. "Then I've helped all I can." The doctor stood and made her way to the door of her office.

"Wait a minute," I called, hurrying after her. "You have to understand. I'm looking out for you."

"Meaning?"

"Meaning I don't want you in any trouble."

She spun around on a dime. "The powder horn is stolen, isn't it?"

"What? Why would you say that? No, I didn't steal it. I found it fair and square. Would've made Indiana Jones proud. But it's valuable and... well..." I turned away as I finished the last inconsequential detail. "There are maybe some people who kinda want it."

She stood there in silence, face tightening, waiting for me to explain. I didn't. No way could I reveal the details to her. Not in a way she'd believe. I got my point across. Either she would help me out or not. So I turned her silence back on her, putting the ball in her court, waiting for her to say something. I could be real stubborn if I wanted to.

In a low voice, she asked me, "Am I in trouble?"

I wasn't taken aback by the question as much as by the fear in her eyes. I reassured her in a neutral tone. "Not at all, Doctor. That's why I haven't brought the Horn in."

She spoke under her breath again. "Maybe it's better if you don't come back."

She tensed as she said it. For some reason, I looked around. "Why are you whispering?" I asked.

Dr. Trinidad shook her head and backpedaled to the entrance. I followed. She opened the door and leaned against the frame.

"You sure you're okay?"

She nodded quickly. "Yes. It's just that weird things have been happening lately."

Weird things? I could relate. "Like what?"

She waved it off. "It's nothing. Ridiculous."

"Tell me," I urged, leaning in. "I can help."

She was conflicted. Her indecision told me that much. She bit her lip and nodded out the doorway. "I have work to do, Mr. Rose," she announced, her voice bolder. Loud in an authoritative way, but polite. "Feel free to return with the powder horn. I'll be available."

She practically pushed me out the door. As soon as I was clear, it shut behind me with a loud click of the lock.

"Academics," I muttered loud enough for her to hear. The doctor was frazzled. Or worse, paranoid. Just like over the phone. But I didn't get it.

I pondered the matter as I made my way down the hall. The curiously empty hall. It was strange, compared to the previous activity. The building was now not only quiet, but serene. I had the feeling I was walking down an abandoned movie set. That didn't make sense because everything was very real. I dragged my finger along the wall to make sure.

Talk about paranoid.

Since nobody was around to judge me, I picked up my pace a wee bit. My cowboy boots echoed on the tiles and the hall dimmed slightly. Not where I looked, but around the edges. The world became a vintage photograph. The faint smell of sulfur filled the air. A door closed in the distance. I spun around but saw no signs of anyone else. Only echoes greeted me.

Maybe Dr. Trinidad was onto something with the whole "weird things" business. Or maybe it was my imagination. Either way, I wasn't sticking around. I hurried to the double doors and pushed the bar.

The mechanism slid in but the door didn't budge. I tried the other. They were locked.

I checked through the reinforced glass to the other side and didn't see anything of note.

Wrong move, Cisco. The only thing of note was behind me. That became exceedingly obvious when something tackled me forward and violently introduced my face to the window.

Chapter 14

Besides the sound of my head bouncing on glass, the attack had been completely silent. A forceful shoulder jammed into my back, pinning me to the door. Hands clamped around my left arm and right leg.

My instinct in these situations is not to hesitate. I didn't. I tried to phase into the shadow, but the hallway was too well lit to accommodate the spellcraft. All my attempt accomplished was to press my body against my perpetrator. Whatever had me wrapped up was strong.

Not impossibly strong, though. My backward shove shifted my attacker's weight. It gave me the sense that I wasn't facing a giant, at least. A grating snarl pierced the silence. It confirmed my fears: my attacker wasn't human. It shoved me forward again, reminding me that it had all the leverage.

Still holding two of my limbs, it ran yet another hand down both sides of my legs to my boots, checking me for weapons.

While it was occupied, I slammed the elbow of my free arm into its gut.

Intense pain jarred my arm. For a second I thought I'd cracked something. My blow was hardly noticed through the armor I'd struck. As I shook the sting away, my attacker found the knife tucked into my waist and tossed it to the floor.

Still wedged into the door, it was my turn to growl. By all accounts, I was at this thing's mercy. Deprived of shadow, unable to maneuver—hell, I didn't even know what I was up against. I forced the panic down. Urged myself to think. The ceremonial blade wouldn't have fared well against armor anyway. I could've rummaged in my belt pouch, but that would be slower than I needed.

Instead, I backed into the thing again. As before, I couldn't shake free, but I was able to loosen enough to sidestep. When it shoved me forward again, I slid free of the door and into the corner wall, where there was a small enough spot of shadow to reach my hand into.

The creature hissed, pinning me into the corner, keeping my face to the wall. Maybe it thought I was out of weapons. Maybe it should think again.

I pulled my trusted sawed off from the darkness and rested the barrel against my hip, aimed backward. The gun kicked as it went off. My back was battered with points of icy fire. I screamed and spun around, suddenly free.

The hallway was empty. My attacker, gone.

Birdshot pellets bounced uselessly on the floor. The tiles at my feet were cracked. At least now I knew why my back was on fire. The shotgun blast had bounced clean off the thing's armor. Most reflected back to me. I ran my fingers under my shirt and didn't feel any holes. Most likely the ricochets weren't forceful enough to pierce my hardened skin. Still stung like a bunch of pissed-off wasps, though.

I readied a heavier load in my shotgun and waited. This

time my back was in the corner. This time I was ready. The smell of sulfur drifted away and the darkened edges of reality dissolved. If there had been an eerie soundtrack of fingernails scraping a chalkboard, that would've ended too. Whatever that thing was, it wasn't coming back.

I bent to recover my knife. Grit scraped under my boot. Something like sand or gravel, leftover from the gunshot. It didn't match the color of the cracked tile.

Was this part of the game? Cisco Suarez, someone's personal cat toy. I figure I'd done more damage to myself than the creature, so I doubt I scared it off. Yet I wasn't dead. The thing had gotten the drop on me. Searched me. I assumed it had been disarming me, but there was frustration in its voice.

I didn't kid myself. That beastie was here for one thing and one thing only. Something I very well might've brought to the museum if I hadn't been suspicious. I'd been ambushed in the hope that I was carrying the Horn of Subjugation. When it was clear I wasn't, my attacker fled.

Not scared. Not defeated. Just biding its time till the next ambush.

This was turning into a doozy of a day.

I flinched as the door beside me opened. A needly man in glasses walked past without giving me a second look. Voices echoed through the hallway from the other end. The training seminar was back. Everything returned to normal. Part of me wondered if I should double-check on Dr. Trinidad. The counter-argument to run like hell was equally strong.

I noped right out of there, an extra skip in my step until I was safe in the pickup. My back was already raw as I leaned into the seat.

Look, Dr. Trinidad had recognized the signs. She'd seen something that had her spooked. But ultimately, if this thing wanted the Horn, there was no reason to harm her. *That* was why Dr. Trinidad had whispered for me not to return. She'd known something was listening. She knew something wanted the Horn.

And there I'd been thinking I was protecting her with euphemisms.

So my thinking as I drove away was that the staff would be safer without me in the museum. Cisco Suarez would be too, and I was kinda partial to that guy.

"What is it?" asked Milena, keying off my silence. "It looks like you've seen a ghost."

I snorted. "Ghosts I can handle. This was something else." I weaved through the afternoon traffic. "Some kind of presence attacked me at the Historical Museum."

"HistoryMiami," she corrected.

I glared. "I'm not calling it that. Ever. But I was right about scrapping my burner phone earlier. Something's following Dr. Trinidad. And it has to be because I showed her pictures of the Horn."

Milena saw how seriously I was taking the threat. "What was it?" she asked flatly.

"Not sure. Not a spirit. More like a creature, but not exactly that either."

"You're not making sense, Cisco."

"I didn't get a look at it. But this thing wasn't flesh and blood. It wasn't just a Netherling playing with magic. One second it was there and the next..."

We both let that sink in. And then Milena decided to

unsettle the situation even more.

"Wait a minute," she added. "If something was following Dr. Trinidad, something that wants the Horn, wouldn't it be following us now?"

In my head I gulped louder than Scooby-Doo. I checked the rear window. Stark daylight outside. No one could follow unnoticed. I sped up anyway, watching my mirrors for any signs of a tail. I watched them more than I watched the road ahead of me, which is a great way to keep your pulse spiked. I just swerved from a third close call when my phone rang.

"Suarez," came Chevalier's precise voice over the phone. "The street has finally spoken. The *Agua Fuego* cartel is meeting this afternoon in the Port of Miami."

The Port of Miami is a world-class port, handling both cargo containers and cruise ships. It's a bustling workplace. Maybe the sort of place where Connor could operate uninhibited.

I turned to Milena. "Did you find anything else on the phone? Anything about the Port of Miami?"

She shook her head. "Nothing like that. Nothing at all, actually. The phone was a waste of a good performance."

I grumbled into my burner. "We haven't dug up anything better. How reliable is the intel?"

"We cannot know until we see it ourselves," answered the bokor.

"'We?'" I asked.

Chevalier was quiet for a moment. "You told me Connor Hatch is the man who had Baptiste killed. Who started the war in Little Haiti."

"He is."

"Then I am obliged to see this through," he said.

I nodded knowingly. "Plus, it doesn't hurt that there'll be lots of cash and drugs on hand."

"Which we will split evenly for every man on the team."

Team. Wait a minute. "Let me guess. You're bringing a few of your Bone Saint buddies."

"Say the word if you would rather I didn't."

I ground my teeth. Jean-Louis Chevalier had me. I couldn't refuse the help, but his numbers against lonely ol' me? They would get the brunt of the spoils. But this wasn't about the score. It was about getting close to Connor Hatch.

What exactly my plan was when I got close was a work in progress. There was so much left between us that I knew we'd figure it out when we saw each other. It was an opportunity I had to take. Chevalier gave me the details and we agreed to meet at the Port in a few hours.

The extra time worked for me. I wasn't too keen on being backed up by a bunch of gangbangers. Chevalier would have his Bone Saints, but I could bring in some people myself. My friend Evan was a Lieutenant in the City of Miami Police Department. He commanded his own team of SWAT-trained detectives. I'd helped him out with intel before. Got him a promotion, even.

It was high time I finally had the police on *my* side.

Chapter 15

Milena whistled as we strolled passed the yellow Corvette in Evan's driveway.

I ground my teeth. "Don't tell me fast things make you swoon."

"Please. Like you don't wanna drive it too." An over-the-top giggle escaped her lips as she ran a finger over the sleek lines. "Check it out. You can feel the wax job."

I ignored the comment and banged on the front door. Milena ogling my best friend's material wealth wasn't putting me in a happy place. Even the welcome mat was perfect. But that wasn't the real reason I was in a sour mood. I was here to cut the cops in on the Connor Hatch heist. Figured I owed them. I could make peace, throw Evan another bone, and come out the good guy.

Except I kinda worked alone. And I didn't consider myself the good guy. Not after the things I'd done.

In contrived Hollywood blockbusters, the heroes overcome their differences. They stand victorious against insurmountable odds. Come together to save the day. Except there were real consequences to involving the police. The DROP team was a unit of elite detectives with SWAT training, but that didn't mean they were experts in supernatural circles. *My* circles.

I banged on the door harder this time.

It was all bullshit. The police weren't the problem. If the deal came with extra baggage, that would only mean I'd get extra goodies too. No, the problem wasn't I didn't work well with others. The problem was I had no idea how to ask for help.

The door swung open at the tail end of my scowl. Cool indoor air washed over my face. I took a breath, expecting to see Emily or Evan, but a five-foot tall nine-year-old greeted me instead.

"I've seen you before," she said. Her tone was somewhere between excited and curious.

"Fran." My tone was somewhere between excited and shell-shocked.

I turned to Milena, hoping she could reteach me how to speak. Mouths form words. Brains organize words into coherent thoughts. Seemed easy enough, but I couldn't stop gawking at the kid.

Flowing brown hair set neatly behind her ears. Large eyes, button nose. She was precious. My eyes flitted to the welcome mat again. I made a show of wiping my boots. Anything to avoid confronting the girl.

We have a history, me and her. Not much of one. Not really. But she's my daughter. I'm her father. Evan's her *dad*, of course. Along with Emily, he's the one that raised her in the wake of my death. But Fran was mine biologically. Yet I'd barely interacted with her.

"What's your name again?" she asked lightly.

"Uh... Cisco. *Fran*-cisco. Suarez."

Milena elbowed me in the stomach. She knew about the

whole secret-daughter thing. I mean, she'd never seen the kid before, but she put two and two together pretty fast. The girl herself had no idea.

I wanted to tell her that I loved her. That I was her father and I'd do anything for her. I had a right to be known, didn't I? And she had a right to know. But I couldn't rip her world apart on a chance visit. Even Cisco Suarez had enough tact to know that much.

"That's a neat getup," I said, pointing to Fran's yellow jersey and green shorts. "What's that for?"

She beamed. "Dad's taking me to soccer practice. I'm the lead scorer."

"Wow," I answered. The joy in my voice surprised me. I was genuinely pleased. I leaned lower. "You know, I was a pretty good goalie in my day," I lied. "Maybe we can practice your penalty kicks."

She gave me the once-over and said, "Piece of cake." I liked her already.

Milena chuckled and leaned against the doorframe with an arched eyebrow and a smile.

"Are you Dad's friend?" asked Fran.

I nodded. "I'm Mom's friend too."

Emily's ears must've been burning because her calm voice came from within. "Who's at the door, honey?"

She stiffened when she saw me. (I have that effect on people.) To Emily's credit, she didn't grimace. (Our relationship's complicated.)

"Cisco," was all she said in way of greeting. Not welcoming or inquisitive, but not damning either. Hey, it was a start.

Emily stroked her blonde hair behind her shoulders and

eyed my guest. "I don't believe we've met."

"Milena Fuentes," she offered, holding out her hand. Emily shook it cordially. "I remember you back when you dated Cisco."

Fran's eyes widened and she looked up at her mom. "You two used to be boyfriend-girlfriend?"

Emily deflated. "That was a long time ago, honey."

To make this a legit crowd, Evan strolled past the entryway with a soccer ball under his arm. He saw the commotion and joined us at the door. He froze when he saw me.

I sighed and looked down at the letters spelling "welcome" under my feet. Cisco Suarez, the doormat standing on a doormat.

Evan laughed it off, a bit too boisterously for my taste. "What a nice *surprise*," he said, putting emphasis on the last word. "Come in, Cisco. And Milena, am I right?"

She nodded and stepped past me. I followed them into the air-conditioned living room. Evan put his hand on his daughter's shoulder. "Fran, where are your cleats?"

"They're in Mom's car."

He handed her a key chain jangling with lots of keys. "Well, you'd better go get them because we're taking my car today."

"The Corvette!" she squealed, putting a little hop into it. She snatched the keys and hurried to the garage, leaving us alone. Which, of course, was Evan's intention.

"Bribery?" I grumbled.

"It *is* a nice car," countered Milena with a wink.

Great. Everyone was against me.

"You should've called," said Evan. "I'm on my way out."

"Sorry. This will only take a minute."

He scoffed. "Any conversation you wanna have is bound to be a long one." Emily crossed her arms silently, but he noticed her gaze and relented. "What's up?"

I got right into it. "I've got a lead on Connor Hatch. He's running a deal in the Port of Miami. I figured I'd do the DROP team another favor."

I immediately had Evan's attention, but a good half of it was blatant skepticism. "The head of the *Agua Fuego* cartel is in Miami?"

"He is or he will be. Real soon."

"You've seen him?"

"Not yet. I just have some street intel."

Evan frowned. "I don't know. The Port of Miami's a bad place for a drug deal. Too much federal and local presence in the water. My guys from Vice say the sketchy stuff comes through the River and the Intracoastal."

"Don't underestimate Connor's connections."

Evan crossed his arms. "Yeah, I get it. The police are a bunch of morons but Cisco's here to save the day."

"I'm not saying that," I told him. "But you're playing checkers and Connor's playing chess."

"Well, gee, that sure does sound like we're morons."

"He's not human, Evan. When are you gonna get it in your head? The police can't fight a jinn."

Emily rested her hand on her husband's arm. She was used to playing referee for me and Evan by now. Ever since I'd returned from the dead, we'd had this rivalry thing going on. It was easy to explain on the surface. He was married to my ex-girlfriend. Raising my child. Hell, he was a police officer and I was a vagrant outlaw. But our friendship was our common ground. That was still strong. We'd just had to work at it lately.

"When's this meeting taking place?" he asked in an even voice.

"Sundown."

Evan eyed me like I just farted rainbows. Then his cynicism returned. My friend stepped closer to me and worked his jaw. "You want me to lead a team of detectives on a raid with zero intel and a few hours' notice?"

So much for the calming hand of his wife.

"I'm just extending the offer," I said. "I've been trying to get close to this guy for months. This is my best chance."

Emily's face hardened. There was no love lost in this family for Connor Hatch. I just hoped she hated him more than she hated me.

Evan rubbed his forehead like a headache was coming on. "You don't want law enforcement, you want backup for an off-the-books drug heist."

I smiled cheekily. "When you put it like that, it sounds like I'm pushing the limits of our friendship."

"You think?"

Fran returned with cleats in her hand. Evan asked her to wait outside. After she was gone again, Evan turned to me.

"I can't help you, Cisco. I could explain how operations like this require more lead time. I could try to convince you that bullshit intel gets people killed. But the real reason I'm not helping you is because you're out of control."

I reared away from him. Milena sat on the couch with her head lowered. Emily avoided my gaze. No one wanted to back me up. "What are you talking about?"

"What am I—?" He laughed. "Collateral damage, Cisco.

Your escapade this morning was all over the news. I don't know which caused more accidents, your car chase or dumping a million in cash on the highway."

I scratched the back of my head. "It was closer to a million and a quarter."

"These drug shootouts are becoming more frequent. They're getting bigger."

"You're talking about bad press?"

He raised his voice. "I'm talking about people. Car accidents. Property damage. You think Miami is your own personal Vice City." He took a breath and added softly, "What happened to your desire to build a relationship with Fran? What happened to the peace you've achieved?"

He was talking about the fact that I'd freed the Covey. Ended the threat against me in Miami. With it, I'd ended the police pursuit as well. I was free and clear in his mind. Ready to move on.

My voice came out gravelly and hard. "I can never be at peace as long as Connor's alive."

Evan scoffed, but nodded like he'd expected my answer. "You know," he said, "at first you were on the defensive, fighting for your life. You came to me scrambling. Now you're fighting for something else. And you're bringing that trouble to the streets of your city. You're bringing strife to everyone close to you."

I pushed the image of Hernan out of my head. The beat-up old man—that's what Evan was talking about. That's what my life was. One long guilt trip, extending breath by miserable breath.

"I've tried to distance myself," I swore. "I've tried. It doesn't work. People I haven't seen in months get assaulted.

Do you want me to just lie down and die?"

"Don't be ridiculous," he said. "I want you to sit this out. I want you to get a job and live a normal life."

"And leave the criminals to the professionals," I finished. "Sorry, Evan. My friends and family are in danger no matter what I do. Because it's not me. It's Connor Hatch." I turned to my ex. "Tell him, Em. The guy needs to be stopped, and the police need my help to do it."

She spoke quickly and precisely, without an ounce of emotion in her words. "I won't tell my husband how to handle police work."

I stood there a moment, feeling the wind go out of my sails. I couldn't believe Emily of all people wouldn't wanna go after the jinn. "At least tell him that Connor needs to be stopped. That we can use our spellcraft for something besides his devious schemes."

She stared at me coldly, but her eyes fluttered when I mentioned spellcraft.

Evan scoffed. "Connor's out of our lives now. All that's behind her. The only magical influence around these days is you, Cisco."

I traded glances with them. Evan didn't know. Emily hadn't revealed her secret to him. She was an animist, like me. Not as talented (I could only assume), but I'd discovered the hard way that she could work light magic. In a way, she was the opposite to my shadow.

A horn honked outside. Fran waiting in the Corvette. Instead of contributing to the conversation, Emily remained quiet. Evan spread his hands, waiting for my comeback. I didn't have one so he hit me again.

"How about this, Cisco? Forget about this business.

Come with me to soccer practice."

"Evan..." warned his wife.

"It's fine, Emily. Cisco can sit next to me on the bleachers. Just two old buddies catching up. I'll even spring for a six-pack of that swill you drink. What do you say?"

My neck tightened. My whole body, really. A strange tingling sensation overtook me. Nerves.

In a way, my friend was offering me everything I wanted. A chance to connect with my daughter. A chance to have something worth having. I turned to Milena. Her eyes shimmered. If I went to Fran's soccer practice, that meant I was letting Hernan down. Still, Milena forced a smile and nodded for me to go. She knew how much it meant to me.

"I can't do that," I said softly.

Emily relaxed her shoulders. The mother of my child didn't want me anywhere near her. What the hell did that say about me?

Evan didn't bother showing relief or disappointment. He'd already known my answer. My friend walked slowly to the front door and then turned. "You're making Miami a more dangerous place, Cisco. And you'll keep doing that as long as you continue fighting your own personal war on drugs."

Every signal in my brain urged me to follow him out that door. I told myself it was for Fran's good. I told myself that it was the wrong time. That I had other commitments.

I didn't believe any of the excuses. I watched him go and collapsed on the couch in defeat.

Chapter 16

Emily had been standing the entire conversation. Now that she was the only one doing so, she sat on the armrest on the couch across from me, next to Milena.

Her motions were careful. Robotic. Normally I would've wondered if something was wrong, but there was plenty wrong and I knew it. Emily had belonged to the Covey, a covert group of mages forcibly led by Connor himself. They hadn't been thralls exactly, not like I was, but they were the next best thing. A powerful artifact had stirred their blood to commit horrible misdeeds. More slaves to the whims of a jinn. It was a lot to own up to.

I didn't have that excuse. Emily's half sister, Kita Mariko, had been under the influence of Connor when she attacked me. It was kill or be killed, and I ended her life. Tough thing for a sister to accept.

So when I looked at Emily now, I knew things weren't okay. The neutral tone when she greeted me at the door had been for her daughter's benefit. Now, without the pretense of friendship, her distaste was clear.

Milena watched me from across the coffee table. She didn't know Emily but she knew the score. She waited for one of us to break the newly formed ice, but Emily and I were stubborn like that. So Milena plucked an apple from the bowl on the table and loudly chomped on it.

I'd always thought those things were just decoration. Who knew people ate random fruit lying around? But maybe she just wanted to make a point. Trust me, if you think awkward silence is uncomfortable, try going through it while Milena chews an apple like a cow. It was unbecoming.

After half-eaten fruit didn't do the trick, she set it down. "So," she said, nodding her head to our host, "you know magic?"

Emily did her best deer-in-headlights impersonation.

"Oh, come on," I said. "It has to be obvious. Especially after what I said. You're telling me Evan doesn't know?"

She pressed her lips together and turned away. "There's no need."

"You should tell him, Em."

"Should I?"

The question was rhetorical but I was never one to pass on a layup. "Of course you should tell him. It's a part of you. A talent you can use for something important. Or just really cool laser light shows."

"I want to give it up," she said bluntly. "The spellcraft... My training was the deal that got me involved with Connor in the first place. Kita introduced us, set the bait, and the rest was history. I was hooked." She frowned at the mention of her sister.

I kept my mouth shut. Even Milena didn't want to touch that live wire.

"She hated our father," continued Emily, softly. "She felt like the redheaded stepchild. Abandoned and uncared for.

Her mother passed away and our father didn't blink an eye. I didn't even know about it. So Kita hated our father. That much is true. But she never would've killed him."

I nodded. That had been the power of the heartstone. To amplify emotion. To create the seed of thought where it didn't exist.

"It seems like such a shame," I offered.

"It's behind us." Emily faced me with piercing eyes. "Don't you see, Cisco? We're free of Connor, but you're not. That's why Evan gets nervous when you're around. He doesn't want targets painted on our backs."

I understood the sentiment well.

"Cisco, you've got to stop gunning for him in the streets. You're asking for more trouble than you can handle."

"It's not about what I'm doing. It's about what I have. The Horn of Subjugation." She didn't say anything. In a fit of anger, I'd revealed to her I had it. That was back when she was Connor's good little slave. He would know whatever she did. I shook my head and took a breath. "Has Connor really left you alone?"

She shrugged. "We're taking it a day at a time, happy for every new sunrise without him."

That was something, I supposed.

"What about you?" asked Emily, studying Milena. "You know magic?"

"Me?" she asked, exasperated. "Oh, no way. I must've missed those electives."

"Cute. I meant what are you doing in my house?"

"Excuse me for helping a friend. You should try it sometime."

"Oh, I get it," said Emily icily. "You're Cisco's new

squeeze. A little young for him, don't you think?"

Milena's eyes narrowed. "Jealousy doesn't look good on you."

"Maybe I'd be more presentable if I had my breasts done too?"

I dropped my face into my hands. "What are we talking about right now?"

"Quiet," they both snapped.

I deserved a lot of bad things, but I didn't deserve this.

Milena sprang to her feet. For a second I thought she would throw down right here, but I should've given her more credit. Some of the old hood was still in Milena—that couldn't be denied—but the woman was in far too much control of herself. She'd overcome too many obstacles to be so easily goaded into losing her temper.

"For your information," said Milena, "Cisco and I are not an item. He's helping me protect my *abuelo* from a bad guy *you* made a deal with. Cisco never had any choice about that. And it's not his fault. So I'm sticking by him. That's what real friends do. Whenever you figure out what the fuck *you* are, let us know. Until then, I have a policy of not staying where I'm not welcome."

Milena brushed past me and slammed the door on the way out. Afterward, the room was so quiet I wished she'd come back and finish her apple. I stared at the scales on my boots for a while. When I leaned back, I noticed Emily's eyes watering.

"I wasn't a zombie," she said softly.

I furrowed my brow. The conversation had passed me by some minutes ago. I figured the best way I could keep up was to shut my mouth and listen.

"You're lucky," continued Emily. "Not being able to remember the bad things you did." She stared at her hands. "The heartstone didn't only leave my memory intact, but it made me believe in everything I did. It made me passionate about betraying friends and lovers. And killing family."

I chewed my lip. Now I *wanted* to say something but had no idea what.

"It's not the bad things I did," she said. "I wasn't in control. I know that. But the way I felt when I did those things, those feelings are still in my head."

I grimaced at the thought. According to Emily, I was fortunate to have been a mindless zombie. And she was right. I killed my parents but didn't remember any of it. She had her father killed and remembered how glorious it felt. There was no accounting for that kind of emotional trauma.

That's why what Emily said was so biting. Just as with Kita's relationship with their dad. That hate might have been engineered—it might've been planted by the jinn as a play for resources—but no matter where the hate came from, it was real. The emotions of the heartstone faded over time, but they shaped their victims no less than any other life experience. That blur, that gray area, was a new experience for Emily to contend with.

"Kita was a tragedy," I said weakly. "That's on me."

"No," she cut in. "My actions prevented you from phasing into the shadows. I blossomed the light in that room to flush you out and force you into a corner. It worked. I was a part of that showdown. I all but guaranteed one of you wouldn't walk away."

I swallowed softly. "Emily, your words are true, but you're only focusing on a tiny part of the whole design. All these little choices, right or wrong, they only mean we're human. The atrocities we committed rest on one man's shoulders. Not a man at all, really. A jinn." I got up and kneeled in front of her. I was even bold enough to clasp her hands in mine. "I know you hate me, Emily. After everything. But I want you to know I'm going to handle Connor. He'll be gone from our lives forever. With or without the police."

Her head remained down, unresponsive to my words. I wanted her to help. I wanted her to give me something. At the same time, I had no idea what I was asking for. I released her hands when they didn't seem to warm. I stood to go.

"It's not you I hate," she said in a whisper, barely audible. "It's me."

"That wasn't you."

"I know. It was Connor. The heartstone. I hear your logic and it makes sense. I know I'm not directly responsible for everything that happened. But how I feel is another matter." She wiped her face. "There's something left behind. Something like..."

"A stain," I finished.

She looked up at me and nodded. "Even though it wasn't me, I feel that I deserve the fallout."

"Residual guilt," I said. "I know about that too. And all I know is that we can't let it paralyze us."

I didn't get a smile. I didn't magically make everything better. By that point, I just wanted to get out of there. I left her sitting in silence, lost in thought, trying to shake away the despair.

How could I help her when I couldn't even help myself?

I kicked the welcome mat angrily on the way out. Sometimes I think spellcraft's less complicated than human emotion.

Chapter 17

Milena waited by the truck. She was on the phone in a heated conversation. It was infectious. Hernan with some family bullshit. I started the pickup and drove in silence, pondering my own family bullshit, until Milena hung up.

After a minute of tense silence, she hissed. "I need to get back to the hospital before they kick my *abuelo* out."

"He has insurance, doesn't he?"

"It's not that. He's causing a commotion. He *wants* to leave."

Tough son of a bitch. A beatdown like that and he didn't even want to spend the night in the hospital.

"He has crazy ideas," she complained. "He hates being away from the house. Thinks someone needs to be there to watch it or something."

I didn't say anything. I learned a long time ago not to try to change the mind of anyone over fifty. After half a century on this spinning ball of rock, they were pretty set in their ways.

I turned north onto 12th Avenue and frowned when a green sedan behind us followed. That was three turns in a row. Still, it could be a coincidence. This was a busy four-lane thoroughfare. Most of Miami was up this way. What was suspicious was that the car had been a speed demon on the side streets, itching to catch up. Now it cruised slowly down two empty lanes of traffic. I slowed to see if it would pass.

"I feel like a third wheel here," Milena confessed.

I threw her a sideways glance. "You do realize there're only two of us."

"So a second wheel then. You can drop me off at the hospital, right?"

Wow. The Russian mob she could take, but an obstinate grandfather was her limit. "Bikes need two wheels," was all I said. She really needed to work on that expression.

Milena waited with a face that was too exhausted to smile.

"Okay," I said. "Maybe the hospital's a good place for you now. It'll give me a little time to prepare for tonight. I can drop you off and figure that out. There's one complication, though."

"What's that?"

"We picked up a tail." I watched the green sedan slow unnaturally to stay behind us. *No one* drives that slow in Miami. "Take the wheel."

She did, with her left hand, but she didn't understand what I was going for.

"Switch with me."

She creased her eyes and looked around, then climbed over me.

Pickups from the seventies aren't small vehicles. There's plenty of space around the bus-sized steering wheel. I slid to the side and Milena sat on my lap, putting both hands on the wheel. She scooted right over me and landed in the driver's seat. I sat facing her, with my back against the passenger door, so I could easily swivel my head front to back.

Milena finally worked it out. "You're not coming," she said flatly.

"I shouldn't be there."

"You could help talk sense into him. He's fond of you."

I took my eyes off the sedan to face Milena. "Hernan's a target because of me, right? They let him live because they think he doesn't know anything else. I should keep my distance for a while."

She chewed her lip. "Not to mention the guy following us." She eyed the rearview mirror. "You think he's from Pop Stars?"

"No way. I would've noticed if someone was on us since then."

She scoffed. "Right. Forgot you were perfect."

I smiled. "No worries. It's easy to forget when you're not perfect."

I got the sassy eye roll I expected. Look at that, a hint of danger and she was getting her groove back. What an adrenaline junkie.

"What about someone from the museum?" she reasoned. "You said something was there."

"That's putting it lightly. But this doesn't feel as sophisticated as that. I wonder if someone was watching Evan's house. Keeping an eye on the family. If that's the case..."

Milena met my glower. "Then whoever's in the car behind us is the guy who roughed up my *abuelo*."

"Bingo."

I wasn't a fan of this business with the Russians and the Ukrainians and the Serbians. It had more moving parts than I could track. Extra security for *Agua Fuego* was one thing, but a personal meeting with Connor Hatch went above and beyond. Then there was the little detail of following my family and friends.

As we approached a red light, I checked up and down the block. A long building hugged the corner. A string of shops with a low red-tile roof.

"Drop me off here."

"You serious?"

"As serious as this sun. There aren't too many pedestrians here. I'll get out and draw him off. I'm the one he's after."

"And if he decides to follow me?"

"Then go up a few blocks, turn around, and pick me up in the alley behind these shops. But he won't follow you. I'll jump out, he'll stop, and you can break off and go see Hernan."

She pressed her lips together. "I don't know about this."

"This is where I need to get off the bus, Milena. I have the mob on my ass and a ticket to a drug deal between them and the biggest cartel operating in Miami."

She nodded as I laid out the full circumstances. Neither of us were letting the old man get hurt again. "Okay."

The light turned green. I hopped out and shut the door.

"Call me if you need something," she called out.

"Ditto."

Milena gassed the truck. I turned away and checked the shops.

The small restaurant was closed, its windows and door

locked tight with security bars. The unit on the corner was empty. A "For Lease" sign hung in the window. That left a single shop in between, thin as a hallway. The front door was propped open with half a cinder block. No display windows, but a faded mannequin stood on the sidewalk wearing a red gown and a sun hat. I pretended to admire the bargain dress to ensure the tail saw me. Then I strolled inside.

The place was a cross between a run-down fashion boutique and a walk-in closet. I squeezed between circular stands of coat hangers and women's clothes. At the far counter, a radio blared lively Cuban music. An older woman moved her shoulders to the beat while filing her nails. The two overhead fans wobbled ineffectually. It was almost as hot in here as it was outside.

I moved deeper into the shop, behind a rack of dresses, and checked the door. The green sedan pulled up halfway onto the sidewalk. The sunlight outside framed one figure in the car. He leaned over and squinted into the shop but couldn't make me out behind the clothes. After a moment's hesitation, he threw the car into park and stepped out.

Why was it these guys were so eager to make public spectacles?

I marched toward the back of the boutique, passed the woman (who never deigned to look at me), and barged through the back door. An alley parking lot, well hidden from the street. Only two cars, both empty. I kicked the two-by-four block jammed between the door and the asphalt. The metal swung closed with a heavy click. Then I waited behind the door for my tail to follow me out.

Waiting's only fun for a minute. Then your nerves start

up. You second-guess the plan, and with good reason. How long did it take to walk through that little shop anyway? Somehow I doubted Mr. Green Sedan was distracting himself with sequins. I considered ending the charade and opening the door myself, but that would give away my position.

He was onto me now, and he knew I was onto him.

My cowboy boots stepped lightly as I began to circle the long building. Past the dumpster and the locked back door of the closed restaurant. Maybe he thought I was running. Maybe instead I'd come up behind him in the car. Catch him off guard while he thought I was rabbiting away.

As far as plans I made went, it was a solid one. Simple and to the point. My confidence in the strategy dissolved when an ear-piercing howl descended on me from above.

Chapter 18

Direct sunlight and shadow magic don't play nice. I could still pull off a trick or two, create manifestations from patches of darkness, but my most powerful spellcraft was quickly neutralized. Sliding through the shadow was my main defense. And impossible from where I was standing.

I leapt away from the wall and caught a glimpse of the figure in the air. He smacked my shoulder with something as I dove. It hurt, but not nearly as much as it would've had my head still been in the way.

I landed roughly on the hot asphalt. Rolled away from the threat. A man stood where I'd been. The fucker had jumped from the roof of the strip mall. Not through the store, but over it.

I took in my attacker. Just a guy, but unlike any Russian mobster I'd ever seen. His black T-shirt and pants were par for the course, but the giant animal skull he wore over his face was a dead giveaway that he wasn't playing a full eighteen holes. The mask was large and long, like a cattle skull, except threatening canines protruded from the bottom. Shaggy gray fur hung over the man's shoulders like some *Game of Thrones* reject. In his hand, a gnarled wooden club. The weapon was so large and twisted that he should've wielded it two-handed, but he was strong enough that he didn't.

"Petrovic?"

Before I could wrap my head around the scene, he lunged at me. I dodged his strike. The massive club took a chunk of rock from the asphalt.

I swung an alligator boot into the fingers holding the weapon. The man yelped like a dog. We were both left in awkward stances but I'd disarmed him. The club hurtled to the ground.

I'm not a lefty but I used what momentum I had. Continuing forward, I shoved my left fist into his chest.

He caught it as easily as the Terminator. Then his knee found my stomach.

I doubled over. Instead of falling to the ground, the blow launched me into the air. The kick literally punted me back a few yards. My skin scraped the ground as I landed from orbit.

I hadn't been hit like that since I got on the bad side of a volcanic elemental. But that was a primal being. This skull-faced brawler was only a man.

I clenched my stomach and hacked my lungs out. He used the time to recover his club. I was too queasy to stand. And still not within reach of shadow. I bought time by pulling one of those plastic Easter eggs from my belt pouch. People usually put candy or toys in these things, but not me.

I beamed it at the freak show. He'd seen my wind up and wasn't only strong, but quick too. The unwieldy club swung in a smooth arc ahead of him and picked the egg right out of the air.

Guess the oversize skull didn't come with an oversize

brain.

The plastic egg exploded open, dispersing white dust. The cloud engulfed him. My opponent paused, confused. Then he swatted at the dust like he was being swarmed by bees.

The powder was weak. A cheap voodoo trick, really. The toxin would dull his senses, slow him down, make him hallucinate if I was lucky. Already I saw the panic setting in.

And then the man lowered his skull and charged forward like a bull.

It should've been easy to sidestep the disoriented attack, but he was inhumanly fast. I barely got out of the way. He rushed past me and shook his skull-head back and forth, trying to clear the fog from his mind. Instead of serving as a distraction, the powder focused his rage on me. This guy was more concerned with me than his own welfare, like a meth addict aware of everything but his own pain. He turned to me again.

I made a break for the dumpster. The lunatic sprinted after me. I executed a baseball slide, shredding my jeans on the asphalt. My hand found what it was looking for. The shadow underneath the dumpster. I pulled my shotgun from its depths and spun around just in time to blast the masked man in the face.

Birdshot shattered the skull. It fell away in three pieces. Under the bones and fur wasn't the monster I expected—just an Eastern European with sand-colored hair. Scraggly and disheveled, his youthful face was marred by weathered lines. Crazed eyes flicked over me erratically. Maybe he was just a tweaked methhead.

The man shook his head, still reeling from the blast.

Blood ran down his forehead, but the wound was superficial. I dug for the first shotgun shell I could find while he charged me again.

Somehow now, without the mask, this dude freaked me out more. He wasn't anything special: average height, lanky. But he fought and moved like no man should. I drew my shotgun up. His club hooked it. The weapon slipped from my fingers as the club reversed direction. It smacked my head and toppled me to the ground.

I paddled forward, elbows and knees on baking asphalt. The man stomped after me. His foot scraped gravel as he readied his next swing. I rolled to the wall. The club shook the ground beside me.

Another near miss. Another quick recovery. But I was getting sick and tired of squirming on the ground.

I drew a tendril of shadow from beneath the dumpster. It locked around the man's ankle. He stopped short with a tug.

"Vukasin Petrovic?" I asked again, scooting back on the ground.

He sneered, but finally spoke. "Vukasin? No, but Vucari."

Where had I heard that before? "Your name's Vucari?"

He chuckled. "My name's Darko. I am Vucari."

He said the last word with reverence, like it was supposed to mean something.

"You Russian?"

Darko spat on the ground. "We take their money, but we are not them."

"Right," I said. "You're Vucari."

Whatever that was, I realized the bouncer in the club hadn't lied to me. These guys, the Vucari, they were

Serbians. A mercenary outfit, maybe. This man wasn't Vukasin Petrovic, but he worked with him maybe. Or *for* him. I was right about him watching Evan's house.

"I've got a bone to pick with you," I said.

Darko glanced at the broken skull on the floor and scowled. Not a fan of wordplay. Fair enough. He tugged his leg and the shadow strained in the sunlight.

"Look familiar?" I asked, flashing the calling card before returning it to my pocket. He smiled at the sight of it. "I want Petrovic," I said gruffly. "Tell me where he is and I'll go easy on you."

Darko scoffed and pressed forward. My line of shadow suddenly snapped. He was free. Not the best interrogation ever.

I growled. "You guys are beating up my family and friends." I pulled my knife and sliced it across my palm. "If you wanted to find me, you should've just asked."

I charged forward before he could ready a swing. My wet fingers snatched at him, the spellcraft already turning the blood, but Darko spun away. I snagged a shag of fur instead.

Instead of attacking with the club, he spun a full one-eighty and elbowed me in the chest. Another body blow that sent me to my knees. He reversed his spin, a ballerina of death, and the club came down hard.

Darko didn't expect me to extend my forearm and catch it, but I did. Instead of snapping my limb in half, the tattoo on my arm flared brilliant blue. My body shuddered at the impact, but a powerful turquoise jolt returned the worst of it. Darko bounced away. Still, the damned methhead came back for more.

He put his foot into my face this time. A quick blow that

jumbled my thoughts for a moment. My vision went blurry and my brain fought to keep up. The club came around again and I ducked away. An engine roared into my scattered thoughts. My pickup truck sped through the alley toward us.

Darko and I watched the out-of-control battering ram for a full second before we scrambled to get out of the way. This time I teased the shadow beneath the dumpster into a spring. As the Serbian rushed to get behind it, I released the projectile. The dumpster collided into him and shoved him into the path of two thousand pounds of Ford steel.

The truck smashed into the dumpster too. The whole train of carnage jostled past me and came to a stop against the wall. The dumpster was dented and the pickup was mostly okay, but poor Darko was pinned between the two of them, leaning forward onto my hood.

Milena unbuckled her seat belt and launched out of the truck.

"What the hell was that?" I shouted, still catching my breath.

She came to my side. "I have no idea!" Her playful expression darkened when she eyed Darko hacking up blood. "Is this the guy?"

"It's not the same one who beat up Hernan," I started.

"Oh, God," she said. Her hand covered her mouth as Darko's head leaked all over my hood.

I spun her away from the sight. "He's one of them, Milena. And even if he wasn't, you still saved my life."

She nodded slowly. Then flinched as the man rasped for air. I couldn't believe the little tweaker was still alive. I approached cautiously.

"Who are you guys?" I asked.

He turned his head with a twitch and froze, just realizing I was there. His eyes were a little less wild now, a little glassy and distant. His breaths came heavy and loud, in hydraulic rhythm. He was in shock.

"Who are you?" I repeated.

"I... am... Vucari," he said with a snarl.

He struggled against the truck like he was invincible. Like it would budge against his efforts and he would walk away from all this. It was impressive, but ultimately feeble. The blood coming from his mouth told the true story.

Vucari. These guys clearly had different motives than the Russian mob. Whatever Connor had planned in the Port of Miami, these guys were playing a separate game.

"Where's Petrovic?" I demanded.

Darko watched me. Bared his teeth but didn't move.

"How do I use this?" I flashed the calling card again. "What do the Vucari want?"

He smiled and coughed, red spilling from his teeth. "Blood," he said. Then his eyes rolled up into his head and he collapsed on the hood.

I stood for a full minute, fuming, watching the blood pool under the pickup. I was pissed that my best lead was dying on me. I was pissed that I couldn't do anything about it. I was pissed that Milena had come back for me. But she had probably saved my life. I'd been unready and outmatched in the sun.

A jet of liquid spattered to the cement. Milena was across the alley keeling over. Her face plainly displayed what was running though her mind. She had never killed anyone before.

"Get in," I said, snatching up my shotgun and taking the wheel of the pickup. I kicked it into reverse and pulled away from the dumpster. Darko's body slumped to the asphalt. "Get in the truck, Milena."

She nodded absently and did so. My tire crushed a piece of skull as we rolled out of the alley.

"He was trying to kill me," I stressed. I didn't feel like conversation but she needed to hear it. "It was either him or me."

She stared blankly ahead, not looking at anything specific. "I still took his life."

"You saved my ass, Milena."

Her eyes fell to her hands in her lap, clasping and unclasping open air.

"What are you gonna do?" she asked.

"I have to go to the Port of Miami. Meet up with Chevalier."

More thinking. "You trust him?"

"No, but I need him. And he's come through for me before. I'll drop you off at the hospital on the way."

She nodded again, but her heart wasn't in it. Damn it. She didn't want me to go. By all accounts, I shouldn't go. Not anymore. I should have stayed with her now, supported her. But it was impossible.

"Look," I assured her. "I'll find the others. I'll do everything I can to help Hernan. You know that. Right now that means keeping on top of Connor."

"Don't worry about me, Cisco," she said. "I'll protect my *abuelo*, whatever it takes. And I know you try hard for your friends and family." She put her hand on my shoulder. "Like you did with Seleste."

Now it was my turn to look away. I stretched in the seat, soreness overtaking my chest and stomach.

Chapter 19

I dropped off Milena and made a pit stop in the Everglades. The idea of taking my own truck to the heist wasn't perfect, but I was running late as it was (and it wasn't like the drug van was an option). The pickup bed was necessary. And to make sure I didn't advertise that I was driving around Miami with stolen contraband, I tied a tarp down over the back.

I considered the lead safe. The wraith would be a powerful ally in the battle ahead. But Connor desperately wanted the Horn. I couldn't risk exposing it to him. I locked up my hideaway and headed out.

The Port of Miami is a bustling island stretch between the beach and the mainland. A flat rock adorned with cement, towering cranes, and cargo containers, it's frequented by hulking cruise ships that sit bow-to-stern in a conga line that runs along the MacArthur Causeway.

Also running off the causeway, and news to me, was the brand new undersea tunnel with direct access to the island. Miami is a city always under construction. I suppose sometimes that construction pays off. As I turned into the tunnel, a slick logo above the entrance proudly displayed the new brand: PortMiami.

"Son of a bitch," I muttered. "It's infectious."

The tunnel, the road it exits to, and the island itself all sit parallel with the causeway to the north. Luckily, my destination was a cargo terminal on the less visible south side. Instead of continuing along the official route, I parked beside a couple work vehicles, hopped out, and pretended I knew what I was doing.

I walked past the highway access and the lampposts. I had to slip off the road and sneak my way by a check-in booth. It wasn't hard. I soon found myself in a field of cement and shipping containers. It was along those alleys of blue, white, and red metal boxes that I strode, hugging their shadows as the sun fell between the skyscrapers of the Miami skyline.

The day was quickly dying. By five the terminals were closed. By six, empty. No cargo ships in port. I wasn't sure if that was standard procedure for an operation like this, but I supposed working the Port was a day job just like fixing cars or stocking warehouses. After that clock's punched, what happens afterward isn't anyone's concern.

The place wasn't a true ghost town, of course—I passed ample workers and security on the way in—but nearing the tip of the island it was looking more and more like the perfect place to make a backroom deal. Figuratively, of course, since the ocean was about as wide open as you could get.

I watched the water carefully. I'm a Miami guy through and through, but the Atlantic unsettles me. Besides the salt content in the water that disrupts my spellcraft, there was a certain mermaid assassin that may or may not want me dead.

It's a long story, but it's enough to say I wouldn't be going for a dip tonight.

But the mermaid was only an afterthought. Tonight, I had two much more pressing concerns.

One was that I was within shouting distance of an illicit deal personally headlined by Connor Hatch. I didn't have an exact location and the Port was huge, but the Bone Saints had given me a bearing. I just needed to find everybody before they found me. In that regard, the shadows were my friend.

Chevalier and the Bone Saints were the other problem. As in, it was a problem I didn't see them. They were supposed to be backing me up out here. At the very least, maybe they had more specific intel to share. Granted, I was late. I hoped they hadn't ducked out of this.

I blew into the silver whistle hanging around my neck. It didn't make an audible sound, but my pet heard me loud and clear. A white bird glided above. By the water, a lot of people might mistake it for a seagull. On closer inspection, they'd probably go with dove. The truth was, the bird was just an albino pigeon. Nothing at all remarkable about it except for the fact that it was dead and I could see though its eyes. I surveyed the grounds until it landed on one of the overhanging arms of a gantry crane.

As I'd hoped, this section of the island was empty. That was a plus as far as onlookers were concerned, but this wouldn't be much of a heist if I couldn't locate Connor. My scout above showed me clear rows of shipping containers, several areas that were private enough for a meeting without drawing eyes, but nobody was around.

Metal scraped quietly. I spun around with my shotgun

ready. Chevalier leaned against a red shipping container. Its door was open enough to let a man at a time squeeze out. In the darkness within, I saw the whites of at least two other men's eyes.

"You sure love making an entrance," I said, dropping the weapon to my side.

The bokor remained stoic. He was dressed in full battle garb: silver gloves and earrings. He wore a loose tunic over his open chest, revealing layers of tattoos that would glow as it grew darker. His face was whited out with the features of a skull. Cracks and shadows under blackened eyes and nose. The teeth painted on his closed lips freaked me out the most. When he smiled, it looked like he had two sets of them, like a shark.

"I am glad you could make it, Suarez," he said.

I hooked my thumb at the shipping container they were hiding in. "Is this how you book group rates to Haiti?"

He didn't laugh. "A collaborative asset among a few gangs," he explained. "And you aren't far from the truth."

A chill went down my spine. I felt the eyes inside watching me. Suddenly I didn't want to know what the Little Haiti gangs used the box for.

He nodded in the direction of a tall stack of crates that formed two walls into an L-shape. The corner pointed our way. "There," he said, "on the other side. They're meeting as we speak."

I frowned. I closed my eyes again to see through the eyes of my pet.

Cement. Just cement. The clearing is clouded with emptiness.

I flicked my eyes open. "Strange," I said to the Bone Saint commander. "I don't see people there, but I don't exactly see nothing either."

He nodded. "They are using a mirage to draw the eye away from them. It is like a blind spot."

"And like all blind spots," I said, closing my eyes again, "you can account for them by looking from a new angle."

The pigeon took flight.

I approach the empty area. A glare flashes across my eyes as I pass. I am too high to penetrate the field of illusion. I return for a second run, gliding lower. The blur shifts. Movement. I—

"Ah!" I yelped, shaking out of my pet's head. I looked up just in time to see a flaming bird fall to the cement like a piece of aircraft wreckage.

"Fire magic," noted the bokor, concerned.

I gritted my teeth. So much for a bird's-eye view. "At least that confirms Connor's here."

Jean-Louis Chevalier turned to me expectantly.

I scratched the back of my head. "Did I forget to mention that the head of the *Agua Fuego* cartel is an ifrit?"

It took a moment for my companion to register the statement. "You said he was a man."

I shrugged. "In a manner of speaking. He's a male jinn."

The bokor traded dour glances with his compatriots in the container. I felt bad for the deception, but he never would've helped me had he known our mutual enemy was a jinn.

"Listen," I stressed. "I'm the one he wants. I need the Bone Saints to handle the security. They're gonna have mercs, probably Russians. Keep them off my back and I'll take care of Connor."

"I have never seen a jinn," he divulged.

"I'm not gonna lie. They're no lightweights. But they're

also limited to affecting only those who have struck a bargain with them. That's how they work, trading favors for servitude. As long as you or your men don't make any deals with him, he can't hurt you."

The Bone Saint commander pondered my words carefully. "Very well, Suarez. It is no matter to us. But if the jinn proves too powerful and overtakes you, we will be forced to retreat. Do not expect us to triumph where you fail."

"Fair enough. Let's go while I still have long shadows to draw from." Once the sun set and twilight hit, the Port would be without shadows for a brief time. Ideally we could've waited until full night, but if the drug dealers had already started their little party, I didn't want to miss it. I motioned to the container. "How many men did you bring?"

"Only two," he said, waving them out. The bokors exited, both wearing white face paint that did a poor job hiding the fact that they were kids. I was momentarily disappointed until the heavy shuffling within the container commenced. A dozen more eyes opened inside the container.

Chevalier flashed a cold smile. "Only two men," he repeated. "The others are men no longer."

A squad of zombies marched out in a disciplined line, each grunting hungrily.

Chapter 20

The undead thralls were no slouches. Men and women, mostly young and black, mean and ready to tear ass. Casualties from the gang war in Little Haiti, I was told. One of the fringe benefits of voodoo was that your dead allies could stand and fight again. Tragic though it was, it was useful as well. The Bone Saints guided their pets toward the target area.

Chevalier was a highly skilled voodoo specialist. His bokor companions... not so much. They were initiates, not unfamiliar with gang life, but new to active contribution to it. It pissed me off to see kids in the grips of violence like that, but I was no saint. The worst person I could think of to save the world was me.

My mission was single minded. It necessitated bad things like death and destruction. As we closed in on our target, I was ready to play the starring role in my own Hollywood blockbuster.

The container grouping was shaped like an L from above. The mirage clouded the area between the two walls, within the half box they formed. We stood at the outside corner. Chevalier took half the thralls to the left and the initiates went right. I jumped straight up a double-stack of containers and pulled a tendril of shadow down from above. The manifestation caught my wrist and heaved me up. My boots rang out against the metal wall as I hoisted myself over.

Muffled voices came from the other side. So much for surprise, but it's not like the zombies wouldn't have raised hell soon enough anyway. Besides, I liked the idea of being the distraction.

The shipping containers were stacked three and four high. I vaulted up to the second level before I could overlook the meeting area. A tingling current of energy coursed over me as I stepped through the haze of the mirage. It was more of a flat sheet than a true volume. Once I crossed it, the illusion was gone.

Below me, on the cement of the shipping yard, were five men. Four wore black gear and held assault rifles. The fifth was Connor Hatch, wearing a sport coat and polo. All were silent but alert, looking up at me.

I smiled. "Aw crap. Was I supposed to wear black?"

Four rifles trained on me in unison. There was no *click-clack* sound like in the movies. These guys were ready with their weapons locked and loaded. My intel from this morning had been correct, too. These weren't the usual *Agua Fuego* mercs. These guys were Russians. I didn't spot the two from the strip club, though.

Even though the shadows were sparse on top of the container, I let the crew know I wasn't afraid of bullets. I stood over them casually, without fear of their pointed weapons. I noted the heavy wooden crate in the center of the clearing, big enough for a coffin maybe. I'd expected this deal to be about a boat, so my curiosity was piqued.

But the real prize of the day was the jinn. Finally, after months of dealing with flunkies, I had my eyes on him.

"Connor Hatch," I announced boldly. "In Miami at last."

The jinn smiled. He had stark features: sharp eyes, an aquiline nose, even sculpted cheekbones. His shaggy mane of red hair and coarse beard softened his demeanor, as did the white polo shirt under his business-casual jacket. Connor wasn't dressed for battle like his security was. Then again, the jinn didn't concern themselves with such trivialities. I couldn't touch him, physically or with spellcraft. Since I hadn't entered a bargain with him, he couldn't touch me either. His men were a different story.

Connor bowed politely as if I'd just commended him for his humanitarian efforts. "Cisco Suarez," he replied plainly. "After this morning's events, I can't say this was entirely unexpected."

"How about this next part?"

My allies flooded out from both sides of the containers, three bokors and six thralls surrounding the group of five. They had a jinn, but we had easy two-to-one odds.

Hey, it felt good to not be the underdog for once.

The Russians spun their rifles to the more immediate threats. The Bone Saints ducked behind their meat shields. Before a single shot was fired, Connor raised a hand and gestured his men to fall back. They sneered but held their fire. Weapons trained, they backed away from the zombies, closing their ranks. The thralls stood at bay, waiting out the standoff. It was one that could erupt at any second.

The jinn took stock of my allies. He still wore that smug expression like a Christmas sweater, but he was surprised.

"The Miami voodoo community," he noted, turning back to me. "You've been holding out on me, Cisco. I wondered whether you would utilize the conquistador, but look at them. They are already your pawns."

Damn it. Chevalier's silver eyes flashed to me. I kept my face a passive mask. The last thing I wanted was for the bokor to know I had the Horn of Subjugation. He'd proven wily before.

Perhaps even more worrying was Connor's knowledge of the Spaniard. To the Covey, the Horn had just been a powerful artifact meant to control death animists. Because of my history, I kind of had a thing against controlling people, so I'd never looked deeply into the wraith's powers of suggestion, but I knew they were scary.

That control was how Connor assumed I'd convinced the Bone Saints to help me. With a single vague statement, the jinn revealed that he knew more about the Horn's purpose. He probably knew more than I did. But it wasn't something I could ask about with the Bone Saints around.

"They're friends," I asserted. "It says a lot about you that your first assumption is that they're slaves."

He didn't blink. "And your failure to use your true power speaks to your weakness. Service is not evil. It's necessary. I, myself, have served many men over many years. The experience grows humility and respect. And, quite often, strength as well. You can attest to that, can you not?"

"You can't get wisdom without choice, Connor. Somehow I doubt the heartstone offered true life lessons. Breaking your little toy made my week."

"And now you will break more." The jinn surveyed the

Bone Saints and snorted. "Friends. They cannot touch me any more than you can. Watch and learn."

Connor Hatch stepped between his guards and approached the nearest zombie. Chevalier took a step backward, surprised at the bold move. His brainless pet showed no hesitation. She was a guard dog, and she took action. Quicker than you'd expect from a corpse, the dead woman pulled a machete from a strap on her leg and swung it at Connor's neck.

The jinn disappeared for a fraction of a second and reappeared in the same stride. It was so quick I thought I blinked. But it was the jinn's power, to blink in and out of this world. To disperse his body into a rush of air, and just as quickly reassemble. The rusty blade whiffed through emptiness, appearing to pass right through him. Connor snatched the neck of the zombie with hooked fingers and squeezed. His other hand held the arm with the machete at bay.

Mankind can't be hurt by the jinn without striking a bargain, but apparently the undead had no such protections. That said, the undead have something else entirely. They're not powered by muscles and nerves. It's spellcraft that animates them. In almost all cases, they are stronger than they look. I suppose the same is true of jinns because Connor held her at bay with only minor effort.

Voice boxes are notoriously breakable. Connor's grip tightened in a sickening crunch. But again, muscles and nerves only matter when you're alive. The dead don't breathe. They don't control their bodies with electrical impulses. Unfazed, the zombie swiped furiously at Connor with her free hand.

Everyone watched the struggle without intervening. The Russians because they were under orders to stand aside. The Bone Saints because they were playing a defensive game, following my lead. And me? Hell, I just wanted to see what would happen.

The jinn's face twisted maniacally. He shook the machete to the ground, then brought both hands up and spun the thrall's head around. The neck snapped and he grinned victoriously.

A strained groan that almost sounded like frustration came from within the thing. Except zombies don't get frustrated and they don't feel pain. She hooked her arms around Connor's. His eyes widened. His hands pressed at her shoulders. Flames squeezed from between his fingers.

I'd never seen Connor fight before. Not really. Not down and dirty. But here he was, grappling with something that wanted to kill him. I knew he wanted to put on a show, but I wondered why.

The zombie's upper body burst into flames. She wasn't done, though. The hardcore bitch grunted with the effort of lifting Connor from the ground.

If this was meant as a display of power, it was backfiring spectacularly. The jinn wasn't truly invincible, he was just really fast. But this zombie had actually done something I could never yet accomplish. She had her hands on him.

He was barely off the floor. His feet touched down as he attempted to shake free. The zombie charged into him and easily took him across the space. The fire spread down her back, but she still barreled ahead, carrying him straight into the wall of shipping containers at full speed.

And then Chevalier's last trick revealed itself. A death

throe from something already dead.

The tangle of bodies and fire exploded in a sickening green jelly. Even though I was above the cloud, I cowered from it, moving farther down my perch. I'd seen the bokor's mastery of sickness and disease before. This wasn't the fog that killed my zombies but something much worse. Pestilence. That little number had put me down for the count. I didn't want to risk getting even a little bit of that goo on me.

Besides the spreading disease, a roar of flame engulfed them. Both groups in the conflict watched as the cloud of mist and smoke dissolved. Charred goop settled on the floor. The zombie had chunked into body parts no larger than a leg.

Connor Hatch cleared his throat. Everybody spun to find him sitting casually on the wooden crate at the center of this deal. "A not entirely disappointing effort," he remarked to the bokors. "Your voodoo is potent. But you show an extreme lack of situational awareness when it comes to the power of the jinn."

The bokor initiates shuffled nervously. Chevalier remained as steely as ever. I'd seen him under fire before and he didn't rattle. But he didn't take stupid chances either. I had to turn Connor's little show around before their resolve went out the window.

"And you can't touch us either," I announced, hopping from the top container and rolling to my knees in landing. "Sure, maybe you can hurt the dead, but not us. Not as long as we don't deal with you." I pointed to the Russians. "It's only these wise guys we need to be worried about."

The gangsters eyed me warily but kept their guns on the

zombies. I took that personally, but I understood their concern. The zombie woman was nothing but charcoal now, but she'd put on a good show. Except now the last thing the Russians wanted to do was open fire. The bullets would spark more contagion.

Connor shrugged noncommittally. "The secret of the jinn is out."

I ignored the jibe and approached. My goal was to ease the concerns of the young bokors. "You can set fire to the dead," I mocked, "but you'll find us all but fireproof. Even if you had a flamethrower."

The jinn stood and I stopped in place. We were ten feet from each other. The four Russians converged behind him and the crate, walling off the Bone Saints, leaving us time to chat.

"Go ahead," I taunted. "Set me on fire. I dare you."

Connor waited, letting me prove my point. I didn't turn into a roasted marshmallow and he didn't try. The young Bone Saints stood more boldly.

"Fair enough, Cisco," concluded the jinn, crossing his arms. "You've made it abundantly clear that we can't directly hurt each other. But—and I hope you don't mind my asking—if we have no power over each other, what is it you hope to accomplish here today?"

The shadows on the floor began to lose their definition. The sun was falling. Maybe Connor was stalling me, waiting for twilight to neuter half my magic.

"The same thing I accomplished this morning," I answered. "And two weeks ago. And the week before that." I approached the jinn again, this time ignoring him and going for the wooden box. I picked up the crowbar that rested on top. "I'll mess up your deals, steal your stuff, and shrug off your army. Little by little you'll feel me taking back the streets. Weakening your influence. Day by day, I won't rest until I destroy your business interests in Miami."

Connor put his hand to his chin to accentuate his frown. "Oh, dear. That sounds serious."

I took the crowbar to the box. Pried the top off and slammed it to the concrete. The Bone Saints widened their eyes at the contents. Not an item, a magical artifact, or anything special, really. Just loads and loads of money. Like a solid bed of it. I couldn't even begin to calculate how much it was, but briefcases and duffel bags wouldn't put a dent in it.

"Cash," I said, clenching my fist. Everyone around me tensed, friend and foe alike. It wasn't because anybody moved. It's just that nobody sees that kind of money and calmly blinks it off. Nobody except Connor, of course. He just watched and waited.

"This isn't the merchandise," I said. "It's your money. Where is it?" I spun around, checking the waterfront again. Looking for more bodies or more containers. Looking for a boat. "What are you buying?" I demanded.

Connor Hatch chuckled. "Not what. Who." The jinn's eyes flashed red. "I'm buying you, Cisco."

Chapter 21

For a moment, no one made a sound. Eventually the bewilderment on my face was too amusing. Connor stifled a laugh.

"What's going on?" I demanded. "What kind of drug meet is this?"

Yeah, I'm a little slow.

The jinn spread his hands and smiled. "There is no meet," he said plainly. "We're here for you."

"No," I said. "The Russians—"

"Don't you get it, Cisco? You didn't find me. I found *you*. I laid the breadcrumbs on the floor—and maybe a family friend too—and led you right to me. I personally invited you to join us, in my own way."

Chevalier gritted his teeth. His men backed up a step. They were getting the same sense I was: we'd walked into a trap.

You see? I catch on given enough time.

I growled and spun again, ready for anything. Connor relished my shock.

"Oh, come on," he said with a hint of derision. "You didn't actually think this was the real meeting location, did you?"

My head snapped to him. "So there *is* a real meeting then."

His mirth evaporated, his face hardened. That confirmed it.

My original intel wasn't bad. Connor Hatch was in town for a secret meeting with the Russians. Somewhere along the way, however, I got sidetracked with the Port of Miami. I was too busy chasing Hernan's attacker to truly look into the *Agua Fuego* deal. Chevalier's kids had heard exactly what Connor had wanted them to hear: that everything was going down here.

Unless... I checked Chevalier's silver eyes. He watched me like a hawk. How much could I really trust him?

But it wasn't possible. The bokor knew where I lived. Besides Milena, he was maybe the only person alive who did. If he was against me, the jinn wouldn't have gone to these lengths to get to me. He could've made a house call whenever it convenienced him.

So this trap was devised. Maybe it was hastily planned after my successful strike in the morning. Maybe Connor had decided to take care of me face to face while he was in town, before his real business commenced. It suddenly made sense why we were all meeting right now when there was still sun in the sky. The real meeting would take place under the cover of night. That meant Connor was on the clock. Once he was finished here, he'd move on to the real thing.

Connor shook his head and approached me. "Don't hurt yourself running the 'how' through your head. You should focus on the 'why.' This," said Connor, tapping the money. "This is why you're here."

"That's a side benefit," I growled. "I'm here for you."

"And I'm here to fix that. Ten million reasons to call off your crusade. One for every year of your service. Unmarked bills from twenties to hundreds. Very spendable. Pay the victims of the Covey. Leave town. See your every whim realized. You can have any life you want, Cisco. Think of this as reparation for the harm I accidentally caused you."

"Accidentally?" I seethed.

"Don't forget," he said. "Tunji Malu created you. You were the vampire's pet."

"I was only on his radar because you set me up to find the Horn."

He shrugged in agreement. "Hence my reparations. It's a lot of money. Take it."

Chevalier stepped closer. "Split four ways," he said in a firm voice.

Connor Hatch arched an eyebrow and turned to me with a smirk. "Friends, you say?"

"What do we need to do for the money?" asked one of the young bokors.

The jinn smiled. "Nothing," he answered. "Nothing at all." He studied me curiously. "It is the easiest thing in the world to let vengeance rest. All you have to do is not do anything. It is literally nothing. Stop gunning down my men. Stop stealing my drugs and my money. With this bounty, you won't need to anymore."

One of the kids licked his lips.

"Of course," added Connor, "I had no idea you'd bring *friends*. I wouldn't want anyone to feel they weren't getting a fair deal, so I'll let you keep the original amount and throw in an equal amount for the voodooists. That's twice the money to walk away."

I sneered at him. "So it's a deal you want to make, right? Where have I heard that before?" I eyed the Bone Saints. "Don't fall for it. The second we agree to his terms, the second we take his money and shake his hands, he can hurt us." Chevalier grimaced but the kids still saw hookers and blow. "He's a drug kingpin. He's not going to give a few gangbangers all this money. He's going to talk trade until he burns you alive. He'll never even wipe the smile off his lips."

The jinn had the audacity to grin even wider at that remark. Like he didn't care about the logical argument because he knew it would be ignored. That much money drove emotion, not constraint. It was like the heartstone all over again. I needed to get the bokors firmly on my side fast.

"You're missing one thing," I told Connor. "Why would we expose ourselves to harm from you? Why would we make a deal for the crate when we already have it? Without you, I count four Russians standing in our way. The money's already ours."

Connor smiled. "How can you steal what is freely given? It *is* yours. You only have to take it."

I swallowed, unsure what to say. Was this some kind of jinn loophole? If we took his money without agreeing to leave him be, that surely didn't constitute a bargain. But what the hell did I know? In truth, I had no clue what governed the limitations of the jinn.

I looked over the faces of my companions. Of the Russians. I locked eyes with Connor. He was clever, I gave him that much. But I hadn't come here wholly unprepared either. The show of force was exactly that. A showing. The Bone Saints were backup to keep the others out of my way by threat of force. And if the Russians did want to throw down, I wouldn't be outnumbered.

In my mind, everyone here besides me and Connor was set dressing. A poorly animated background crowd in our *Street Fighter II* championship match. Except I couldn't hurt Connor, and Connor couldn't hurt me.

Reciprocity between jinnkind and man is uneven but equal. It was the jinn's law that prevented him from harming me, but it was his power that prevented me from harming him. But I'd figured out how to counter both those protections in one fell swoop. I would strike a deal with the jinn so that he could hurt me. But the deal he'd agree to would be to not blink away from my attacks. To remain and fight.

"I've got a counteroffer," I said, stepping into Connor's face and giving my voice an edge. "You want a deal? How about this one? You and me. Right here, right now. No one else jumps in."

Everybody watched quietly. Connor's cheek twitched as the full ramifications of my offer dawned on him.

"That's right," I said. "With that bargain, you'd be able to hurt me. You'd get what you want. But you'd need to follow the terms. You agree to fight me like a man, face to face. None of that disappearing bullshit. I won't escape into the shadows either. We both stand our ground and do our worst to each other." I clenched my fist and dark wisps of shadow burned up my forearm. "We agree to finish this, here and now," I said. "*That's* my deal."

The jinn's eyes burned, angry at being called out so

plainly. It would've been so easy to agree. If he was as confident as he let on, he could have the Cisco Suarez problem wrapped up by dinnertime. But his eyes showed the fury of his impotence. Jinns didn't live a long time by taking useless risks. And they weren't so easily goaded.

Connor chuckled after a moment, smiling ear to ear and adding levity to his voice. "You seem to be under the delusion that you're the one calling the shots." He pantomimed a look at everybody. "Is anyone else here the head of a Caribbean drug cartel? Anybody else fuck-you rich?" He played to the crowd and his men guffawed. When Connor finally settled his eyes on me, he was dead serious. "I don't play games unless I make the rules, Cisco. That's why I always win."

I couldn't believe it. After all the damage I'd caused him over the months, he wouldn't take the chance to fight me. "So you're gonna back down, then? Tuck your tail between your legs and run like the coward you are?"

"Such heated emotion," remarked Connor offhandedly. "Humans really are strange creatures. More heart than brains. Let me put it plainly then. I don't accept your terms. Accept mine, or die."

The shadow flicked up my arm in waves. I was putting on my best show, trying to look as intimidating as possible, but I couldn't touch Connor so he didn't care. My only answer to the jinn was a low grumble. He sighed, and motioned his head to one of the Russians.

The man in skintight black gear moved so fast the zombies didn't have time to react. He stepped forward and raised his gun, popping automatic rounds at my head.

I slipped straight into them, *through* them, falling into

the shadow and rematerializing right beside the startled goon. My shadow-cloaked fist rammed into his side so hard I felt ribs crack. He took flight, crashed headfirst into the wall of shipping containers, and crumpled to the floor.

Because the other three Russians hadn't moved yet, the bokors and zombies held their ground. Another show. Another test. I wouldn't even call it a fight 'cause it was over within a second.

"You're gonna have to try harder than that," I taunted.

The three Russians began to laugh—guttural booms from deep within their bellies. They all looked above me. The top of the shipping containers, where I'd been. I followed their eyes. Another man dressed in combat gear. This one was short but broad like an oak tree. Bald head. Black beard. And a symbol tattooed over his scorn-filled face.

"Vukasin Petrovic," I growled.

The men laughed harder. Then the grunt I'd smashed into the container joined in, bellowing above the others. Even crazier. He stood and swiveled to me slowly. His face was malformed, not just ugly or beat up. There was something wrong with him. As he laughed, his face stretched. His jaw ripped open, revealing an elongated mouth with large canines. His ears pointed and his nose blackened and fur sprouted from his skin.

"They're not Russians," I said to myself. "They're Serbians."

Like Darko. Without the skull masks, I hadn't made the connection. I watched the whole contingent sprout new heads, bloody chunks of flesh falling away to reveal their real selves. The skull masks incarnate. I'd call them werewolves except it was only their heads that transformed. They panted in anticipation, fingering their assault rifles.

"It's about time you figured it out, shadow witch," said Connor, pleased with the reversal. "You didn't think I led you into a trap without teeth, did you? Let me introduce you to the Vucari."

Chapter 22

It made sense now, what I was dealing with. These men, they were human, but they were cursed. Whether through spellcraft or infection, the result was the same. They weren't human anymore. Most people called them subhumans, but that wasn't accurate. That implied they were below us. And I knew from firsthand experience that these wolf men were way stronger than me.

There went my two-to-one odds. Petrovic was only one extra man, but the subhuman factor changed the game completely. Zombies were inhumanly strong, no doubt, but that scrap with Darko had opened my eyes to what strength was. *And he was skinnier than these five.*

Things were about to start hurting.

Vukasin hopped to the floor. A hungry howl escaped his wolf jaws. His four companions growled deeply. And then all hell broke loose.

Automatic fire laid into the zombies. The Vucari were afraid of the poison, but it was better than being ripped apart. Contagion didn't burst from the bodies of the charging horde, however. The two crews crashed into each other, fist against claw, blade against bite.

And Connor? He was already gone.

The Vucari I'd downed charged me. It was an easy thing to drift by him. I didn't go for another punch this time. I scooped up his dropped rifle and turned it on him. Holes shredded across his back. He yelped and rolled into the brawling crowd. I released the trigger. I couldn't risk firing upon the Bone Saints.

For what it was worth, those guys were holding their own. The three bokors stood at the rear of their minions, intently gesturing silver fetishes and giving orders. A few of the thralls leaked where magazines had emptied into them, but the Vucari couldn't reload fast enough. The zombies closed the distance, swatting the empty weapons away. One particularly bright zombie used the rifle as a club, holding the barrel and smacking a wolf face with the stock.

When my wounded opponent joined the fray, it was an even five-versus-five scrap. The zombies were rugged but the wolves were tenacious, and they were stronger to boot.

I stood dumbfounded. Did everybody really just forget about me?

I shifted through the shadow, to the center of the scrum, and emerged with my weapon pointed at Petrovic's head. A fist from behind forced me down. I rolled over to my back, wiggling away from stomping enemies. They all seemed too tall from this angle. To me, that meant they were excellent targets.

Next to me, a Vucari grappled a zombie, using good technique and superior strength to lift it above his head and howl triumphantly. I emptied my rifle into his belly. The Vucari buckled to his knees and dropped his prize, clutching his stomach. If landing on the cement was painful, the zombie didn't show it. It stood up and began bashing the vulnerable wolf's head to a bloody pulp.

The Serbians rallied, knocking a couple thralls to the floor and ganging up. Two of them grabbed the stoutest zombie fighter and held him down, ripping his limbs asunder.

I slipped away from an attack and grabbed another assault rifle. Empty. Another one close by had a bent barrel. I couldn't track the last. I would've been more relieved to confirm it was out of play, but it wasn't an immediate threat. And I had firepower of my own.

My hand slipped through the cement on the floor, into the shadow, and emerged with a sawed-off shotgun. I usually kept it loaded with plain-old birdshot, but with this meeting in mind I'd slapped a shell of fireshot in there. Voodoo spark powder that burned hotter than normal fire. I aimed at the two Vucari and the zombie they tore apart and the shotgun boomed. A cone of fire swept over them like a wave.

Both wolves lost their footing. One of them recovered quickly, without thinking. He flipped to his feet and growled at me. Then he realized he was on fire. He screeched, high-tailed it to the ocean, and dove in.

His friend hadn't fared so well. The direct hit had opened him up. He rocked on the ground, in pain. The zombie also wouldn't take death for an answer. A stub of an arm scraped at the ground in a fruitless attempt to right himself. Neither of them were going anywhere for a while.

The odds were starting to look better. Two remaining Vucari, Petrovic and a real ugly motherfucker. Sizing up their four zombie opponents, they weren't scared as much as enraged. Just as I had seen in Darko's eyes right before he bled out, these guys had no instinct for self-preservation. Their only instinct was for blood.

Chevalier sent a minion at the two Serbians. Petrovic swung a giant wooden club and took the thing's head off. Contagion spurted out in what Crayola would've named puke-green. I'd been waiting for this trick, but I supposed Chevalier hadn't been able to poison them all.

The two Vucari were caught in the sandstorm of pestilence. They roared and shook and stomped around like angry bulls. The explosion of movement shocked the bokors. Petrovic had taken the brunt of the spellcraft in the face. He should've been hurling his guts on the floor. Instead he was more infuriated than ever. I'd never seen anyone shrug off that attack before. From the looks on Chevalier's face, he hadn't either.

First time for everything.

From what I pieced together, the Vucari fought with a sort of berserker style. It was both their asset and their vice. Hallucinogens, poisons—they only seemed to inflame them. But they weren't completely useless gestures. The key was to use the Vucari's power against them.

Given the right tools and preparation, rabid dogs aren't hard to put down. And at my count they were still outnumbered. The three remaining zombies lumbered toward their prey with emotionless faces.

Then a lance of flame pierced through a zombie from behind, arcing up and cutting it in half like a stick of butter. Connor joined his hands and outstretched fingers, sending another spear at the next thrall. It did its best I-Can't-Believe-It's-Not-Butter impression.

The final zombie charged the ifrit, but he only made it

halfway before disintegrating in a burst of flames. The ashes washed over Connor as he clapped his hands clean, smiling at his brutal handiwork.

I cracked my shotgun in half and slid another fire round into the barrel. "Too bad you can't touch us," I taunted. But my hand was shaking. I hadn't witnessed lethal efficiency like that in a while. I was afraid to imagine what a fair fight between us would look like.

"Don't be so sure," he said, then clapped his hands together.

A burst of fire roared my way, eating up the shadows at my feet. I recoiled as the searing flames enveloped me. I was unhurt. The fire was a magic show, a special effect. It wasn't even hot.

So we were still immune to the jinn. Why would he waste the effort?

"Watch your back, Suarez!" called out the bokor.

The fire. It was a distraction.

I spun and drew up the sawed off. I couldn't see through the dying flames encircling me, but I aimed at the Vucari's previous position. Vukasin Petrovic crashed into me. The gun barked wide, sending flames of my own dancing in the air. I was hefted from my feet and slung over his shoulder in an instant. Petrovic leaned low and charged forward.

I took a harried breath, coughing when the contagion plastering his face got too close to me. My mind reeled. I turned away. We were going fifty miles per hour right into a red shipping container.

Right before we hit, I fell into the shadow. I couldn't slip Petrovic—his grip was too tight—so we plunged into the darkness together. Thing is, we still had a metric shitload of inertia, and there wasn't enough clearance to slide under the container.

I angled us up instead, along the wall. Ignoring gravity, the mass of darkness crawled upward in an instant. At the top of the third container, where there was a surface to stand on, I hopped from the shadow and pulled down. Petrovic still held me but was no longer in control. The sudden and inextricable movement was jarring. He was quick, but he was used to obeying the laws of physics. Now thrust into a different position, he was disoriented. I slammed an elbow into the back of his head, wiggled free, and dropped under him, planting my boot in his chest and tugging on his arm as I rolled on my back.

The Vucari sailed into the air and was greeted with a crack on the cement a few stories below.

I turned to my allies. They were playing Keep Away with the last Serbian. He was covered in cuts from Chevalier's silver claws while the kids distracted him with bone dust.

Connor stood between the containers, his arms crossed as he pondered his losing proposition. My eyes met his.

"Cut out this proxy war," I yelled.

"Proxy wars are how I fight."

The bloody Vucari retreated from Chevalier. They let him go. He disappeared toward the highway, leaving his friends behind.

"This isn't a fight," I countered.

Connor blinked. One moment he was standing on the dock, the next he was beside me on the shipping container. "Don't think I couldn't wipe the floor with you, Cisco," he said calmly. "It's just that doing so is a bigger risk than necessary. It's easy for a man like you—in your prime, one foot in the grave—to act rashly. Your life is short. It's all downhill from here. But the jinn live interminably long. We value patience over immediate satisfaction."

My face was covered in sweat and blood. "Then watch patiently as I spend the rest of my short life destroying everything you've built."

His cheek twitched, but he didn't want to show me his anger. He was determined to prove himself superior to man. "You punch above your weight class, Cisco. I'll give you that. And holding onto the Horn is impressive. Tell me. Where was it hidden all these years?"

I showed the jinn my teeth. "In cosmic irony, it was safe in a hiding place of your own creation. My grave."

Connor's eyes twitched now. "That bitch Martine..."

"I told you," barked Petrovic from below. The lunatic was on his feet again. He had a thick accent and used just enough words to get his point across. "Roughing up the old man not enough."

I worked my jaw. He was talking about Hernan.

Connor rolled his eyes at the insolence. On one hand, maybe the Vucari were useful to him. On the other, it would be fun to vaporize them. But he sighed and nodded. "You're right, of course." He turned to me. "I was going easy on you before, Cisco. Professional courtesy. But all bets are off now. You just made me take you seriously." He looked down and addressed Petrovic. "Your leash is officially removed. Do what you have to do to rein in the shadow witch."

Connor Hatch spread his arms wide and raised his gaze to the heavens. A guttural scream reverberated through his chest as he was consumed with hot fire. In a wisp of air, he vanished, stray flames licking out in the sky. I swiped at him uselessly, but he was gone.

That was no blink. Connor had returned to the Aether. He was out of reach again.

Below me, Petrovic howled.

"Finally!" he cackled. "The Vucari are coming for you, Cisco. No more beating up old men."

My face darkened. The shadow cloaked me, running up both arms and my back.

"You're not safe," he yelled. "Your friends not safe."

I grumbled and tugged at shadow, invoking my patron, Opiyel. Tapping more power than was comfortable or healthy. If this guy thought he was getting another shot at my people, he was dead wrong.

Petrovic yipped and paced below in anticipation. "Fight me now," he taunted. "Or I see you another day. Maybe I get down and dirty. I make this real personal."

I sneered at the waste of oxygen below me. I brought my hand up in a fist and braced myself against the shadow. "You're not gonna do anything," I said flatly. Then the shipping container beside me screeched off its supports and crashed on top of Petrovic.

Chapter 23

The collision shook the ground. I wobbled to my knees as a mushroom cloud of dirt shot into the air. On a man-made island in the middle of the Bay, the commotion was swallowed up. Silence fell over the shipping yard.

Behind me, within the container wall, the Bone Saint initiates watched me warily. Just as they'd watched the jinn. But it wasn't lasting. Chevalier did a status check on his thralls while his companions went for the money. The elder bokor began teasing one back to life, which is something I'd never been able to do. But that's how it was with specialists. Voodoo was his whole life; I was just a dabbler.

I guess, in a way, we all surprised each other with our power.

My eyes fell on the toppled shipping container outside the wall, opposite my allies. It scraped faintly against the concrete. Was it possible? Vukasin Petrovic was struggling to free himself from beneath it.

"Let's get out of here," I announced to the Bone Saints. Chevalier nodded but kept working on the dead.

I hopped down on the far side and skirted the large container I'd used as a weapon. The last remaining Vucari was pinned. His wolf head and human chest were free. The rest of his body was crushed. Yet he struggled. As Darko had. Apparently the Vucari didn't like to die.

"All your strength," I said tersely, "and you go after old men."

It was just him and me here now. No one else in sight. His eyes quivered, fear for the first time entering his animal brain.

Then the shadows of the world fell away. The surroundings shifted to a state of in-betweenness. My familiar cloak disappeared.

The sun had finally set. The remaining light in the sky was substantial, but it was just the afterglow in the atmosphere. Twilight, an omnidirectional luminance that cast no shadows. That meant, for the next several minutes, my spellcraft was in check.

That was all right. I didn't need spellcraft to end Petrovic. I reached for the bronze knife at my belt.

"Now!" came a cry from deeper in the alley.

I had time to swivel towards the oncoming threat. A man and a woman in the distance. That was all I saw before being swept into the air by an unseen force.

It didn't hurt. It wasn't a physical blow or any sort of collision. And I wasn't buffeted by wind and forced into the air like a kite. I was simply drawn into flight without warning. Fifty yards from the point of takeoff, I slammed into a shipping container.

That was the part that hurt.

I didn't have time to assess the damage. Reeling from the collision, I scrambled to escape my attackers' line of sight.

"Incoming!" I yelled to Chevalier.

I approached my attackers from the other side of the

container grouping. Rushed past the Bone Saints. The bokors had reattached the top of the crate and two dilapidated zombies were hauling it. One was missing its head.

I scooped up my shotgun and reloaded. I didn't have a full arsenal of fire rounds but I made sure to use one now. I peeked around the container and saw them quickly converging.

Two animists. The man was Chinese, in his twenties, clean-cut with short hair gelled into spikes. He wore a dapper suit and metallic red tie.

The girl was even younger. A teenager, maybe, with a short bob of bright red hair. She wore a dark gray blouse over skinny jeans. A collection of colorful gummy bracelets ran up her arm and some kind of wraparound scarf hung around her neck.

In her hand was a statuette. A fetish, no doubt. The man didn't carry anything so arcane. His pistol swept ahead of him, searching for me.

I didn't blink. I raised my shotgun and fired.

A cone of spark powder consumed him. He flinched, but didn't fall. Then they both flickered out.

An illusion. And not like the weak mirage from before. That had just been a trick of the light. This was a full-on constructed fabrication of reality. It wasn't sourceless, though. It likely represented who I was up against. Just not in the same location.

In answer to my question, pistol reports rang out. Sparks cascaded off the metal beside me. I threw my hand up. The turquoise shield flared brilliantly, catching the last round before it pegged me.

These animists were prepared. Not only had they come for me, but they knew to wait until twilight hit. When my shadow would be negated. I didn't have the luxury of waiting another twenty minutes till true night.

Not only that, but they knew to wait until Connor was gone. They hadn't interfered with the meeting or helped the Vucari, which meant they weren't working for the jinn.

The guy in the suit slapped a new mag in his pistol before I could reload. Modern firearms, what can I say? I threw my shield up and snapped the shotgun closed one-handed as he fired.

Everything was going dandy until the witch raised her fetish. The invisible force returned. This time, it jerked my left arm to the side, dragging my shield with it. Hollow-points peppered my chest.

"Shen!" cried the witch. "Look out!"

His eagerness to empty his magazine slowed him down. The invisible force released my hand. I slumped to the ground. The girl turned and pointed her figurine to their flank, but it was too late.

A headless thrall barreled into Shen. He was no illusion this time. They both hit the cement and his gun skidded from his grip. They tumbled over each other, but Chevalier's zombie was stronger, head or not. The thrall took top position and rained punches down on the illusionist. It was all Shen could do to protect his face.

It was all *I* could do to gasp for breath. Every time something floored me, I was finding it harder and harder to get up. I'd been pelted with lead this time. I ran my hand over my chest. The first two spots were sore but the rounds hadn't penetrated my charmed skin (thanks to my upgraded zombie option package). Too bad I didn't have dulled zombie nerves. The pain was brutal. But I could live with that. I was just happy he wasn't using enchanted bullets.

My finger brushed over a hole in the third hit area. So much for Superman. The wound wasn't deep. I hooked out the pieces of shattered lead but didn't have time for much more.

The girl focused on her companion. The headless zombie over him slowed as if underwater. The thrall kept pressing his advantage, though. The witch gritted her teeth. She leaned forward with both arms outstretched and muttered an incantation under her breath.

Interesting. I didn't know what kind of witch she was, but she could fling me around like a rag doll. The zombie, however, was giving her trouble. I wondered if her mojo worked great on physical things but couldn't manipulate that powered by spellcraft.

With enough exertion, she appeared to overpower it. The zombie released Shen and actually floated up in the air several feet. A weird flapping sound escaped its neckhole as it viciously spat against the magic keeping it at bay.

Shen deftly rolled to his feet. I raised my sawed off. This time I aimed for the young witch. She was a perfect target. Probably the most powerful of the two. In the distance, Chevalier's crew retreated, shoving the box of money over the ground. The Bone Saints cleared out. But they'd left me a parting gift.

I adjusted the aim of my weapon and pulled the trigger. The fireshot ripped the floating thrall apart, instantly incinerating it. The expulsion from its body was unaffected. Contagion detonated over Shen and the girl with explosive force. He flickered out but reappeared only a few feet away, not having had enough time to separate from his illusory double. He keeled over and hacked at the sickening substance that ruined his fine clothes.

The witch had protected herself. Although she coughed, her raised statue had managed to redirect the majority of the fluid. She fought through nausea and began telekinetically separating her partner from the goop that clung to him. Too little, too late. He rolled on the ground, puking.

I was hurting in different ways. My allies had booked it. And the bitch was strong. I took off like a rabbit, darting past them and making for the Port entrance.

The witch turned to stop me. I fired a load of birdshot at her. The little statuette froze all the pellets before they found their mark, but the effort had shifted her from offense to defense. I successfully rounded the corner and escaped into another alley of shipping containers. Out of sight.

I raced down the Port of Miami as fast as I could push myself. Light posts along the road activated in the failing sun. It was still twilight, but I found limited shadow to work with. I skipped ahead where I could. I wasn't sure if they were on my ass, but I didn't take chances.

Behind the wheel of my pickup, I shoved a small squeeze bottle into my wound and pushed out the thick gray gel. I bit down at the pain of the poison. It would numb me and keep the wound from going septic. I shoved a cotton ball over the top and hit the gas. Before long I was speeding down I-95, free and clear.

Free and clear. Right. Not only did I have Connor and the Russian mob to worry about, but the Vucari were completely separate players. They didn't concern themselves with drugs and deals. They just wanted me. Throw in whatever was at the Historical Museum, then these two knuckleheads at the Port, and Cisco Suarez was a popular guy these days.

Wasn't there anybody I *hadn't* pissed off?

Chapter 24

I wasn't exactly bulletproof, but I was pretty close. Soft-nosed and hollow-point bullets, specifically, had trouble penetrating my toughened skin. Unfortunately, the zombie curse didn't do a damn thing for pain. It felt like a rib was cracked. Moving any of the muscles on my chest, stomach, or back hurt like hell. (For the record, it's nearly impossible to do anything without those muscles but sleep and watch TV.)

I steered the pickup with my arms at the bottom of the wheel, carefully checking my mirrors as I rolled into the Everglades. I was in no condition to be followed. It was nice and dark finally, so that was some comfort. Still, I didn't take chances. I overshot my turns and looped around and did everything I could to make sure I was alone.

I dialed Milena. I told her I'd met Petrovic and he was still alive and he was gonna go after them. She'd convinced Hernan to spend the night in the hospital, so they had that going for them. She was staying with him too. I recounted what happened at the Port and assured her I was still working on the situation, even though all I wanted to do was crawl in my bedroll and sleep it off. Milena wanted to meet up but agreed that watching her grandfather was more important until we had a substantive lead. I was fine with that. By the end of the call, it was obvious she was distracted.

"Milena," I started softly. "Are you holding up okay?"

She blew into the phone. "Sure I am. Why do you ask?"

I shook my head to myself. "I don't know. You sound a little off."

"I'm just exhausted. It's been a hell of a day. To think I was supposed to be on vacation."

"Vacation," I laughed. "What's that?"

She gave me half a snort. That was it. "I'd better go, Cisco. Call me if something happens."

She ended the call quickly. The thing with her grandfather was really wearing her out. The way I saw it, the best thing she could do was pass out in a chair next to him. Sleep it off. Relax. That was the point of vacation anyway.

Rest wasn't a bad idea for me either. But I couldn't afford it just yet. There was plenty on my mind that needed marinating.

The more I thought about it, the more I was sure the Vucari served different ends than the Russians. I should've paid more attention to the bouncer at Pop Stars. The Russians looked down on the Serbians. The Serbians resented the Russians.

The Vucari weren't mobsters. They were a crazed pack of I-didn't-know-whats. Smaller, supernaturally inclined, and likely the more dangerous of the two groups.

Which was scary seeing as how the Russians weren't a bunch of nobodies.

Pop Stars was a sleazy dive, but the men who ran it were

connected to dark dealings. Despite not finding any hard evidence linking them to Connor, I still had a gut feeling they were working on something. The jinn had slipped that there was a genuine meeting in Miami, after all.

The problem? After all my bruising and sleuthing, I still had no idea what Connor was really doing in Miami.

When I pulled up to my hideaway, I found Chevalier's black work van backed up on the grass. The back doors were open. The crate of money rested inside next to a brain-dead zombie. The two bokors walked from boathouse to van, transferring duffel bags from this morning's haul. One of them favored a bloody arm, but he looked all right. I nodded as I walked past and found Chevalier inside.

"I'm surprised you're here," I said.

"Me too, Suarez." He flashed a grim smile. "But we had a deal."

I crossed my arms and leaned against the wall. "That deal involve you hightailing it and leaving me to deal with an animist ambush?"

His face darkened. "You failed to mention the jinn," he reminded me. "Perhaps there was more you left unsaid."

"I don't know anything about them."

He nodded once. "Then now you do. There are powerful people after you, Suarez." He cocked his head curiously. "It's as if you have something they desire."

I forced myself not to glance at the safe. "That's between me and them."

"And any you recruit to assist you," he said pointedly.

I frowned instead of saying anything.

"I did not know it was a trap, Suarez," he offered after a moment. "The Port of Miami was whispered in the streets.

That information was left for us to find."

"I know. I'm just glad you didn't take the jinn's offer."

"It was tempting."

"About as tempting as a lethal injection."

Chevalier strolled to the open back doors of the drug van in the boathouse. I was hoping they'd dispose of the vehicle for me too but no dice. The bokors had scavenged all the cocaine except for the dusty layer that coated the interior. Two garbage bags now replaced them. Those were new.

"Twenty-five percent of the take," he said, holding open a bag with silver gauntlets. "As agreed."

"I'm surprised you're not cutting in the zombies," I muttered.

He raised an eyebrow.

"I mean thanks," I said. "You earned it. Really."

I took in the messy piles of cash. Had to be more than a million per bag. Cisco Suarez was officially a multimillionaire. The thought frightened me.

The leader of the Bone Saints took my hand and shook fiercely. "You know, Suarez. If you weren't such a dangerous man, I might actually enjoy your company." He left me in the boathouse. The muffled sounds of his van faded into the distance.

I stared at the garbage bags and snickered. I now had more money than I could ever spend. At least something good had come from this clusterfuck. Thing is, people have a habit of focusing on the failures. In that I was no exception. I had utterly failed to achieve my goals. Connor Hatch was loose. Vukasin Petrovic was a threat. The Russian deal was happening. And everywhere I turned, I picked up more trouble.

I flipped Petrovic's calling card in my fingers.

"*Kree*," I said unemphatically.

I should just figure out how to use it and get it over with already. By avoiding the calling card, I had just traded one ambush for another. There I'd been, believing I was subverting Petrovic's plans, and he'd been tugging on my leash the whole time.

At least Connor didn't know the location of my hideout, or I'd really be screwed.

My gator growled. The alarm wasn't long enough to give me a sense of anything. One second I felt it, and then it was gone.

I lifted my silver whistle to my lips. Damn it. Chevalier's pompous entrance had decimated my security staff. The gator was my last thrall. Without him I was dry.

I drew the shadows close and slipped outside, massing a glove around my fist. No more vehicles out here. Nothing approached from the road. Everything was quiet, but eerily so. In the darkness I expected splashes from the swamp and rustles in the grass. Birds. Frogs. Nature sounds. Everybody refers to awkward silence as "crickets" but, you know what? Crickets are a comforting constant. If you're out in the Everglades and don't hear crickets you've got a problem.

But I was greeted with absolute stillness.

I crept around my truck, my boots twisting in the dirt. My pet gator was on the ground, lying on his back, head crushed, insides ripped out. Something had done this so fast I didn't even feel it.

"Does *everybody* know the location of my secret hideout?" I complained.

The tarp over the back of my pickup had been ripped

off. Something had been under there. I'd been so concerned about keeping an eye on the street behind me that I hadn't even checked my truck bed. I'd freaking driven something right to my doorstep.

Deep scratches scuffed the metal cargo bed. I ran my fingers along them and came up with granular dust. When I caught the whiff of sulfur, I knew exactly what was going down.

Chapter 25

I phased into shadow a split second before a stone hand punched through me from behind. The fist put a dent in the side of my pickup, rocking the vehicle violently. I didn't stop to collect insurance information. I slipped under the truck and landed on the other side, facing my attacker. A bony, demonic face trained on me. The head peeked just over the top of the bed, two horn stubs pointing out at angles, gray skin like mottled stone, rows of tiny sharp incisors in its mouth. The beast's dull appearance was broken only by its glowing golden eyes.

It raised two clawed hands and shoved them against the truck. The backside skidded toward me in a stationary fishtail. I hopped away to easily avoid the attack.

The thing snarled and vaulted into the pickup between us, but I snagged its leg with a tentacle of shadow. It fought against the grip of spellcraft, stretching its entire body over me. I was amazed at the creature's full form.

The beast was humanoid but fairly small, maybe two-thirds my height standing straight. Folded leathery wings and a serpentine tail extended from its back. Hands and feet ended in vicious claws. Pointed ears twitched angrily. It was about the size of a giant dog (and growled at me like one) but something told me it was intelligent.

I swung my shotgun up to blast it in the teeth but held off at the last second. My instincts were working faster than my brain, but I'd just caught up. This was a gargoyle. A true-to-life creature of stone. That explained the traces of dust I'd been finding. This was the thing that ambushed me in the museum. I'd emptied a load of birdshot into its belly at point-blank range and was rewarded with a confetti of ricochets. Better not try that again.

Armored or not, the gargoyle retreated from my weapon. Instead of struggling against the shadow, it pulled back with it, disappearing behind the truck bed.

I bent open my sawed off and let the regular shell fall to the ground. I loaded in one with spark powder. The shadow suddenly tugged away from me like hair pulled from its roots. With a leap, the gargoyle took to the air ten feet above and extended its full wingspan.

The stature of the creature didn't look so underwhelming from this vantage. It was smaller than me, but this was an arcane creature built for flight. A cross between a bat and a man, with the limb tactility of a monkey.

Protracted fingers and toes descended on me. I gave it a proper Fourth of July welcome with the sawed off. Streaks of red light bounced overhead and rained down on me. The flames ate up my shadow so I ducked and rolled back under the truck the old-fashioned way. Stone claws ripped into the earth where I'd been standing.

I slid to the other side of the truck. My ears rang from the blast. The flames licked out and the darkness returned so I shifted to my feet, playing Keep Away with a bat out of hell.

I moved around the back of the truck and caught the beast rolling away. It crouched on all fours, ready to pounce. One of my more powerful attacks had just glanced off the thing causing little more than pained annoyance.

I loaded another round in my shotty. This was another of my homebrew specials. Bone dust grinded into a gluey paste, activated by the heat of the blast. I drew the boomstick up but the creature was faster. It knocked me aside with a vicious backhand.

Luckily, the gargoyle had been more concerned with the shotgun than goring me. I tumbled and lost my grip. The gun juggled in and out of my fingers, airborne and just out of reach. It landed in the dirt. The gargoyle and I both leaped for it.

I was closer but it was faster. My fingers reached the wooden grip of my antique shotgun. At nearly the same instant, a clawed foot smashed into the barrel. The beast pounded a furrow in the ground. The shotgun, however, was gone. I'd chosen to release it into the shadow rather than lose it.

The gargoyle roared. I sprang up to one knee right beside it, waiting.

The beast swiped downward. I held up my forearm and blocked his overhead blow. While the rune flared blue, I tapped Opiyel through the spiked dog collar on my wrist. Gotcha. I shoved his arm away and decked him right in the chest with a fistful of shadow.

The gargoyle tumbled backward a good ten yards, clawed the dirt, and skidded to a stop. For just a moment, it wheezed and stared at me in disbelief, then it showed tiny rows of teeth and charged.

I waved my hand and thickened the shadow on the ground, gumming up the terrain. The beast nearly tripped but deftly caught itself on all fours, snarling in the darkness. My spellcraft wouldn't keep it stuck but it wasn't meant to. Slowing it down removed its speed advantage.

The gargoyle screeched and extended its full wingspan, readying to take flight. My shadows couldn't slow him in the air. Ground speed was a worrying factor; flight was a whole other category. I was close enough to the boathouse. As it jumped into the sky, I retreated inside.

The beast roared. Metal clanged above me. Bangs and knocks navigated over the corrugated metal roof of my hideaway. My eyes tracked where I thought it might be. I backed up, realizing that it could crash through the roof at any second. In fact, the thin sheet of metal shouldn't even be enough to support the gargoyle's weight. Unless...

A blow slammed against the back of my neck and jarred my entire body forward. Something clicked as I attempted to take to the shadow. Pain pinched against my throat. Suffocated me. I found myself stuck in the material world, choking, something cold gripping my neck.

I fell to my knees and struggled to shake the hold. A boot against my back shoved me forward. I caught the floor with my hands. Then someone behind me clasped a handcuff around one of my wrists.

I was collared, with a boot forcing my body down but a leash pulling my arm and neck backward. The steel prevented me from escaping into the shadows. Immaterial things like spirits don't mesh with iron. I was now trapped.

The person jerked my arm behind my back. Reached a

shackle for my other wrist. Everything in my body told me not to move my hand, to keep pressing it against the concrete floor so I wouldn't choke to death. But that reflex was pinning me down, making my wrist an easy target.

I took a breath and yanked my hand to my waist, reaching for my knife. My weight fell forward and I immediately regretted the decision. A crushing force pushed against my larynx. My air supply was cut off. My gasps came out as desperate little coughs of air.

But I'd only needed that second.

With my arm still free, I plunged the knife behind me, hoping to hit something vital. A woman released a sharp groan. Suddenly I was weightless. At least, that's what it felt like the second before my face hit the cement.

I didn't care, though. I could breathe again. I twisted around. A woman in biker leathers grasped her side. Her pants were skin tight, but her jacket was a hefty thing. As my knife clattered to the floor, I realized the thick leather had deflected the blow. She spread her oversized boots to either side of her body, catching herself in a wide split stance, coiled to attack. She watched me as I did her.

I recognized her. She was the same short woman with the sharp, punky haircut I'd seen in the museum leaving Dr. Trinidad's office. She was cute, too. But I wasn't about to let that spoil a good fight.

My free hand went to my belt pouch. It was odd that she wasn't making a move for a weapon. She just waited.

"About time," she said tersely. Her eyes flicked behind me, and I knew I was screwed.

Four heavy limbs pounded into my back and dropped me to the floor quicker than I could think. This time when my head hit the cement, something jarred loose in my brain. The world spun. I ground my teeth together, staving off unconsciousness.

My captor stomped toward me with heavy boots, yanked my free hand behind my back, and snapped the shackle closed. I was her prisoner.

Chapter 26

Voices and movement swirled through my head like fog, apparent but unreadable. A good concussion will do that. But I hadn't been knocked out. I might have been captured, but no one could say Cisco Suarez had a glass jaw.

My awareness came back in stages: The drool in my mouth. No, that was blood. Wait, did I detect a sprinkle of Everglades dirt as well?

I spit on the concrete floor of the boathouse, which was easy because it was only an inch away from my face. I was pinned to the floor. My wrists were shackled together behind my back with a length of chain running to the collar around my neck. Oh, and there was either a gargoyle sitting on my back or I literally had the weight of the world on my shoulders. I turned my head at the soft whiff whiff of leather. Skinny legs in clunky biker boots paced around me in a circle.

"Cisco Suarez," she said with dry satisfaction. "You're a hard man to find."

"I'm even harder to kill so don't get any ideas."

"Are you trying to impress me?" The woman lowered to her haunches in front of me, leather straining against her hips. Up close, she was a bit older than she first looked. Still pretty, but experienced. She practically straddled my head with her legs.

"Are you trying to turn me on?" I countered.

She ignored the jab and whispered in my ear. "I'll admit your tradecraft is interesting, at least."

Tough crowd. I thought about clamping my teeth down on her inner thigh and seeing if she'd be impressed with that. Hey, I knew it was a dirty move, but she'd brought a gargoyle to the fight. How fair was that?

I twisted around and managed to catch the stone creature in my peripheral vision. "Ditto," I forced out between clamped teeth. "You must be a summoner of some sort, right? Can't say I've seen a real gargoyle before. You mind calling him off? This is less comfortable than it looks."

The biker chick stood. "Knowledgeable. Calm under fire. You *are* trying to impress me." She began pacing around me again, each boot stomp echoing in my hideaway, each an agonizing refusal of my request.

"You're a proficient necromancer too. And somewhat toughened by a voodoo curse, if the stories are true. Nordic protection tats."

"Hey, what do you say we quit the small talk and just bang already?"

Instead of getting a rise out of her, the gargoyle's toothy grin appeared beside my face. He spoke with an elegant voice of sophistication that had no business coming from his Nosferatu face. "Speaking of banging, shall I introduce your head to the floor again?"

I widened my eyes, not sure if the teeth startled me more than the fact that it could talk.

"You're British?"

"Not exactly," he answered, "though I did spend ages there."

I stared at the beast but addressed his master. "Cool trick. You taught him to talk. Why don't you call him off, like a good dog? Or better yet, tell him to play dead."

His tail rapped my head sharply. What was meant as a minor reproach nearly cracked my skull. I groaned and reminded myself: rock equals hard.

"Bernard," snapped the summoner. "Don't kill him. We're here for the Horn."

A hiss seethed from my lips. Of course they were. "Connor Hatch hired you," I spat.

Damn, between the Vucari and the summoner, everybody wanted a piece of Cisco Suarez today. I'd been so worried about the jinn that I hadn't adequately defended myself against his minions. I recalled what Connor said at the Port. The last thing he wanted was a fair fight. Call him a coward, sure, but don't call him stupid. He'd been a busy little bee behind the scenes.

"What's the going rate these days for selling your soul to a drug lord?" I asked.

"Everybody I steal from has it coming," she said with an indignant sneer. "I choose the work that I can live with. Lucky for you, I've got two rules. I don't kill anyone, and I don't screw over drug lords. Seems to me you've been doing plenty of both, so I wouldn't go throwing stones."

I chewed my lip. Was she really not going to kill me? I shifted my head to a position that put less strain on my neck. "If Connor could send you, why not just send an assassin instead?"

She shrugged. "Who's to say he didn't? I'm not a party

to his affairs. I'm just an independent contractor. He's just a client."

Call me crazy, but I thought she might actually be telling the truth. The Vucari were the assassins. Brutes who shoved people around with the elegance of a garbage truck. The other animists at the dock were another team. They tried to kill me too. But Biker Chick wasn't like that. She was a cat burglar. A thief with finesse. And a three-hundred-pound gargoyle named Bernard.

"So where is it?" she asked.

I turned away. "I don't know what you're talking about."

The gargoyle shoved me. "Shall I flay him?" he asked. Then he leaned in to me. "I detest blood under my nails, but for you I might make an exception."

I smiled. If Biker Chick had a no-killing rule, I didn't think she'd give her pet free reign to spill blood. Still, better not to antagonize him. I kept quiet.

The woman sighed and stepped away from us to study my lodgings. "This humidity is frizzing my hair," she complained nonchalantly.

I watched her in amusement. "It's eighty degrees outside. What're you wearing all that leather for?"

Biker Chick shrugged. "I'm a West Coast gal. What can I say?"

Jeez, a professional thief from across the country. Connor had spared no expense.

"So," I said, working it out, "you started with museums, looking for signs of Taíno artifacts. You somehow got word of Dr. Trinidad's side project and put pressure on her to get the Horn from me. That it?" All the pieces fit. That was why the gargoyle had jumped me in the hallway. They were hoping I'd brought the artifact in for study.

The summoner paced around me and out of my vision. I flipped my head to the other side but still couldn't see her.

"I put a trace on your phone and had her call you," she admitted, "but it seems like you destroyed it."

"So you snuck into my pickup after the meet with Connor. Smart."

At least that meant I hadn't been followed. After my earlier conversation with Milena, she would never let me live that down. Not that I'd tell her about this. My arm tingled with pins and needles. I shifted my weight to ease the pressure.

"So?" she asked impatiently. "It's not in your truck. It's not in your van. It's not on your shelf of curios."

I clamped my mouth shut. The veneer of shadow that clung to the lead safe was unnatural but inconspicuous. It wasn't a real illusion and anything as simple as a flashlight could dispel it, but apparently Biker Chick hadn't found it.

"By the way," I asked, "What's your name? Otherwise I have to keep calling you Biker Chick in my head."

"This one is insolent," growled the gargoyle. He jumped off me, which hurt more than expected but at least returned the flow of blood to my body. The ensuing relief was short-lived. Bernard tugged the neck chain a foot in the air. I had to roll to my side to breathe.

"Don't assume I have the same qualms about killing as she does," he warned.

"Aren't gargoyles supposed to be protectors of mankind or something?" I asked.

"You tell me," he answered. The beast cupped the top of my head with clawed fingers and began to squeeze. I suddenly felt like I'd been doing vodka shots for a week straight.

"You've got to be shitting me," said the summoner, holding up her hand passively.

Thankfully, the gargoyle released me. Biker Chick was staring past my bedroll at the dark corner in the room. What did I say? It was a weak camouflage. More of a party trick, really. Animists with skill could pick it apart. Oversized boots clunked across the room to my safe.

"It's not even closed," she said, almost disappointed.

"You don't wanna do that," I warned.

She turned and reached for the broken door.

"Do something!" I yelled, appealing to the Spaniard who had thus far remained silent.

The door of the safe creaked open. The summoner pulled out the double-wide briefcase and set it on the floor. "What have we here?" she said to herself.

What the...

I watched her surprise when she realized the case didn't close properly. Some outlaw I was. A safe that couldn't lock and a briefcase of cash that couldn't close. She flipped the top open. Her features went hard. She flung the briefcase against the wall. Bricks of cash bounced to the floor.

"Where is it?" she demanded, turning to me.

Behind her, the safe was empty.

No, seriously. What the—?

My head spun to the road, to where Chevalier had driven off just moments before. That son of a bastard had taken off with more than just cash and cocaine.

"It's not here?" asked the gargoyle.

Biker Chick caught my gaze. I pulled it away but it was

too late. She understood. "The gangbanger," she cried in frustration. "The damned Haitians have the Horn."

Her panic turned to anger. I meekly shrugged in mock sympathy. "Hey, I'm a victim too."

I'd expected another snarl from the gargoyle, but even Biker Chick had her limits. Her heavy boots stomped toward me so fast I didn't have time to regret the comment. An armored boot hit me square in the head.

Glass jaw or not, no chance staying conscious for that one.

Chapter 27

I had a dream I was rocking in shallow waves on a beach, choking on the foamy surf. I woke up confused. Found it hard to breathe. I remembered the collar around my neck and eased my arms higher so I wouldn't tug on it. I was lying on my stomach on a metal floor. This wasn't my boathouse. I was in some kind of vehicle, rumbling shakily in the Miami night.

My chains clinked as I turned. Half my face was plastered in powder. I coughed and a cloud of cocaine swirled away.

I was in the damn drug van.

The summoner drove while her pet sat on the floor behind the passenger seat. Watching me. His golden eyes flickered when I stirred.

"Shyla," he called, countless teeth frowning. "He's not dead." I think he was disappointed.

She swiveled around while she drove to check on me. I couldn't see where we were from the floor but assumed we were after Chevalier. Biker Chick—excuse me, Shyla—wanted to find the Horn. Why I was here was anybody's guess. I suppose you hold onto insurance for as long as you can.

"He's not going anywhere," she said dismissively.

I rested my chin on the floor of the van. "Shyla, is it?" I asked, all smiles and charm. "I'm Cisco. I know you know that, but I figured we could start over, you know?"

No answer.

"How much is Connor paying you for this gig? Maybe I could outbid him."

"I doubt you could afford it," she said.

I grinned with confident machismo. "You'd be surprised. I came into some money recently and—" I paused, noticing the two garbage bags that sandwiched me. "Hey! That's my money!"

Shyla snickered. "Like I said, you can't afford it."

The smile fled my face. "You don't get to keep that, you know. That's Connor Hatch's money. I don't think he'd appreciate you appropriating it."

She shrugged. "Count your blessings. I left you the scraps you had in that briefcase."

Scraps? That was three-quarters of a million dollars in there. Maybe she hadn't realized the bills were all hundreds.

"Only because we were in a hurry," added Bernard. He turned to the road ahead and yawned. Great. Even the gargoyle was getting bored with me.

"Hey," I said. He ignored me. "Hey!"

He turned.

"Where are you from anyway? The Nether?"

He smiled. "The World Below, human." His voice was calm. Even though he wanted to rip my head off, he came off stately.

My forehead crinkled. "The Nether *is* below."

"You must imagine even further, then. Below your

dreaded steppes."

My face darkened. I couldn't believe what I was hearing. "You're a hellion?"

He snickered and looked away.

I feel inclined to point out that I don't really believe in hell. But why juggle semantics while staring at a demon? This thing qualified for that moniker more than anything I'd ever seen. Suddenly I could understand the beliefs of millions of people worldwide. The idea of a wicked place far below ours.

I needed get out of this mess, stat.

I repositioned on my side to get a look around. I was being watched, of course, but I kept my movements slow and casual. A grunt as I stretched my neck. Just getting comfortable.

When Shyla had listed off my talents at the boathouse, she hadn't mentioned metallurgy. Maybe she knew about it and maybe she didn't. It was my weakest angle, really. Nearly useless. With focused, uninterrupted effort, I could break simple metals, as long as they weren't reinforced.

The shackles on my wrists and neck were no joke. Cartoon-sized bars of steel. Those things weren't going anywhere. The chain connecting them was more reasonable.

Within my capacity to break, however? Probably not. Like I said, this was my weakest spellcraft. The things I could snap apart were mostly breakable anyway. A novelty pair of handcuffs were no problem to slip. Police-grade gave me problems. My current shackles? Judging by their weight, I was going with rhinoceros-grade. I cursed my lack of metallurgy practice, but I only had myself to blame.

I tried anyway. I awkwardly wrapped my fingers around a single central link that connected the cuffs with the neck chain, focused the flow of the Intrinsics into that band of metal, and pulled. My face must've turned beet red with the effort.

The gargoyle chortled. "Keep still, human." He rapped my head lightly with a foot. "Lightly" is relative.

"Don't hurt him," ordered Shyla. "He's my prisoner."

"Not if we kill him," he grumbled under his breath.

"Besides," she said. "We've got him. The black van, up ahead."

All eyes went to the windshield, including mine. I strained to raise my head. We passed through an intersection and I caught a glimpse of the Miami Avenue sign. I didn't see the cross street but it was a good bet we were headed to Little Haiti. And the black van meant she'd found Chevalier.

I wondered how she'd managed that. The bokors should've been way ahead of us (unless they'd stopped for churros). Managing to catch them en route was impressive. Or maybe it just showed what a sad fight I'd put up.

"I'm gonna run him off the road," said Shyla. "As soon as they hit the curb, jump out the back and subdue the bokor."

"With pleasure," answered Bernard, licking his lips.

"Get in their van if you can," she added. "I don't want undue exposure."

He nodded as she placed her phone on the center console. It had a map up with a waypoint—some kind of tracking program. That was how she found him. She'd mentioned trying to track my burners. There was a good bet Chevalier wasn't as careful with his phone as I was. I tried to get eyes on the Bone Saints ahead of us, but I couldn't see anything at ground level.

"Here we go," said Shyla. The drug van accelerated. Bernard's claws tightened around the headrest of the passenger seat.

The van pulled alongside the bokor's. Chevalier turned to look out his open window. We swerved into him.

We jerked to the side as the vans collided. I skipped across the floor and hit the wall with a grunt. The van slowed as Shyla corrected her steering.

This was the distraction I needed. I tightened my jaw and kept trying to break the shackles.

The gargoyle hissed as Shyla gunned the accelerator again. Tires squealed on the street ahead. We swerved back and forth. Chevalier was taking evasive maneuvers now, making it difficult for the summoner to pull beside him. It was hard for me to brace myself since I couldn't see the chase and anticipate our turns.

"Have it your way," muttered Shyla. She rammed right into the back of the other van.

I jolted forward, pulling my knees to my chin and scrunching up like a ball to protect my head. It wasn't just me shooting around like a pinball, but the various other loose objects in the van. The bags of money were the least of my concern. Compared to everything else, they were giant pillows. The stone gargoyle was a static obstacle, but various metal implements like an empty rifle, tackle box, and bolt cutters were all dangerous in their own right.

Hold up a minute. Was I sliding around the back of this van with a pair of bolt cutters? Thank you, Manolo.

At the next swerve, I kicked my boot out and scooped

them toward me. I rolled around to hide them behind my back. The gargoyle checked on me but didn't seem overly concerned.

I grabbed the bolt cutters. Fitted the teeth around the chain. Only then did I realize my predicament. My wrists were right next to the link that needed snapping. There was no way my hands would have enough leverage.

I pulled my feet up and tried pressing them over the handle, but the alligator boots kept slipping. I couldn't get a good grip.

We swerved a couple more times and I got a bright idea. I propped the bolt cutters against my back and the wall of the van, teeth tightened over the link. I pressed into the wall, trying to get enough force to snap the chain.

Without warning, the van suddenly jerked to the side and hit something. Metal crunched. The right window shattered. Outside, Chevalier's black van spun sideways. Then I realized it was us spinning. We were out of control. Shyla steered into the turn but we slid off the street backward. The floor rocked up as we hit a curb. I bounced to the other side of the van and lost the bolt cutters. The engine cut out and we rolled to a stop.

"Shit!" cried the summoner, trying and failing to restart the van.

"He's getting away," reminded Bernard. All the power to summon a creature from another world and you get insight like that. The gargoyle looked me over to make sure I was still being a good little animist and then turned away when the van started again. All three of us jostled as the tires bounced back onto the street. The van gathered speed again as Shyla rushed to catch up.

I slid over, grabbed the bolt cutters behind my back, and rolled to the wall. As I tried to put it in position, the gargoyle narrowed his eyes.

"Shadow charmer," he growled. "What are you up to?"

I relaxed. "Oh, you know, just waiting for you to uncuff me so I can kick your ass."

A long tongue slipped between his lips as he hissed. "Insolent human."

"I gotta tell you, that hurts, coming from a walking cinder block."

The gargoyle reached for me but a sudden siren made him freeze. Outside. Behind us. It had blared suddenly but now settled into a protracted series of crescendos.

I never thought I'd be so happy to hear the cops.

Chapter 28

"Not good," remarked Shyla, checking her side mirror. Maybe her pet gargoyle gets the stating-the-obvious stuff from her.

She faced us, looking for advice maybe. Stoney and I had blank expressions. That seemed to frazzle her more. As she considered her options, I waited with the bolt cutters behind my back, considering mine.

I mean, it was good the police were after us, right? What kidnappee *doesn't* want to hear those sirens? And it wasn't like I was a fugitive anymore. The police knew about the drug hits, but they weren't wise to me. I didn't have ID. If worse came to worse I could always give them the ol' me-no-speakee-English bit. Evan told me they love that.

Then again, I was currently in a van from one of said drug hits. Hell, the interior was lined with cocaine. At this point, so was I. The back windows were tinted but spiderwebbed with cracks. One observant police officer would figure things out real quick. And that was if the van wasn't already on their radar. (Somehow, I kinda doubted it was. What drug dealer in their right mind reports their drug van stolen?)

"Okay," said Shyla after gathering herself. "We're gonna

pull over."

The gargoyle smiled. "I can handle the officer."

"No," she said. "We don't want trouble. I was speeding. He'll write me a ticket and be on his way."

I snorted. "Not if you can't show him registration. Look, get me out of these chains, unsummon your pet, and I'll pull the shadow over us. The cop won't see anyone inside and will search the area, thinking we ditched. No one gets hurt and we all win."

She tightened her lips and pondered my offer. There were complications with my plan, of course, but I didn't point those out. I just wanted to get her on my side. In the meantime, the van slowed and turned down a dark side street. She stopped a block in, pulling the cop out of sight. Just in case she needed to handle him.

Shyla turned to me. "No. I'm gonna talk or bribe my way out of this. If you make a sound, I'll have no choice but to hurt him." She locked eyes with the gargoyle. "If he opens the back, we need to subdue him. But no killing."

The beast grumbled. I suspected she constantly muzzled his bloodthirsty inclinations.

Shyla shifted the van into park. Red and blue lighting reflected off the telephone pole and building ahead. We waited in tense silence for a minute. The cop was running the plate. Was the van stolen?

"Screw this," said the summoner, and jumped out. As soon as she slammed the door, a loudspeaker blared.

"Stay in the van!" ordered the officer.

Her voice was muted. "It's just that—"

"Stay in the v— Too late. Hands against the van. Now."

The gargoyle released a guttural breath and listened. I'm

sure he felt helpless back here. Ducking down, we couldn't see anything.

A door opened but didn't close. Just one cop, I thought.

"I'm sorry, Officer, I thought you wanted me to get out."

"That's okay," came a voice. "Just don't move. Is anyone else in the van?"

"No," she said. "Just me."

Bernard leaned close and ran his tongue over rows of teeth. "Remember," he whispered. "If you make a sound, I'll kill him."

Shyla didn't want bodies, but letting something like this loose was reckless. The hellion played rough, plain and simple. One overeager swipe of a tail could cave the officer's skull in. I clenched my jaw. Not a lot of options here. I slowly fit the teeth of the bolt cutters around the link I needed to break.

"You know," said Shyla outside. "This is actually my boss' van. I checked the glove box but I have no idea where the registration is. I can call him, if you like."

"That's okay. Just stay there. Keep your hands where I can see them."

A flashlight beam shone through the driver's window. It swept over the dash and the seats. The gargoyle leaned in and huddled his wings over us as the light angled to the back. I had chains on which meant I couldn't slip into shadow, and manifestations were tough with my hands bound, but that didn't mean I couldn't tweak the darkness some. I blanketed it over us, even though the flashlight would illuminate anything it directly pointed at.

"That, uh, some kind of statue?" asked the officer.

"Yeah," she answered. "I'm delivering it to a client."

The flashlight disappeared. I looked up and saw the gargoyle had closed his eyes, hiding their repulsive glow. Damn, he did look just like a statue.

"Can you open it up, ma'am?"

"What? Why?"

"Open it up," repeated the officer with indifference.

"Come on," said Shyla. "I know I was speeding a little, but searching my vehicle like I'm a criminal—"

"Are you carrying any weapons, ma'am?" he interrupted.

The gargoyle growled again. Their conversation was heading downhill and we both knew it. Bernard pulled away from me as they spoke, careful not to rock the van. He scowled at the back doors.

"Ma'am, are you aware you have bullet holes in your vehicle?"

"Uh, no..."

"Then either open the back doors of the vehicle or I'm gonna need to detain you."

"Okay!" she snapped, but then lightened her voice. Mildly annoyed, but compliant. "I'll open the van, if that's what you want, but I think this is all unnecessary."

With surprising silence, the beast leaned away from me and readied to pounce on all fours.

Shit. I couldn't let this go down. That cop would never know what hit him. I shifted my back against the wall to prop the bolt cutters between it and me, but it was impossible to do it silently. The metal tool scraped against the indents in the floor and the gargoyle's head snapped to me.

"Let's go, ma'am," said the cop outside.

Bernard kept his focus on me. "What are you hiding

back there?" he asked slyly.

I feigned confusion. "What do you mean?"

He growled and grabbed my shoulder, forcing me to my stomach. When my hands came into view, instead of finding the tool, he discovered a sawed off aiming at his chest.

The back doors flung open and Shyla jumped out of the way. An officer in a blue uniform held a flashlight with one hand and rested his other on his holstered service weapon.

The gargoyle leapt from the vehicle, partly to attack the cop, partly to avoid my weapon. With my arm twisted around, I pulled the trigger. The gun kicked out of my awkward grip but a cone of glue staggered the startled beast. He stumbled to the pavement outside the van as the dust liquefied and hardened in an instant, pinning him to the street.

"What the fuck!" cried the officer, pulling his gun.

I rolled back against the wall and balanced the bolt cutters in place. Then I brought my boot out and kicked it backward into the handle, snapping the link.

At the same time, Shyla's heavy boot connected with the officer's hand and sent his weapon flying. He deflected another kick and yelled into a radio clipped to his shoulder.

"Officer needs assistance! Miami Avenue and Northwest Two-Five Street."

He took a punch but managed to pull a Taser from his belt. Shyla tried to bat his arm away, but his finger found the trigger. Two hooks caught her stomach between her unzipped jacket. Thin wires delivered fifty-thousand volts in a flash. She straightened and fell to the floor, muscles tensed.

I sat up and stretched my arms, showing my chains.

"Thanks, Officer. I thought she was gonna kill me."

He jumped and peered into the van, wondering how many more of us were gonna surprise him. His eyes went to the gargoyle, pinned under a layer of glue. Then he seemed to remember he had a pistol somewhere. The poor dude had twenty things running through his head at once and seemed to be in shock.

I hurried to the front seat of the van.

"Nobody move!" he ordered.

"Actually," I said. "It looks like you have everything in hand here, Officer. I'll leave you to it."

He scrambled to find his gun. Shyla was on the floor blinking. She turned to her gargoyle, surprised to see him down. With a wave of her hand, Bernard disintegrated into charcoal dust that splashed out in all directions. Then she worked up a quick conjuration with her fingers. Something flashed. I smelled burnt hemlock. Visible power flowed into her. Any confusion that she'd had from being jolted to the floor vanished. Shyla hopped lightly to her feet. She stretched her neck and extended her arms like something alien feeling out the world.

"Stay down!" yelled the cop. He pressed the stun gun trigger again. The two wires were still connected to Shyla. They delivered a second shock. The summoner laughed and tore the hooks from her skin. Something was different about her. She had an air of bloodlust about her. Like the gargoyle, but out of control. Shyla picked up the cop and slammed him on the hood of his car.

I looked back from the driver's seat reluctantly. "Aw, hell."

The summoner grunted and shook the officer up and

down. Whatever spell she'd used had given her more than renewed strength. The larger man couldn't wrest himself free. Shyla raised a fist to the sky.

I pulled the action on my shotgun and rested it against the back of her head. "Stop right there."

She froze. The cop stared up at us, breathing heavily.

"What is that?" I asked her. "Some kind of summoning?"

She clenched her jaw, fighting for control. I tapped the short barrel on her head. She nodded. "Internal."

Another trick I hadn't seen before. She'd basically possessed herself with something she summoned. That was one way to go, I figured.

"Let's say bye-bye," I ordered.

She scowled but, seeing no other option, did as she was told. The presence flushed from within her. The summoner gulped for breath as if she'd been underwater.

My eyes strayed to the officer. He was a young guy with a shaved head. Scared. Probably just a rookie. The poor guy was definitely having one of those days. I drew my index finger to my lips. With a wink, I said, "Shh."

I dragged Shyla by the collar to the passenger door of the van. I shoved inside after her and pushed her into the driver's seat.

"Drive," I ordered, holding my gun steady. "Before that rookie finds his gun. And don't even think about any of that summoning mumbo jumbo or my boomstick goes boom."

She grimaced and shifted into gear.

Chapter 29

"Not too fast," I told Shyla. "We don't want to attract the attention of the cops again."

She laughed coarsely. "Sure, because there's not already a BOLO matching our exact description out there."

Her sarcasm was tainted with uncertainty. Fear. It was obvious she wasn't used to having a gun to her head. Not that she couldn't fight, but it was a good bet that her pets were the ones who got dirty. That was the way with summoners. I knew because the same was often true for necromancers.

"Get off the main road," I instructed. "Turn here."

Nervous or not, she took direction well.

"You have any weapons on you?" I asked.

"No."

I reached into her open leather jacket. She pulled away. I jiggled the gun at her ear. She clenched her teeth as I slid my hand along the waist of her pants. She leaned forward as I checked the small of her back.

"What's this?" I asked, pulling a retractable metal baton from a strap on her left leg.

"It's just an ASP."

"That's a weapon, lady."

She shrugged.

I tossed it to the back of the van. I ran my hands down her leather pants, checking for hidden pockets. Her muscles tensed as I did so. Confident she was clean, I then checked her jacket pockets. Car keys.

"Any of these unlock my chains?" I asked.

She shook her head.

"Where's the key then?"

"I don't have it."

"I don't believe you."

She let out a hiss. "I swear." A stray hair fell over her face and she blew at it over and over before brushing it away with her hand.

I stared into her eyes. Still nervous. And she'd lied about the ASP. But I didn't find it on her and the van wasn't hers.

"You know," I said. "You're pretty cute for an untrustworthy demon summoner."

"I hate being called cute."

Tough crowd. I grabbed her phone from the console. "You following Chevalier's cell signal?"

"I dropped a tracker on his van at the Port. Just in case."

Damn. She'd covered all the angles. Shyla grumbled when I slipped the phone into my back pocket.

My wrists and neck had solid bars of steel clamped around them. Oversized fashion accessories. Who knew I was on the leading edge of cool? The hanging chain was loose so I could move about freely, but the closed links kept me from phasing into shadow. That was a big problem for me. I tried the key chain. Each of the three cuffs had a keyhole, and none of the keys fit. Shyla watched until I gave up and tossed the keys into the cup holder.

I checked the mirrors for police and frowned, wondering if we'd be able to make it back to the Everglades or Little Haiti. I wasn't optimistic about either option.

"Why'd you take me with you?" she asked suddenly.

I turned to her, wondering the same thing myself. "I guess I like to hold onto insurance as long as I can."

"Insurance for what?"

"That cop was just doing his job," I said, changing the subject. "He didn't deserve to die just because you were dumb enough to kidnap me in a stolen drug van riddled with bullet holes and broken windows."

"I wouldn't have hurt him."

I snorted. "Yeah, I forgot. The thief with a conscience."

"Don't laugh. I bet you have some kind of moral code too."

"Well, it didn't look very moral to me while you were denting the hood of the police car with his head."

She turned to the street, lips pouting. "It's... That one's hard to control."

I frowned. She'd summoned a dark power to herself without being sure of her ability to contain it. Why did that sound familiar? I lowered the shotgun to my lap.

"So you don't like summoning it," I said. "But you didn't hesitate to avoid jail."

"It wasn't like that."

"Hey, I'm not judging you. I'm not a good person. I've killed people." I sat back in the seat. "Even innocents."

She watched me again, waiting for me to bare my soul, probably. I showed her I was the silent type. We stopped at a small intersection and heard a siren in the distance. It was Fire Rescue. We sat at the stop sign until it passed us, and then continued.

"Wanna tell me about it?" she offered.

Me and Biker Chick. Fast friends.

"Enough with the chitchat, Shyla." I squeezed the gun to her waist. "Who else are you working with?"

A stoic expression overtook her face. "You saw my pet. I don't work with anyone else."

"Cut the shit."

"I told you, I'm an independent contractor. That's why I backed off at the Port and stowed away in your truck alone." She sighed. "Bringing in the Horn would've been a huge payday for me. Now I'm gonna head back to LA empty-handed."

My face soured. "Cry me a river, lady. You think you can steal for a living without getting a few fingers chopped off?"

She widened her eyes in horror.

"It's an expression."

That only partially relieved her. I pulled the hammer of the shotgun dramatically.

"Where's Connor Hatch?"

"I don't know that."

"He hired you, didn't he?"

She pressed her lips together. "I'm supposed to call him when I get the Horn."

I patted my back pocket. "On this thing?"

"No," she said quickly. "That's mine. He supplied me with a separate phone. It's at my base of operations."

"Where's that?"

She frowned and I jammed the gun into her side.

"Where?"

"Close, actually."

"And what exactly constitutes a base?"

"It's just a warehouse with some supplies," she answered. "I stashed my ride there before heading to the Port."

I nodded, liking the sound of this. "That wouldn't happen to be where the key to my shackles is, would it?"

She worked her jaw then nodded.

I checked her phone again. A GPS blip displayed Chevalier's location. I wanted the Horn back more than anything. The quickest path between two points is a line, but that's not always the smartest.

"Okay," I announced, pulling the sawed off back and enjoying the ride. "Here's the plan. We need to get off the street. We're ditching this van in your warehouse. We're gonna take your car, get my Horn back, and then we're gonna call up Connor Hatch. Tell him you found it. You do everything I say and I let you walk away. You can even keep whatever cash he brings you."

She furrowed her brow and wet her lips. "That sounds dangerous."

"You're the one who wanted a payday."

Shyla was right. Her base of operations was close. We had to turn around and head to the outskirts of Downtown. A police car raced by us in the other direction flashing lights and siren, but he wasn't after us. When we pulled up to the warehouse, we both breathed a sigh of relief.

She stopped in front of a sliding garage door. "We need to open it manually. You wanna do the honors?"

"And leave you alone in the van?"

She shrugged. "I could get out."

Actually, I didn't like the sound of that either. I wiped my lips and glanced up and down the block, working out the logistics. "How about this?" I shut the van off and pulled the keys. "You sit tight. I'll open the door and come back. We'll drive in together."

Shyla frowned, but it was the only deal on the table. I reached over her and rolled the window down. Then I exited my side and circled the vehicle from the front, stopping beside her.

"Don't forget this," she said, dropping her keys in my hand. "It's the gold one."

I nodded and stepped away. "Remember, no incantations or I'll be forced to fight back."

She stuck her jaw out and faced forward, hands on ten and two.

I moved to the lock without taking my eyes off her. The key slipped in easily. The lock fell open. I dropped it on the asphalt and drew the garage door high.

As I did, the door of the van slammed.

I spun around with my shotgun ready. Shyla stood outside with her hands in the air.

"I said to stay in the van!"

"I'm sorry," she said, gulping down a whimper. "I didn't want it to go down this way, but you left me no choice."

I arched an eyebrow. The van was empty. None of her pets were swooping down on top of me. As far as I could tell, she hadn't used any spellcraft at all.

Suddenly, my right arm shot above my head, fingers unclasped. The shotgun fell lax, still looped around my finger. I managed to spin around halfway before my body encountered stiff resistance, like the air was sludge.

The two animists from the Port were inside. The teenage girl gripped her statuette fetish in both arms, locking me up tight.

Chapter 30

"Cisco Suarez!" cried the excited voice of the illusionist. He hadn't been as fast as the witch, but by now he had a pistol drawn on me. He'd changed to a new suit. Just as debonair as the first, less covered in vile pestilence. Same red tie, though. Same exacting look. "Get him in here, Darcy. Before someone sees us."

The witch tugged on my arm with her invisible power. I fought against it. The last thing I wanted was to get locked inside a warehouse with a bunch of animists. Darcy struggled to drag me in. She was young and was no doubt still mastering her skills.

It didn't matter because a stiff boot shoved to my back did the job. Shyla recovered both sets of keys, idled the van inside, and rolled the door down.

Getting captured was really getting tiresome.

"You've met Darcy," said the illusionist, only in his late twenties himself. "My name's Shen Santos. And you're here courtesy of the Society."

My face slackened as it dawned on me. The Society was a group of animists who looked out for each other's business interests. A legal cartel, I called them. I'd run into one of their experienced enforcers before and had found myself on the short end of that fight. These two kids weren't at that level yet, but they'd been well trained.

I turned my head to Shyla. "So much for working alone."

She crossed her arms defiantly and turned to Shen. "My job's done. Pay me so I can get out of this muggy city."

The illusionist waved the gun to a cubby behind him. "The red bag."

Shyla hefted it to the hood of a convertible BMW. So the little wizard alliance had hired her to find the Horn. Even though Connor was a participating member of that cartel, these guys had tried to scoop me up outside of his influence. That meant there was no cell phone here that could contact the jinn. Shyla unzipped the bag, quickly checked through the contents, and tossed it into the trunk.

Well, at least she'd been telling the truth about being an independent contractor. She wasn't part of the Society. She didn't work for Connor Hatch, either. I was liking her more by the minute.

The Connor Hatch thing had been an assumption on my part. One she hadn't dispelled. Smart of her. And since she wasn't in service to the jinn, she had no obligation to return his money. Double win. Shyla strolled to the van and hefted the two garbage bags out, one at a time. They joined her payment in the trunk.

"I guess honorable thieves don't have qualms about taking money," I said with a sigh.

She smiled tersely. "If it was really yours, I'd leave you with it. But you stole it too, didn't you?" The summoner remotely unlocked her car with a double beep.

"Not so fast," said Shen. "You still need to deliver the Horn."

She swallowed slowly. "I'm delivering him, not the artifact."

Shen's face tightened. He lowered the gun to his side and turned to her, but she knew he was wondering whether he should point it her way.

With the illusionist's attention (and the gun) off me, I turned to the girl. Darcy. She had short red hair and ripped skinny jeans and held her statuette in both hands with conviction. From this close I could see it was an honorific for Hecate, the Greek goddess of witches.

"Isn't Hecate a bit too trendy these days?" I teased.

She narrowed her eyes but her grip wavered. It had to be taxing to keep a hold on me like that. It was only my right arm that she pinned up in the air, but I was kinda attached to it so I didn't have a lot of room to maneuver. Coupled with the steel links around me, I was fairly boned. But my shotgun still hung limp around my trigger finger.

In the meantime, Shyla and Shen had erupted into an argument.

"The job was either him or the Horn," she insisted.

His tone was more calm but melodramatic. "And you assured us you would focus on the Horn."

She shrugged defensively, arms spread to her sides. "Shit happens. I can still get it for you, but if you want me to deliver double, you need to pay double."

Shen snorted. "Your price is too high."

She relaxed a bit, trying to steer the argument into a business negotiation, but I could see she wanted out. "That's the price," she said firmly. She waited in silence, not pressing the issue.

The illusionist crossed his arms. Darcy turned to him.

That was my opening. I reached my left hand up and unhooked the shotgun from my frozen arm. Holding the barrel, I flipped it lightly to catch the handle. Before the antique wood hit my palm, a tide of force shoved me back into the wall. The sawed off bounced on the floor.

Darcy sighed. "Don't try anything else. We're too strong and have you outnumbered."

I grimaced. Luckily, Shen seemed to have missed the whole show. He waved his hand dismissively at Shyla. "No more payments. We have what we want. Your job is done."

The summoner was pleased with the decision. She quickly went to the garage door and jerked it up. "Whatever you say."

"Where'd you find him?" asked Darcy. I stiffened.

Shyla hiked a shoulder. "On the street. I followed him from the Port."

"And the artifact?"

The summoner played off the question with casual disregard. "No idea."

I sighed under my breath. I had more pressing concerns at the moment, but I didn't want to add the-Society-knowing-the-location-of-my-hideaway to the list. And a secret group of manipulative animists getting their hands on the Horn would be a disaster.

I had to admit, though, it was strange that Shyla kept the information from them. Maybe she was protecting me, in a way. Or maybe it was as simple as job security. Why tell them where they could find me or the Horn for free? If I escaped they'd need to hire her all over again. Mercenary instincts, right there.

"What about the key to the chains?" asked Shen.

"That's right," she said. She reached into her boot and tossed him a shiny silver key attached to a thin chain. He smiled and hung it around his neck. Cisco Suarez, the complete sucker.

Shyla considered me for a moment, eyes revealing that she had done her best to help me. "For what it's worth, Cisco, I really am sorry. You seem like a nice enough guy. If I'd recovered the Horn, you wouldn't be here. I don't like leaving poor saps to these animals."

"Yeah," I grumbled, facing away. She was a survivor. And as she hopped into her Beamer and drove off, we both knew she had successfully survived another day.

My horoscope was a bit less certain.

Chapter 31

Between Darcy the Teen Witch and the steel band around my neck, it wasn't hard to secure me. They stuffed me in an isolated back room. It was like a walk-in closet with steel shelves, but the walls were only eight-feet high, disconnected from the warehouse's high ceiling. A row of windows lined the outer walls along the ceiling. Metal rafters crisscrossed in between. It was a nice view for a storage room but I wasn't going anywhere.

They looped my neck chain around the industrial shelving's corner support beam. This wasn't your typical IKEA setup. It was solid steel. They clicked it down with a Master Lock and that was that.

The two animists stripped my spell tokens. The pouch on my belt, my ceremonial bronze knife—they even took my dog-collar bracelet. They didn't see the silver whistle because the neck shackle covered the black twine. They missed the belt buckle too, but it didn't do me a whole lot of good in this situation.

My hands were free. Shackled, of course, but loose. That was enough to work most shadow magic, but I couldn't create physical manifestations without my bracelet.

Shen checked my pockets. A burner phone. That was

useless to him. And Shyla's phone too, still in my back pocket. It was interesting that she forgot it. Then again, it was apparent she'd wanted to leave ASAP. I held a blank face as Shen checked it out, hoping he didn't realize the significance of the GPS locator.

"Two phones?" he snickered. "What are you, a drug dealer?" He laughed at his own joke.

I gave him a half-assed smile to keep him happy. Hopefully he'd be so pleased he wouldn't notice the—

"Whoa. A tracking program."

Crap. If they had that then they as good as had the Horn.

"What is this?" he asked. The screen refreshed and the GPS location disappeared. A notification popped up. "Coordinate Charlie deleted. What the fuck?"

All the air went out of my lungs. Shyla must've realized she'd left her phone with me. She was remotely erasing her tracks. The one shred of hope I had of recovering the Horn had just vanished with a pop-up message.

"What're you doing?" growled Shen. He rammed his hand to my throat. I shook him away and growled louder.

"That's not mine. I took it off your thief. She left a tracker on my car. Her job's done so she doesn't need it anymore."

He frowned, trying to poke a hole in the story. He must've been satisfied because he shut the phone off and tossed it with the rest of my stuff. On the far shelf, just ten feet from me. All my power was frustratingly close.

Then they basically let me be. Darcy kept watch in silence. Shen wandered in and out, making a few phone calls. They pretended I wasn't there but barely left me alone for more than a minute.

I got tired of struggling eventually. My position was uncomfortable. My neck was chained high enough that I couldn't sit on the floor but too low for me to properly stand. My thighs burned.

I remained quiet. I went through everything I had. Everything I needed. I tried to play out every available angle in my head, so that I'd be ready for anything.

After an extended absence, Shen Santos returned. Darcy hopped to her feet expectantly.

"Anything?" she asked.

He shook his head. "No word. Has to be any minute though."

"I don't like sitting here alone with this guy." She turned to me with an apologetic shrug. "He just watches me like a lion, completely calm, waiting for the perfect moment to bite my face off."

I snapped my teeth just to mess with her nerves. She gave me the finger.

"Bring that finger a little closer and see what happens," I said.

She pulled her hand away and tucked it under her elbow.

I considered these two in a new light. They were capable animists, but they weren't in charge. Darcy acted like she was working the Burger King register and was counting the hours till she could clock out. Shen, well, he was enjoying himself enough. He was confident too. Maybe he'd been promoted to shift manager and got to wear a little paper hat. But he wasn't the boss. Both of them were worker bees in a grander design.

"Look at Mulder and Scully here," I commented,

eyebrows raised in mock admiration.

Shen turned to me quizzically. "I'm Chinese."

I shrugged. Clean-cut confidence was close enough. And Darcy had the hairdo.

"Who's Mulder and Scully?" she asked.

"Really?" I shot back. "How old are you?"

"Seventeen."

I did the math. "Wow, as much as I hate to admit it, it literally was before your time."

"They're on Netflix," offered Shen. "Even the new ones, I think."

Darcy scowled. "Netflix is for old people. I watch YouTube."

Shen and Darcy got into a debate on the merits of user-generated content and corporate media overlords.

"Whoa," I cut in. "Slow down, guys. I was kinda dead for ten years so I'm not up on current events. You need to take it slow with me. Also—hold up. Did you just say there were new X-Files episodes? Do Mulder and Scully finally hook up?"

Shen opened his mouth to answer but someone spoke over him. "What is this, a high school reunion?"

We all turned to the metal closet door.

"Crap," I muttered.

Simon Feigelstock smiled. "What, you'll chum it up with these two strangers but you don't have anything nice to say to an old friend?"

Simon was in his mid forties, dressed to the nines in a power suit, and threatening to go bald any day now. He was also an accomplished channeler of thunder and lightning. The two kids holding me hostage had power, but they were young and brash. You wanna talk pure combat experience, I had the edge on them.

But Simon Feigelstock was a different story. I'd gotten into a tangle with him before and, well, I'm too proud to admit he kicked my ass, so let's just say I was sore the next morning.

"Cisco Suarez, the shadow charmer," said Simon, strolling casually closer. I may have been a patient lion, but I was a wounded one, and he was that wily hyena who was hungry enough to take a bite out of me. Simon stopped short and tapped his polished wing tips on the unfinished concrete. "You've been making business with Connor progressively more difficult these days."

"Aw, you noticed," I said as insincerely as possible. "That's kinda the point, Simon. Make him more of a liability than an asset. Even to his friends."

He glanced at his associates in amusement then spun back to me. "This has nothing to do with friends. This is business."

"That's what—"

I didn't have time to finish my quippy rejoinder because Simon hit me with his lightning special, courtesy of his fingertips.

Everything went white. A fleeting moment of absolutely no pain or self-awareness. Then it all rushed back in a surge of pins and needles and a contact burn. I couldn't even scream until he let up.

"Son of a bitch!" I grunted. "You didn't even ask for the Horn yet."

He chuckled. "You're not complaining about that little shock, are you? That wasn't part of the interrogation. That was payback for Rudi Alvarez. You do remember Rudi Alvarez, don't you?"

I did. Another scumbag Miami politician doing the Covey's dirty work. Rudi enjoyed a good run for a while there, even being primed for the mayor's office, until I exposed his illegal dealings. Last I heard, he escaped any prison time, but he left the city in ruins. Some of his ruin was financial because his accounts had been frozen and his assets seized, but most of it was his reputation. The man would never hold a public office again. If you ask me, he got off light.

I grimaced as Simon leaned closer to me. "I recall asking you to leave our political connections alone."

I gritted my teeth. "And I recall telling you to go fuck yourself."

He zapped me again. I was a sucker for punishment, or maybe just a good one-liner. I didn't think either was a crime, but Simon seemed to disagree. He clamped his hands around my face and pushed me back into the shelves.

"You. Shouldn't. Have. Messed. With. Our. Business."

We stared at each other for a minute. He released me, only to pound my head into the pole when I slackened.

I grunted. "Simon, I don't give a shit what you and the wizard cartel do in your spare time. When your conspiracies involve killing me and my entire family, you can't blame me for making things personal."

Shen and Darcy traded uncertain glances. Simon just clenched his jaw. He could do this all day if he needed to. Me? I could at least make sure he didn't get any sleep tonight.

"Wait outside," he ordered. Shen reluctantly complied.

Darcy was happy to leave the room.

Simon took a menacing step toward me before his phone rang. He pulled it from his pocket and frowned.

"Saved by the bell," I muttered.

Simon silenced the call and returned the cell to his pocket. Uh-oh.

"The thing is, Cisco," he said, pacing past me with his hands crossed, "people like you have to be shown." He turned to me. "I get it. I do. You grew up in the streets where it's all about posturing and puffing out your chest and talking a big game. That's where you get your power." He snapped his fingers together and a blinding crackle of light sparked between them. "Power isn't always subtle," he said. "We both know that. We both can respect that."

Simon crouched in front of me, face to face. "But sometimes we need to acknowledge power greater than ours. That is what channeling the patrons is about, after all. And in this case, Cisco, you're just one man. Me? I represent a collective of the best and brightest animists on the east coast. Our plays have been in motion for decades. We're shaping the country, even if we need to get in bed with people like Connor Hatch once in a while. That's how we move mountains. And you? Right now you're wondering if you can knock me out with a quick headbutt."

He moved away quickly before I could follow through. I hissed. "Actually, I was wondering if I could cave your head in."

He showed his teeth. "Close enough. And far from the point."

"Yeah? Are you gonna get to it one day?"

"The point is that we are better bearers of the Horn of

Subjugation than you are."

My eyes narrowed to meet his.

"It's only a matter of time before you lose it, Cisco. You don't have the resources to do more than that. Do you really want Connor to end up with it? 'Cause that's where this is heading."

Something about his appeal struck me as odd, but just like him it was out of my reach. Maybe I was too electrified to get it. Or maybe he was testing me. Either way, there was something unsaid in his words. I suddenly asked myself why he'd sent Shen and Darcy out.

The metal door to the room screeched open. An older woman with a head of short gray hair entered. "That will be enough," she said, glooming at Simon's handiwork. I wondered what I looked like to deserve that expression.

Simon straightened and nodded to his superior as a few other agents mingled behind her.

The enforcer smirked and leaned in conspiratorially. "You're gonna get it now," he warned under his breath. "The Gray Lady's here."

Chapter 32

Several assistants filled the room. They all wore the same unassuming black clothes. Long sleeves, gloves. Each had some kind of hood over their heads. Gray cashmere, maybe. Thick. Definitely not transparent. They moved around with precision even though their faces were completely covered.

One stuck his head around me. Studying me. He didn't say a word. It was creepy. Two more stood by the door, one inside and one outside. Another carried a chair in from the main warehouse. He set it down beside the Gray Lady, facing me.

The older woman, who was clearly the boss, kicked the chair toward me.

"Where's mine?" she asked impatiently.

The assistant hurried out and retrieved another. I dragged my chair closer with my boot and sat. Joy. It was the perfect height. For the first time in over an hour, I could relax without suffocating pressure on my neck.

Despite having a chair herself, the older woman remained standing with her arms clasped behind her back. Whether or not she meant for me to catch my breath, I jumped at the opportunity.

Darcy peeked in through the open doorway. As Simon

left the room, he pulled her with him. The chair carrier left and shut the door. All that remained was a single anonymous assistant, waiting at the back wall. Within reach but out of the picture. Only then did the boss sit.

She was a bulldog of a woman. Pale cheeks, sagging, worn with age and hard lines. Dark and mysterious eyes. Her scruffy white hair was cropped more for convenience than appearance. She wore a long gray sweater and pants. Matching cashmere, I thought. It must've been a killer in the Miami heat.

"You are Francisco Suarez," she noted, not quite a question. When she spoke, it was firm and direct. "You are the one who killed the vampire, Tunji Malu?"

I cleared my throat. "I am."

She tightened her lips and sized me up, answering with a terse nod. "I'm sorry to meet under these circumstances."

"Are you?"

Her lips twitched. "Believe it or not, your death isn't our goal. The thief was tasked with recovering an artifact you have no business possessing."

"Finders keepers."

The Gray Lady sat back and crossed her arms with a sigh. "I've been keeping abreast of your activities. We've only known about you for a few short months. Crossing paths with Simon first was unfortunate." She leaned toward me. "He is exceedingly good at his job, but he often does it mindlessly." She shrugged. "Maybe that's why he's so good at it. In this business, a conscience can get in the way."

"This is an awful supervillain speech," I said.

Something resembling a chuckle escaped her lips. A smile followed, but her eyes were glass. Clear but impassive.

"So that's it," she said, her voice softer but still stern. "You believe we're villains."

I shrugged. "While chained up and electrocuted, the thought had crossed my mind."

"Not a careless jump in logic," she agreed with another twitch of her lips. "But that is because you don't know us yet."

"I know you're in bed with drug lords. That you twist politicians under your thumb."

"Rudi Alvarez was Connor's project," she said.

"Simon seemed awfully invested in the *project* when he kidnapped a silvan princess to protect him."

The woman's breath caught for a moment. She didn't like being talked back to, but she also understood my point of view.

"This is an ugly world, Francisco. There are ugly people in it. Usually they're the ones who end up in positions of power. Leadership doesn't just fall into anybody's lap. It needs to be taken. And only those with both the desire and ability to take that power get it."

"Lady, you're making my point for me."

She chewed her lip brusquely. "My name is Margo Gray. And I'm not just some lady. Lady Gray, if you like. But most who fear my power simply go with the Gray Lady." She paused on that note to let it sink in. "There's that word again. Power. It's true that I've worked hard for mine, and it's true that such proclivities put me in touch with many bad people. How is that any different from your black magic pursuits?"

I remained silent, wondering where she was going with this.

Margo looked past me wistfully. "In the days when this country first formed, the air was turbulent. The common folk were both the biggest troublemakers and the strongest assets of this land. Much was built on their backs. And much ugliness was necessary." She focused on me again. "Nations are not birthed by smiles, Francisco. It takes blood to bear something so robust."

Damn, she was talking about the dawn of America. A part of me wondered if she'd been around for it, but people don't live that long.

"The Society of Free Thinkers was formed at a time when the only other choice was extermination. Extinction. And yes, our collective didn't shy from battlegrounds. The only way to get anything done back then was to fight for it."

"And now?" I asked.

"I won't debate moralities with a thug. The Society is no longer an army. We no longer preach Manifest Destiny. In today's world, being territorial means having influence. We will always make sure our ilk has influence."

"I'm still waiting for the part where you explain why Connor Hatch is a necessary evil."

Margo lifted her chin. "I wouldn't expect such a coarse instrument as yourself to understand the delicate surgery with which we affect the world, but it is sufficient to know that we didn't create Connor Hatch. Whatever or whoever took control of the Caribbean would've been a big enough player to participate in open dialog with the Society, because we, like you, are a casualty of circumstance."

"Circumstance didn't make me, Lady Gray."

"Perhaps," she hedged. "But then, circumstance hasn't made us enemies, either. That is the result of your doing.

But it doesn't need to be so."

I was dying to get to the point, but I knew Margo had to do things her way. I waited. It's not that I bought into the good-cop act. A chair and civilized conversation weren't gonna flip my perspective, but at least I wasn't getting tortured.

The door cracked open. The man in black spun around and warded off the intruder, but Simon scowled and pushed past.

"Ma'am," he called, holding up a phone. *My* phone.

"What is it?"

"A call," he said, "for our guest."

She turned to me. I shrugged. Margo held her hand over her shoulder and waved him forward.

The enforcer stomped up to me, wondering what designs I had. But there were no tricks—at least not yet. I knew what was going on less than they did. He handed me the phone and backed away.

"Uh... Hello?" I said, holding the phone a couple inches from my ear in case this was some sort of practical joke.

"Cisco!" cried Milena, relieved to hear my voice. "You didn't have anything to do with this, did you?"

Margo and Simon watched me curiously. I pulled the phone flush to my ear. "With what?"

"Where are you?" she asked.

"I... I can't really get into that right now. Did I have anything to do with what?"

"*Dios mío*. You don't know?"

"Know what, Milena?"

Her voice hitched. "It's all over the news, Cisco. Your daughter, Fran—she's been kidnapped!"

My heart flushed with heat. It turned over on a spit. "What?"

"It's on the news right now," she said. "I only noticed because I saw Evan's picture. They're saying a police officer's daughter was stolen right from her bedroom as she was going to sleep. Nobody saw anyone or knows what could've happened. I thought..." Her words turned to stutters.

My grip on the phone tightened. "Petrovic." I said plainly.

That was what Petrovic had referenced back at the Port. He'd been attacking ancillary connections to me, like Hernan. Apparently he hadn't had the go ahead to go after the Covey. But I'd backed the jinn into a corner. Made him desperate. He'd taken his gang of assassins off their leash.

Emily had given the last ten years of her life to the drug lord. She'd been an unwilling participant, a victim of the heartstone. She'd sacrificed everything for him. Including her sister. And Connor Hatch had just green-lit her daughter.

I shook against my chains. Simon hopped backward but Margo just watched. They were all inconsequential. I barely registered them. All I saw was blood and blackness seeping over my thoughts.

"How's Hernan?" I asked.

"He's okay. But you shouldn't worry about me right now. You should worry about your daughter. Evan and Emily."

"Get to their house as soon as possible," I told her. "Tell Emily I'm on my way."

"Whatever you need." She paused a moment. "I'm

scared, Cisco."

My fist began to shake in my white-knuckled grip. "They're the ones who should be scared."

Simon tried to pry the phone away. The call was over and he didn't want me getting worked up. He leveraged both arms against me. I released the phone and lifted my head square with Margo.

"I need to get out of here," I said flatly.

She studied me in silence.

Simon backed away, checking the phone number. "Sorry, buddy. It ain't gonna happen."

I growled. "I'm leaving here with or without your blessing."

He snickered and looked at Margo. "What did I tell you about this guy? Cockiest son of a bitch I've met." He leaned toward me (but made sure to keep out of my reach). "Explain it to me. How're you gonna meet this girl when you're locked up here?"

If I could hurt with my eyes, he would've been pushing daisies. "They kidnapped my friend's nine-year-old daughter."

Their eyes widened. It was the first time I'd seen an emotion on the Gray Lady's face. Simon backed away and cleared his throat, but he shook it off. His rationalizations returned.

"Sick fucks. It wouldn't have been *my* course of action—even I'm not that much of an animal—but you did screw with a jinn. What did you think was gonna happen?"

I lunged at him. He was close and I was fast, but he was faster. The streaks of lightning darted from his fingers and engulfed me. I screamed as they met my flesh. I tried to bowl through them. I didn't care how much it hurt as long as I got to this asshole. For a second, I thought I could make it.

Then my head jerked backward as the steel around my neck caught. I stumbled and kicked out my legs anyway. It was a feeble shot that barely brushed the lightning wizard.

Everything was too much, then. The choking. The strain of his spellcraft. I collapsed backward, breaking the chair as I fell on it.

"Simon!" snapped Margo sharply. Her nameless assistant was already at her side, attempting to pull her away. She stood and brushed off further attempts at retreat.

I hung close to the floor, trying to roll over and catch my breath. As I did, Simon pitched my burner to the concrete. It shattered. Then he stomped it under his wingtips until it exploded into circuits and plastic.

"You can't..." I snarled, pushing to my feet. "The Society doesn't want to be a party to this kidnapping."

Margo crossed her arms firmly. "We certainly do not, Francisco. I give you my word that we had nothing to do with this. Like I've said, there are plenty of bad people in this world without us."

"Your word's not good enough," I returned. "You need to let me go. I need to deal with them."

The Gray Lady lifted her eyebrows. "I don't *need* to do anything," she corrected.

"You told me you weren't villains. You told me we didn't need to be enemies. Prove it. Let me go and we can pick this up later."

She frowned at the broken phone on the floor. Then considered me. "I'm afraid I can't do that." She moved for the exit. Simon and the man in black followed.

"You have to let me out of here!" I screamed. The Gray Lady didn't even turn around. They left the room and locked it tight, leaving me in isolation.

Harried conversation erupted on the other side of the door. I couldn't make it out. I couldn't hear any of it.

My thoughts were too loud now. They were berating me for letting this happen. Wailing for being too dumb, too slow, too tainted.

Me. My family. My friends. They all suffered because of me.

And it was happening all over again.

Chapter 33

My chains didn't break. The beam didn't budge. My metallurgy was useless. I struggled in vain for what seemed like forever but was probably ten minutes. Then I fell against the shelving. My body was exhausted but my mind was racing. By the time the metal door opened again, I was a broken wreck squinting against the light.

The Gray Lady marched in followed by the troupe of Society animists. Something was up. They stopped a good six feet away. Instead of causing a scene, I quietly lifted my head.

"I see that you've composed yourself," she said.

Composed. That was a funny way to put it considering the mess I was in. Blood staining my shirt. My neck and wrists bruised to hell. Char marks dotting my flesh. I was soaking in a sheen of my own sweat, half exhausted and probably half dead.

"I have a solution for you," she started. "No one wants to see a child harmed. We'll bargain with Connor on your behalf."

I spat on the floor. Not out of contempt, but because there was too much bloody saliva in my mouth. I would've choked otherwise. "Out of the goodness of your heart, huh?"

"Out of common decency," she returned. "But we need to know we can trust you. That we are allies." She cocked her head. "If you provide us with some form of trust, we'll know we can rely on you. Say, the Horn of Subjugation?"

I laughed hysterically. The tracking program pop-up flashed in my mind. "Well, I hate to disappoint you, but I don't have it."

The air in the room went bad. As if the stink of sweat and blood wasn't enough, now their desperation and disappointment added to the mix.

Simon scoffed. "You're all talk, aren't you? You thumb your nose at the greedy and corrupt, but here you are, playing your cards close to your chest when a child's life is on the line."

I laughed again. Perfect. They didn't believe me. Of course they didn't believe me.

It was clear they weren't going to let me just walk out of here. But then, I'd already figured that part out.

"You really wanna help me find her?" I asked.

"Yes," answered Darcy quickly.

Margo glared at her sharply for speaking out of turn and then turned to me and resumed her smile. "We can try."

I reached into my back pocket for my ace. When I was searched, Shen hadn't noticed it because it was paper thin. He couldn't feel it against my jeans. I flashed Petrovic's card between my fingers.

"You know what this is?"

Simon went to grab it but I snatched my hand away. He teetered on the edge of my reach, unwilling to get closer. After a grumble, he glared at the doorway. Darcy had already left the room. Shen realized his failure to properly search me. He kept his eyes down and retreated to the corner. He sat and crossed his legs. Simon muttered something about kids and finding good help. Then he turned to me cautiously.

"What is that?"

I held the symbol up to the light so they could see. "*Kree*," I said.

Margo's eyes widened. "The Vucari."

"Yeah," I answered. "You know who they are?"

"Of course. Do you, Francisco?"

I grimaced against the chains. "Slavic reject mercenaries."

"That is *what* they are, not *who*." She studied the card carefully. "They were human once, from a line of Slavic pagans. They honored several patrons as gods. The sect worshipped Dažbog in its early days, but a fringe group fractured the line and took over. The new Vucari call themselves the Sons of Van."

I furrowed my brow and mouthed the word, wondering if it was useful to me. "Van."

She smiled politely and continued when she didn't see recognition on my face. "Van is the scorned son of Dažbog. Caught between a stringent father and a bitter mother, he was often used as a pawn. Van is the son of Life and Death. Loved by neither, empowered by both. Devout followers of Van reject that anything on this planet is meaningful. Everything is expendable. Nothing is sacred."

I ground my teeth hard.

Simon shook his head in mock sympathy. "Sounds like you got a real psychopath on your hands, brother."

I remained perfectly still, but my eyes found him. I waved the card in the air.

The enforcer slowly raised his hand, like he was facing a gun. "Hold it, now. That's a lodestar. A beacon. If you use it, you'll rain hell on all of us."

I glowered. "Maybe that's what we all deserve."

Simon's face slackened. He turned to the Gray Lady. She narrowed her eyes. "You wouldn't."

"I don't have a lot to lose, lady." I stood, leaning sideways so as not to pressure my neck. "You left me with a lot of time to think," I told her. "And not a lot of possessions. You took my fetishes, my weapons, but you didn't take the card. So I thought about it. The character, *Kree*. It's Proto-Slavic for blood. At first I thought it was a threat, like things would get bloody if I didn't show myself. True enough, but I realized it was simpler than that. More direct."

They both took a hesitant step away from me.

"This is a calling card," I explained. "Activated by my blood. And thanks to your friends, there's plenty of that to go around." I spat on the floor again. It wasn't enough blood but it made my point.

Simon grasped for the card again. I drew it away. Protected it with my body. Let him shock me all he wanted but I was gonna hold onto that card.

I stared him down. "Give me the key to get out of here and none of us needs to find out what hell feels like."

Simon froze. The Gray Lady lifted her chin. "Impossible."

I hissed. I didn't have a lot of time and the old lady was stubborn. "Give me my dog collar then."

Simon snorted. "That's not gonna save you, brother. Now look, if you don't give me that card I'm gonna take it." He was talking tough, but hesitation weakened his voice.

"Try it and the signal fire goes out," I warned.

The enforcer nodded and chuckled as a nervous release.

"Do it," said the Gray Lady.

He turned to her, puzzled.

"Do it," she repeated. "The steel will keep him bound. His shadows are nothing to me."

Simon took a moment to show his displeasure but went to the shelf and grabbed the dog fetish. "Even trade," he said. "We both hand it over at the same time, right hand to left. No tricks."

"No tricks," I agreed.

I held the card out. He lifted his hand to take it and offered the fetish. We snatched the objects from each other.

"Stupid prick!" he yelled in relief. He backed away and flipped the card in his hand, examining it. I hastily wrapped the collar around my wrist.

"It's genuine too," he continued. Simon ripped the paper card and let the shreds flutter to the floor. "Well, that was your chance." He scattered the paper with his shoes. "You're not getting that back."

I bedeviled him with a smile. I lifted my shirt and showed them my side. A long cut ran across my ribs, deep enough to well with considerable blood. "Then it's a good thing I activated it ten minutes ago."

All the tart smugness in his face dried up. Their eyes darted to the piece of circuit board on the floor. A piece of my phone. I had sliced myself open with it.

Cracking glass echoed in the large warehouse. Within

seconds it was followed by others. The windows along the street were breaking. The Vucari were here.

Chapter 34

Shen sprang to his feet. The door swung open. The animists spun around, their hands at the ready. Darcy and two men in black rushed in with pistols drawn. Margo motioned them to cover the door, and they wordlessly obeyed. Their fire was precise and coordinated.

"Get me out of here," I urged. "I can help you fight."

Simon scoffed. "You made this bed, partner."

One of the men at the door tumbled backward, tackled by a flash of movement. It was unlike anything I'd ever seen. A foggy, translucent darkness, dotted with sparkles. It reminded me of the night sky and twinkling stars, except this image came in the shape of a raging wolf. The beast moved in a blur. It ripped the assistant's throat out.

So the Sons of Van had spellcraft of their own. Pagan animists, Margo had said. They were some kind of Serbian wolf cult and we were now seeing what they were capable of firsthand.

Another hooded figure fired at the manifestation. His bullets didn't harm the magical being. It spun to face the new threat.

Darcy thrust her statue forward and catapulted the animal back through the door. Multiple howls came from outside.

"Spectral wolves!" announced Margo. "Fight them with spellcraft! Drive them out into the night, where they can be dispelled!"

Simon fell in at her side, working up a wall of white-hot energy to cover their movement. They charged through the open doorway. Shen Santos readied at their back.

I struggled against the steel. "Shen. Let me help you."

The illusionist paused and turned to me. Unlike the more experienced animists, he was scared. He worked his jaw. Then he shook his head. He followed Darcy to the exit. Shen was the last of the group heading out.

"So be it," I muttered.

I raised my right arm, now sporting my studded dog collar. A tendril of shadow caught Shen's neck and jerked him toward me, slamming him on the floor. I reeled him in like a panicking fish without his companions noticing.

Suddenly, Shen disappeared. He flashed out and three versions of him stood over me, pulling pistols.

I shut my eyes. I reached for the tip of my shadow until my hands clasped the man's shoulders. That was real. Everything else was his illusion, trying to throw me off.

I scratched at him, feeling for his neck. A stray kick caught my side. I leaned into him as much as my collar allowed. Keeping my eyes shut, my grip came up with his tie. I yanked him into me and slammed my forehead into his.

The kicking stopped.

I looked again. The multiple Shens were gone. Now he was just a dazed man in my arms. I found Shyla's key dangling on a chain around his neck. Then I realized someone was watching and spun toward the door again.

Darcy stood boldly, eyes wide, Hecate pointed at me.

I froze, but it was of my own volition.

Slowly, I rested Shen on the floor. Gently. He rolled over, stunned like a grounded boxer. I waited another moment, the chain dangling from my fingers. Darcy had the statuette drawn but wasn't making a move. Once I realized that, I lifted the key to the bar on my neck and twisted it open.

The witch waved her hand. Shen slid along the floor to her. She planted her shoulder under his and helped him up. She made it look ridiculously easy. I assumed her spellcraft was assisting. She locked eyes with me once more and nodded. I returned the nod and undid my arm bars. Darcy walked Shen from the room to join her team.

When the last shackle fell to the floor, I was already across the room scooping my items from the shelf. I dropped my shotgun into the shadow. I refastened my belt pouch. I considered following everybody out the door, but I looked up and had a better idea.

The closet was one of several subrooms, a collection of divider walls with doors. The open ceiling above gave me an alternate escape. I used the metal shelves as a ladder and climbed to the top. It rewarded me a nice vantage of the carnage.

The Society was formidable, but I counted five spectral wolves. The beings hunted like their animal counterparts, using pack tactics and focusing on the weaker enemies. Another man in black was dead and another was wounded.

Darcy and Simon held off the wolves with their powerful magic. Margo worked her hands, but I couldn't see what kind of spellcraft she channeled. And with Shen in the mix, I couldn't trust my eyes out there anymore.

Despite the sudden ambush, the animists were driving the astral attack back. Darcy flung the garage door open. Shen masked his team's location. Already they were forming a line to maneuver the beasts outside.

The damned Vucari. They didn't even show up to their own appointment. They were counting on cult magic and a death squad of magical beasts to handle their business. That meant there was no one here to interrogate. To ask about Fran. Kasper had been right. This had all been a trap.

Then again, I'd figured as much. This was a fight I didn't need to join.

I scurried over the top of the shelf to the back wall, where high windows lined the ceiling. They were angled open to let the heat out. It wasn't big enough for a person to squeeze through, but without my chains I was once again free to phase. I leapt at the window, became shadow, and landed twelve feet below in the alley outside.

It was a bit of a tumble, but by that point I was used to that kind of thing. What mattered was Cisco Suarez was free again.

And he was hella pissed too.

Chapter 35

The taxi slowed as it rounded a parked police car. Evan's entire block was lined with them, each silently strobing red and blue. The driver dropped me off a few houses away. I paid while eyeing the crowd of uniforms milling in Evan's yard.

Holy hell. This was what it looked like when one of the City of Miami's own got victimized.

The taxi pulled away without me. I swallowed nervously. This wasn't exactly my cup of tea. I was an outlaw and this house was crawling with badges. Whether or not I had an active warrant, I had to go in there. Fran was in danger. Nothing could back me down.

I stepped through their ranks, keeping my head down, hoping nobody noticed the guy in the bloody tank top.

Yeah, right.

All eyes were on Cisco Suarez. I stood out like a virus pushing through white blood cells, each ready to strike in unison if alerted.

"What's your business here?" asked the man at the door.

"Just a friend," I answered. I stepped lightly onto the porch.

He shoved me back down. Not violently, but assertively.

"No visitors tonight."

I shook my head. "I don't have time for this. I need to talk to Evan and Emily now. This is private property and you can't stop me."

"I can't what?" asked the officer in challenge.

"Hold up," came a voice to our side. Just my luck. Of all the cops in all the world, it was the skinhead rookie Shyla knocked around a couple hours earlier. He converged on us quickly with his hand on his gun belt.

I watched him passively. Calmly. Not giving him a reason to pull his weapon. He still had his uniform on. I figured he'd be decked up in a hospital suite, but maybe his injuries weren't that bad. For all I knew he was clocked out and showing support for Evan. I took a slow breath while he looked me over. He was wondering what to do. I was wondering how to get outta here without hurting him.

"You know the lieutenant?" asked the rookie.

"Since elementary school," I said carefully.

He worked his brow. I wondered if he'd told anybody what he'd seen on Miami Avenue. Hard to fit in as the new guy when you start seeing demons.

The rookie slapped the doorman on the shoulder. "This guy's okay," he said.

The other officer narrowed his eyes and wanted to say something. Laziness won out and he shrugged instead. "It's your ass," he told the rookie, and then proceeded to pretend I wasn't there. No apology or anything, but he wasn't in my way anymore. I gave the rookie a silent nod and stepped inside.

There was a lot of blue in the house. Cops leaning against walls and sitting on extra chairs. This wasn't a crime scene so much as a hub for emotional support. Close friends. Some of these guys didn't have uniforms on, but I could tell they were cops by the way they stood and spoke. No doubt they'd come over as soon as they heard the news. Beside the kitchen, a crowd huddled around Evan.

"Thank God!" cried Milena as she bore down on me. She clasped me tightly. "I don't know what I'm doing here. I feel like a fiftieth wheel."

I tried to smile. "I see you've finally got that expression down." She pulled away, eager for a serious answer. "It's important that you're here," I told her. "We're all facing the same threat."

"Facing?" she asked. "Cisco, I *killed* someone!"

"Shh!" I pulled her away from the ears of Miami's finest. Milena didn't seem to care.

"He wasn't even the right one," she said. "I killed the wrong guy. And now look what happened."

"Don't do this to yourself, Milena. Listen to me. Darko was a piece of shit. He would've done the same thing Petrovic did. He wasn't even human, so don't beat yourself up about it."

She swallowed, dejected. "He sure looked human enough."

"Maybe he was once. Like a vampire or a zombie. But he wasn't human anymore." I waited until she digested that and met my eyes. "He was a monster, Milena. And Petrovic taking Fran had nothing to do with Darko."

She just shrugged. It didn't matter.

I shook my head and surveyed the room. "Where's Emily?"

Milena led me by the hand. We went upstairs, where it

was quieter. This was the private space. The family space. Emily sat on her bed in a dim room. Her eyes softened as Milena returned, like she was welcome company. I guess, given the circumstances, they'd dropped their defenses against each other.

When Emily saw me, I could tell she was conflicted. Would she lean on me or knock me over? She stood abruptly. "They took her, Cisco."

"I know," I said. I hugged her tight. She didn't push away. "Tell me what happened."

"It was so quick," she started, speaking with a strange emotional detachment. "Evan and I were downstairs watching a movie and Fran screamed. Evan went to check on her. I saw a man in the backyard running away. I panicked. I figured we had a stalker or something and Fran got scared. I ran up after Evan. But she was already gone." Emily dropped her head. "I should have gone after that intruder. We did, afterwards. But it was too late. There was nothing, Cisco... There was nothing..."

I held her and said, "We'll get her back." I knew it in my bones to be true. I needed her to know it too.

Emily stood straight and wiped her face. "I tried to track her," she offered, showing me a crystal ball on the bed.

"You can scry?"

"Not technically, but light magic has illuminative properties."

I peeked into the ball but just saw my big dumb upside-down reflection. She snatched it from me.

"You shouldn't touch that."

I brushed the comment away. "So what are you saying? You should be able to find Fran in there?"

She sat on the bed again. "Yes. The people close to me, the ones that share my living space and see me every day—you could say I'm attuned to them."

"Evan and Fran."

She nodded.

"And what do you see?"

"That's just it. I— I'm not like you, Cisco. Or my sister either. I'm not brave. I didn't know what to do in the face of it all. I'd give my life for Fran but when the time came, I just panicked."

"Don't say that. This was a coordinated strike."

She didn't want to hear it so she moved on. "Evan contacted the police and ran around outside. By the time I found some time alone to consult the crystal, there was nothing left to see."

The room fell silent. It was a heavy thing. Suffocating. I was afraid to speak, but I had to know.

"Does that mean—"

"I should still see her," stressed Emily. "If she was..."

I released a heavy breath. "Okay, so that means they're blocking her somehow. Jamming the Intrinsics. That's not so bad."

We all pretended to be comforted.

"Tell him what they left," urged Milena.

"Of course." Emily pointed to the dresser. To a calling card with the same plaid backing.

I flipped it over. Instead of a Proto-Slavic character, a skull was pictured on the face.

"It's not active," said Emily. "Milena told me about your other card, that it was meant to contact them." She swallowed. "This one isn't enchanted. It's just a message. A taunt. I think they're gonna kill her, Cisco."

I shook my head. "No way." I took the card to a dark corner of the room and let the shadow seep into my irises. I didn't see a glow. I didn't see anything. I wasn't a scribe like Kasper but, as far as I could tell, this was just a piece of thick paper stock.

"But you can use the other card," suggested Milena. "Right?"

"I activated it already," I said. "It was worthless. A trap, like we thought."

Emily covered her face again. "Then we have nothing."

"No. I know who these people are. And I know what they want." I placed the card on the bed. "That skull is pre-printed, but the eyes are filled in with a red marker. Glowing red eyes. It's the Spaniard."

Milena flashed recognition. "They want the Horn."

"Bingo. That's what they've always wanted, from the beginning. That's why we met in the first place, Emily."

The gears in Emily's head starting turning. I could see the scenarios playing out across her face. The anticipation of getting Fran back. "You have the Horn," she whispered, excitement tingeing her voice. "You have the Horn." She sprang from the bed. "You have to give it to them!"

I steadied her shoulders and closed my eyes. My mouth twitched. "I would, Em. In a heartbeat. But I don't have it right now."

When I looked again, the hope in her expression had cracked like an antiquated mask. Like it hadn't been there for hundreds of years. Panic shone beneath.

The bedroom door opened slowly. Evan Cross blinked in disbelief.

"Of all the people to show their face here," he said, voice moribund. "I didn't think you had the balls, Cisco."

I sighed in frustration. That was the bell for Round Two.

Chapter 36

Evan stomped toward me, but he wasn't looking for a fight. He stopped sharp. Frowned at his wife. My friend was worn out. Worry lines marred his face, aged in just a few short hours. In the absence of anything else productive to do, his hands shot to the sky in futility.

"I told you," he said. "I told you. Was it too much to ask, Cisco?"

I took a breath. "Evan..."

"Was it too much to ask to lie low? To not piss off drug dealers?" He raised his voice and it cracked. "To *not* get Fran abducted?"

I bit down hard. Evan and Emily were friends. I hated seeing them like this. But this wasn't a situation I could've walked away from. As much as I liked blaming myself, I wasn't convinced this was my fault. Maybe I couldn't accept that it was.

"I didn't do this, Evan."

He laughed my objection away. "Don't tell me that. You're the only one perpetrating violence in the streets. You're the only one going outside the law and pressing the cartel."

My eyes met his. "I'm not the one who brought Connor

Hatch into the mix. Emily did," I yelled.

I froze, realizing I hadn't meant to accuse her. I mean, it was true, but I wasn't heartless. We didn't need to be throwing around blame right now. But maybe it was the truth that needed to be said. If everybody else could be an emotional wreck once in a while, why couldn't I? I had feelings. I'd been wronged. So I bit back my apology and waited.

But then I lightened my tone. "Look, we all know the history of the Covey here. Kita got Emily involved, in over her head, before I ever met her. Connor Hatch was pulling those strings before Fran was ever conceived. Emily, Fran—they were always gonna be leverage to him."

Evan crossed his arms and hardened his features. He knew I wasn't wrong. For her part, Emily didn't object. No doubt she'd been telling herself worse than anything I could say anyway. Connor's overarching plans may have screwed up our relationships forever, but I wasn't gonna let him mess up my daughter's life.

"He's right, Evan," said Emily. "And it's worse than that." She dropped her head in shame. "Fran's conception was by Connor's order."

My face twisted just as Evan's did. "What?" we both said.

"It was always that way with Connor. Dividing us against our parents. Orphaning us so we only had him to turn to. Classic psychological manipulation. No doubt he had plans for Fran as well."

I could barely stomach that. The jinn had run the Covey like a cult. Taking advantage of adult animists was one thing, but starting on children?

"Connor won't stop," she said unequivocally. "We need to deal with him. For the sake of our family." She shook her head. "It's all my fault."

"That's not the point now," I said. "You guys, you're my family. All of you. You're all I have left."

Evan turned away. I still couldn't get a read on Emily, but at least Milena smiled.

"We've all been through the shit," I told them. "We've all been forced into lives we hadn't planned. But we're here now. We're together. We can work together."

My best friend met my eyes. I could see the struggle within him. The conflicting loyalties, the attempt to resolve our hijacked pasts. When he teared up, it was evident how worried he was for Fran. How helpless he felt.

How much he loved my daughter. Because she was his daughter too.

I fought off watery eyes with him. I had nothing but respect for this man.

"Evan," I said slowly, "buddy. There's only one way to end this oppression. There's only one way to free ourselves from Connor Hatch. I hate to say it, but it doesn't involve a bunch of guys in blue uniforms."

"They can help," he insisted.

I nodded. "And maybe we can use that. But we're talking about spellcraft here. If the law doesn't recognize magic, it can't possibly serve justice to those who abuse it."

He didn't answer.

"What about his island?" offered Emily. "He's kidnapped people there before."

"Maybe," I reasoned. "Although I have reason to believe he's still in Miami."

"He's a jinn," Milena cut in. "Can't he just blink over there?"

"Not with Fran. Anybody or anything that goes with him will hold him back. I've seen teleportation magic before, but that package was used by a Society enforcer. And they're not in on this."

Evan grinded his teeth. "Society?"

I sighed. "You're not gonna believe this, but they're essentially a group of animist lobbyists."

"Like a fucking wizard's guild?" He was incredulous. "Like some Harry Potter shit?"

"They have a business relationship with Connor, but that's all I know. They won't help us so we can't worry about them right now."

Evan grumbled. "I can't believe this is all going on behind the scenes. Unchecked."

It must be hard on him. He lived in a world of law and order. He'd seen those rules bent and broken, but spellcraft had its own rules. He had no idea how to deal with that. Faced with the possibility of never seeing his daughter again, it was finally sinking in.

"No one knows about the Society," I explained, "so no one targets them. That's exactly the way these guys want it. But you guys have me for that. You need every hand on deck here. You need every dirty trick I can muster. You need me here, and you know it."

My friend lifted his chin, mulling it over. "What do you have in mind?"

"First off, if Emily forged some kind of link with Fran, we need to keep working that angle." I turned to her. "What I don't understand is how your crystal ball can't get a fix on her at all. If you can track her then shouldn't there be some sort of footprint left behind? I mean, I get that you didn't start the spell until it was too late and she was hidden, but shouldn't your light magic reveal an afterimage of the Intrinsics? Can't you start with her echo in this house?"

I stood at the ready, feeling I'd put together a solid metaphysical argument, but three blank faces stared back at me. Emily scooped the crystal ball into her lap. Milena swiveled her head in alarm.

"Uh," I ventured. "Was it something I said?"

Evan slowly turned to his wife. "What is he talking about, light magic?"

I slapped my forehead. "You didn't tell him," I said flatly. My friend's face went beet red. He glanced my way. I stepped away and shrugged. "Sorry, bro. She had us both fooled. I only recently found out she was an animist myself."

"You?" he asked his wife, like he was charging her with murder. "You can use magic?"

She grinned meekly. "Remember when I said there were parts of me I wanted to forget?"

"Yeah. I thought you meant your family. I thought you meant—" He stumbled on his words as his brain tried to catch up. "Magic?"

Evan collapsed to the bed. After everything that had happened—his boss being a criminal, Kita Mariko revealed as family, his wife's involvement with the Covey—Evan had a lot of things to come to terms with. The fact that Emily had been under the suggestion of a heartstone alleviated matters. It really did. But now, learning that his wife was an animist in her own right, he went quiet and broody. Emily leaned into her husband's chest, but neither of them could muster their voice.

I put my hands on my hips and turned away. Milena shook her head. "Smooth move, Cisco."

I avoided eye contact with the moping couple. I pitched my voice, hopeful. "The truth will set them free?"

She was not amused.

I waved it off. "We don't have time for this. Anyway, this whole thing is simpler than we thought. There are lots of players but we don't need to handle them all."

Evan and Emily didn't stir but at least Milena was listening. I continued.

"We can forget about Connor for now. We don't need to worry about the Society. What matters right now is who has Fran. That's Petrovic's card. The same guy who beat up Hernan. Our primary concern is the Vucari."

Milena chewed her lip. "Vucari... Where have I heard that before?"

I looked at my boot. "It was, uh, what Darko said before he died."

Milena's eyes narrowed.

"Listen," I said. "I know this isn't your fight."

"Are you kidding me right now?" she asked.

"Okay, maybe I could've phrased that better. All I mean is that Connor doesn't have his hooks into you."

She jutted her chin out. "He came after my family too, Cisco. And just in case you haven't noticed, I've got your back."

I stopped arguing and smiled. "Yes," I said, "you always do."

"Then I'm in."

I beamed. Milena rested her palm on my shoulder and

rubbed lightly.

"But that's not where I remember the word Vucari from," she noted, pulling out the phone she'd swiped from the Russian strip club owner. She scrolled through the contacts and showed me the entry.

"Vucari."

Chapter 37

Evan snapped out of his funk. "You have a contact number?"

Milena tossed the phone to his lap.

"Vucari," he read. "These are Connor's people?"

I crossed my arms. "They're a fringe group of Serbians who do odd jobs for the Russian mob. Right now, both of them have contracts with Connor. To be honest, I still don't know how the plain-old Russians fit in, but the Vucari are the ones actively hunting me. And the Horn."

Evan looked puzzled.

"It's a long story," I said. "Emily can catch you up sometime. It's an artifact they want that I don't have."

My friend turned to his wife. He almost said something. Then he rubbed his eyes and shook it off. "I think," he said, gently pushing Emily away, "everyone needs to get their heads out of their asses. Including me." He stood and gave his wife a sideways glance. "We can settle accounts later. For now we have a lead. We need to move fast."

I set my jaw. "Damn straight."

"I know a guy in Felony Apprehension who can get me a location on this."

"Except we don't know who's on the other end of that

line," said Milena.

"It's a lead," he shot back.

"True," I interjected, "but these guys aren't human. They're super strong and grow canine heads and summon spectral wolves. Like I said, it's not a job for your friendly neighborhood police."

Evan made a face like I was speaking Greek. "But guns should hurt them?"

"Probably. They shrug off damage pretty well, but they can be pounded down."

"Good enough for me," he concluded. "I can set up a dummy call if I need to. But we can get a fix from the towers without that." He stormed out of the room with a new mission.

I was glad to set him on something, but I had a feeling spellcraft was a better bet. "Emily?"

She shook away her destitute gaze. "Yes?"

"Your magic?" I reminded, shutting the door again.

"I tried." She presented the crystal ball. "Those signatures are too faint. I can get a flickering of activity in the house, but anything further gets washed out by the noise of the city."

"Washed out?"

She inhaled sharply and focused her thoughts. "Yes. The Intrinsics shift all around us. You know that. Miami's too densely populated to fixate on a single fading trail. There's too much light."

"Too much light you say?" I licked my lips and cracked my knuckles. "Emily, you've come to the right man. What if I could filter that light? Apply a layer of darkness to your scrying?" She raised a skeptical eyebrow. "Seriously. Right now it's like you're stargazing in the middle of the day. Let me make it night."

She folded her lip under her teeth. "That might actually work."

We got to it. Emily explained her process with the crystal. It wasn't infused with magic itself, but it served as a lens for her to bend light through. She molded it into a reflection of the world.

At least, she did her best to. Varying degrees of talents can execute all sorts of tricks with crystal. Many look for echoes of the past or visions of the future. It's easiest to focus on people or objects you're close to. Even then, it's sometimes a crapshoot as to which perspective will be reflected back at you.

Emily had been trained by some bad people, but she was essentially a white witch. Though her power wasn't finely honed yet, it had impressive potential. I believed she could find Fran. She pulled out her crystal ball again.

"No," I said. "Let's start at the source."

Emily swallowed as if afraid to comply. But she nodded and led us into my daughter's room.

I felt extreme warmth and sadness at the same time. Fran wasn't yet into the stage where music posters plastered her walls. She hadn't given up her stuffed animal collection either, but they'd graduated from the bed to a place on the bookshelf. I was happy to see fantasy novels beside them. Taking after her old man. The fairy doll I'd given her was on the shelf too. It was the only pink thing in the entire room, but she'd kept it for some reason. In some ways, this glimpse of her personal sanctuary was the closest I'd been to seeing who Fran really was. But the room was just a place. It was empty.

Emily placed the crystal on a square of black felt in the center of the bed. Her fingers cupped the air on either side of it. Light danced between her palms. This wasn't like Simon's lightning—crackling and vulgar. This was subtle. An aura of feeling more than a special effect. The swirls of color within the glass orb, however, were most definitely not subtle.

Staring into the crystal was like drifting outside our bodies, looking down on ourselves. Emily isolated the glow around us. Keyed in on it. We wafted higher, bringing multiple rooms of the house into view without the roof obstructing us. The faint trail led through the hall and out an upstairs window.

But Emily was right. Once exposed to the madness of the city, the trail washed out. Dizzying streaks rushed past us. Blinding coronas consumed the distant skyline. It became a struggle to make anything out, much less concentrate.

I reminded myself that this wasn't the world, just a reflection within glass. I empowered the darkness. Like a virus, it multiplied, blackening the edges of the vision and crowding out the glare. Emily pushed back, teasing Fran's footprint into the foreground.

It was back and forth like that a bit, one long pointless argument, except Emily managed to follow the path north.

I bit down as we followed, nurturing the darkness as she energized the light. Confirming my suspicions, the trail had a westerly drift. If the Vucari had meant to escape the city, they would've headed to the highway or to the coast. Instead the path turned sharply inland.

And then we lost it. Neither Emily nor I could make out anything else, and the vision abruptly popped out.

I blinked away the magic. Evan was with us now, peering over my shoulder with Milena. Emily jumped when she saw her husband there. He considered her carefully, like a stranger.

"It's not much," I said. "We couldn't pinpoint a destination or current location."

"It's more than I had before," said Emily.

Evan held up the Russian cell. "The phone's a bust. Whoever used that number was last pinged at towers around the Port of Miami several hours ago, but their phone's been off since."

"The Vucari ambushed me over there. Maybe the phone dropped in the drink or they went dark or something. But what if they're still there?"

Evan didn't buy it. "The Port is too secure. It wouldn't make sense to stage anything there."

"That's 'cause you weren't there several hours ago. Trust me. They could bypass any security with spellcraft."

"But you're talking a whole boat," he said. "Could they hide that? Trust *me*, Cisco. Especially with that battle earlier, there's no way they're going back there. Besides, didn't Emily's magic just prove they didn't?"

He was right about one thing, at least. The Port of Miami had been a trap. "Connor let slide there was a real meeting somewhere," I said. "It's possible the Vucari are holing up with him at the real location. I heard a rumor about casino boats. But if not the Port, if not the coast..."

"The Miami River," concluded Evan. "The river mouth is wide enough and deep enough for just about any vessel. If you go past the hotels and yacht clubs, there're all kinds of sketchy marinas out there."

"The pictures," exclaimed Milena. She snatched the Russian phone from Evan's hand and showed him the photographs of dockside properties. They were sprinkled among loads of other unassuming pictures. We'd figured them for Russian real estate interests, but maybe the mob was scouting locations.

Evan swiped through the photos. "I don't know where this is but it's the River," he agreed.

"Okay," I said, coming around. "That has to be where they are."

They turned to me, beaming.

"But," I cautioned, "this means we're not just dealing with the Vucari. This all but confirms Connor will be there too. And if any of my intel today has been true, the Russian mob is in on this boat deal with the *Agua Fuego* cartel."

Everybody huddled together in a circle.

"We got that phone from Pop Stars," I explained. "Which is Russian territory, not Vucari. The Sons of Van were hired for a single purpose: to catch and kill me. But they answer to the jinn. If the Vucari are taking Fran to him, then maybe everybody's in the same place at the same time."

Evan let out a low whistle as we all pondered the logistics. "We need to get boots on the ground," he said. "I'll mobilize the DROP team. Finding the shipyard that matches those photos shouldn't be too difficult. And my team's supposed to log a training exercise this month anyway."

"Training," I said. "That sounds awfully close to an off-the-books operation."

Evan glared at me. He didn't say anything. I didn't push the matter.

"I'm going out there," Emily said.

"Not on your life," said Evan.

She squared her shoulders. "This is my fault and I'm fixing it."

"It's too dangerous."

"First of all," she countered, "it's too dangerous for *you*. I'm an animist. You know that now. My spellcraft will come in handy. Even if it's just to get a fix on Fran. Second, I'm the only person here who knows Connor Hatch well. I was never as tight as the rest of the Covey members, but it counts for something. Besides, I am NOT sitting at home while someone has our daughter."

I cocked my head. "I probably wouldn't argue with her on that point, buddy."

Evan winced. "You'll ride in my squad car then. Cisco?"

"You do your thing. I took a taxi here so I'm gonna hitch a ride with Milena."

She grinned. "Hopefully we don't get ambushed by poltergeists this time."

They furrowed their brows.

"Long story," I told them again. "Let me know as soon as you get word of where she is. My phone's busted but Milena's works."

"I'm not waiting," said Evan. "If I have a lead on Fran I'm taking it."

I glowered at him. It wasn't ideal, but I knew just as well as he did that every second counted. "Just give me the heads up as soon as possible. If your guys go in without me, it'll get ugly." I made for the door. "Hell, it'll get ugly anyway."

"And where will you be?" asked Emily.

I grinned. "I gotta see a girl about a Horn."

Chapter 38

"The airport?" asked Milena as she drove.

I leaned back as far as I could in her cramped hatchback. "Sure. It's close to the marinas. As soon as Evan locates our target, we'll be minutes away."

"Okay," she conceded. "But why the airport?"

"What would you do if you had three giant bags of money, lived in LA, and found yourself in the middle of a drug cartel dispute?"

She turned to me. "Get the hell out of Miami?"

"Give the nice lady a prize," I announced.

She remained skeptical. "It's a stretch, Cisco. MIA is huge. You need to be at the right terminal at the right time. How are you supposed to figure that out?"

I brought up Shyla's phone. "Let's see what Shyla's online check-in confirmation says." The thief had deleted the GPS coordinates, but she'd forgotten to delete her email. I was still logged into her inbox. We had her exact flight and boarding time.

Milena slapped my shoulder playfully. "Here I thought you were Sherlocking the hell out of this problem. Turns out it's all smoke and mirrors."

I smiled. "For my next trick, I'll help a Nigerian prince

smuggle his riches out of Africa."

She arched an eyebrow my way.

I shrugged. "She doesn't have a good spam filter."

Milena rolled her eyes. "Aren't you glossing over the fact that this demonic cat burglar nearly killed you?"

"Eh. It's not a perfect plan. But she seemed to have a code of honor. She felt bad about leaving me in the hands of the Society psychopaths."

"Wow. Sounds like an upstanding citizen."

I ignored her. My lifestyle involved lots of risk. I saw this as one of my less dangerous gambles.

The departure intake was clear. Milena dropped me off and turned into a short-term parking lot. I sprinted to the terminal. The flight wasn't departing for another two hours but I needed to be early to catch her before she went through security.

With my daughter in immediate danger, waiting really sucked. I leaned against the back wall watching the self-check-in terminals and the counter. Shyla had to come through here. As the minutes ticked by, I wondered if she already had. Milena joined me and we made each other even more antsy.

Then a woman in a leather jacket casually strolled into the check-in line. She put tags on two brand-new suitcases wrapped in clear plastic. I waited as she finished in the line. Then she wheeled the luggage to a separate attendant who checked them. I approached her from behind and caught her just as she turned.

"Boo," I said.

Shyla nearly recoiled out of her boots. We were surrounded by a sea of people. No one paid us any mind, but we'd have more witnesses than we could count if we didn't play nice. Shyla relaxed her outward appearance. Her eyes busily scanned the terminal, falling on Milena's approach. Once it was clear she wasn't surrounded, Shyla spoke calmly.

"Got away from those bastards, did you?"

I nodded. "You basically got paid for nothing."

Shyla crossed her arms. "You have to admit, it kinda worked out for both of us."

"I wouldn't be here if it did," I said firmly.

She gulped nervously and nodded. "The money."

I snorted. "Where is it, by the way? Those suitcases aren't big enough to hold your score."

"Trade secret," she answered. "I fly first class. The money has alternate accommodations."

Lucky for me, too. Those accommodations had delayed Shyla's arrival at the airport, allowing me to catch her.

"I need the Horn back," I said plainly. "I know you can still track it."

She worked her lips for a moment as she considered Milena, who only glared back. Then Shyla relaxed. "How much is it worth to you?"

"Oh, I don't know," I said, annoyed. "How about two giant garbage bags full of money? Unlike the Society, I expect value for my cash."

She chuckled, half relieved. "Fair enough." The summoner pulled out a duplicate phone and typed in the location. Her old phone buzzed in my pocket. I checked the tracking program and Coordinate Charlie was once again live.

"I'm on the next flight out of this humid paradise," she

said. "I'm putting Miami on my no-go list. You're free to chase down that artifact all you want."

"You know you gotta take off those giant boots to go through security, right?"

She smiled and studied me a moment. Shyla took a slow step backward. "If not money, what are you doing all this for, Cisco Suarez?"

I shrugged. "Everything's not about a new pair of shoes, Shyla."

"You know me so well already." Her eyes flitted down my body. "But that maxim's coming from a guy wearing cowboy boots. Seriously, what are you getting out of this?"

"It's simple," I answered. "I have to protect me and mine."

Her eyebrow twitched approvingly. "If that's what makes you happy. It was nice to meet you, Cisco." Shyla turned and disappeared into the crowd.

Milena groaned. "You didn't tell me she was pretty."

I grinned and checked the phone again. Chevalier's signal was active. Close, even. But there was a problem. I knew the location. Intimately. And if we didn't get to him fast, he was gonna blow my whole plan sky high.

Chapter 39

We pulled into the empty parking lot of Saint Martin's Cemetery. Empty because it was midnight, and nobody but necromancers and grave robbers have any business around cemeteries at midnight. This one, specifically, was special to me. It was where I was supposed to be buried.

For a decade, I hadn't rested in peace as everybody else had thought, but that hadn't meant my six-feet-deep home was unoccupied. The Spaniard had been there, buried with the Horn of Subjugation, lying in wait for me to find him. My best guess was that Chevalier wanted to put him back where he couldn't hurt anyone.

"Check it out," said Milena, pointing to the grassy area outside the distant gate. Chevalier's black van was parked behind some brush, invisible from the street.

"You might wanna stay out of their way," I said.

She gave me a chiding look and reached for the glove compartment. Before I could tell her not to bother with the stun gun, she produced a pistol.

"Is that—" I started.

"Okay, so I stole this from the van that you stole from the drug dealers."

The gun she had pulled on the bokor in the boathouse. I

didn't know what to say. "Do you know how to use that thing?"

She gave me that look again.

I shrugged it off and stretched my legs outside the Fiat. She followed me to the gate. I scooped her off the floor in both arms and carried her *Gone with the Wind* style. Then I phased forward through the shadow, pulling her with me. When we solidified on the other side of the gate, her eyes were frozen mid surprise. Then she gazed at me with wonder. This close, with her face inches from mine—it was a lovely feeling.

"Wow. You can do that all the time?"

I winked. "Perks of being me."

I eased her to the floor, disappointed that her soft body had to disengage from me.

"Follow me from a distance," I instructed. "Watch my back. Only show yourself if you need to."

She didn't look at me funny this time so I assumed she agreed with the plan. I plowed ahead, not worrying about stealth or silence, until I saw the huddled figures around my family plot.

Jean-Louis Chevalier and the two bokor initiates crouched in a semicircle facing my grave. A twice-dead zombie stood behind them at the ready. I sliced open my palm with my knife, scooped up cemetery dirt, and stomped toward them.

Ten feet away, one of the bokors turned his head to me. Chevalier spun around, startled, and rose to his feet.

"Suarez!"

I lunged sideways and wrapped the zombie around the neck. My open fist shoved bloody dirt into his mouth and I whispered in his ear. "Shh."

The corpse flopped unceremoniously to the ground.

Chevalier sighed in annoyance. "Now I have to clean that up."

He wouldn't be able to reanimate the body. After a necromancer dispels zombie magic with proper graveyard dirt, that husk is done for good. I assumed whoever the corpse was in life could be tied to Little Haiti and the Bone Saints. So yeah, Chevalier would need to dispose of the body now or leave it as evidence.

"We had a deal," I growled.

All three gangbangers readied for violence. One of the initiates drew a pistol. None, however, made a move.

"I held my end," protested Chevalier.

"You didn't say anything about stealing the Horn."

"And you didn't say anything about possessing it."

I sidestepped them to check how deep they were into my grave. The answer was not very. Only a small pit was dug from the center of my plot, a bowl a couple feet wide and eight inches deep. A small contraption of sticks in the shape of a man was staked into the hole. The twigs and dried thistles were wrapped around the Horn of Subjugation like a cage.

Necromantic circles like ours had various strategies for dealing with the dead. I'd assumed the Bone Saints were attempting to hide the artifact, but I immediately recognized the truth.

This was an offering. A pyre. A miniature wicker man.

"You aren't trying to hide the Horn," I said, face darkening. "You're trying to destroy it."

Chevalier raised his head proudly, silver earrings

swinging with the sudden movement. "Do you not wonder, Suarez, if maybe this world is better without it?"

"I wonder that all the time."

I leaned down and snatched the wicker man from the pit. The kids got antsy. The one with the gun raised it. Chevalier held up a silver-covered finger. They paused.

So did I. I was confident I could take the bokors if it came down to it, but that didn't mean they weren't dangerous.

"You have a gun on your back," called out Milena from behind a tree. She was twenty yards away. I was afraid she'd hit me if she fired, but the threat was more important.

Chevalier ground his teeth. "We make a good team, Suarez. This wouldn't be the first time we eradicated evil together."

"Killing is easier than solving problems," I said.

A hint of anger overtook his features. "Don't you know what the Horn can do?"

"Subjugation," I answered, not missing a beat. "I don't have any delusions that the Spaniard was a noble man in life. But I'm not looking to control Miami's voodoo elite. You have nothing to fear."

"It is not just control," he argued. "The Horn's power can enslave those gifted in the black arts. Assimilate them. The islanders speak of the wraith as a parasite. He doesn't just absorb our magic; he eats us alive. Corrupts our souls until we are something not quite living but not quite dead."

A shiver ran up my spine. A foot in both worlds. That didn't sound at all pleasant.

"I need the Horn to take down Connor."

Chevalier showed his teeth. "One man's quest for

vengeance is not worth the lives of my people."

I averted my eyes to the ground. "They have my daughter, Jean-Louis."

The men watched me blankly, but I felt the tide turn.

"Ever since I got on the jinn's radar," I explained, "death has followed me. Family, friends—it didn't matter. People I loved died over and over. I won't let the same thing happen to my daughter. I can't."

Moments passed under the scrutiny of the bokor. Under the winding oak tree shadowing my grave. Eventually Chevalier lowered his arm. "I cannot stand in the way of family," he said.

I nodded and snapped the wicker man over my knees. As soon as I had the Horn in my hands, the Spaniard appeared beside me in full regalia. His red eyes blazed like wildfires. The bokors shrank away in horror. One of the kids dropped to his knees in reverence.

"I shall dispatch them!" roared the Spaniard.

"You shall not," I said firmly.

The apparition turned to me, anger evident.

After consideration, I added, "They're friends."

The wraith scoffed, but he was powerless without my blessing. He did nothing.

I tossed the remaining twigs on my grave. It was a shame. The grass had just grown in after the last time I'd dug it up. Now a pit marred the green.

"You cannot let the Horn fall into the wrong hands," warned Chevalier.

"Put my grave back the way you found it," I said. I stomped away from the defeated huddle and called out with my back to them. "And some flowers would be nice."

I caught up with Milena. We encountered no trouble getting back to the Fiat.

"Nice work," I said, wrapping the Horn in a length of cloth and hitching it to my belt.

"We needed to hurry it up," she answered, showing me her phone. "Evan texted us. We have an address."

Chapter 40

"Where are they?" I asked.

Milena started her car. "Looks like small docks and a shipping yard not too far from here. The DROP team's on the way."

"Let's beat them to it," I urged. "Let's finish this."

She sat still a moment, refusing to shift into drive. "You think Petrovic's there?"

"I know it."

Milena grew introspective again. She was thinking about Hernan. Darko. What she was willing to do to protect family. Maybe what she wished she hadn't done.

"We have to go, Milena."

I understood her reluctance. She was the toughest person I knew. But she'd never killed before. This world I'd thrust her into, it was alien to her. I wondered if she belonged in it. I wondered if letting her come along was a mistake.

But Fran didn't have time for wondering.

"We have to go," I repeated.

Milena huffed, shifted into gear, and peeled out of the cemetery lot.

"You know the way?" I asked.

She nodded silently.

The Miami streets at night are almost magical. Even in the bad neighborhoods. The contrast of the illuminated lines on fresh blacktop. The glow of the city skyline. The charged tension in the air. This is the city of hurricanes and cocaine cowboys. Residents live on the razor's edge between order and lawlessness, ripe with the appreciation that it could all be blown away at any time. Tonight, the city was more radiant than ever.

"Stop moping," I said curtly.

Milena turned to me with the evil eye.

"Not you," I said.

Seconds later, the wraith appeared in the back seat. "You should have let me kill them," he rasped.

"The Bone Saints aren't the bad guys."

"They wished to destroy me." His eyes smoldered. "I doubt the efficacy of their efforts, but it would not have been pleasant. Their intent was clearly an attempt on my life."

"You don't have a life," I snapped. "You're dead. And they're afraid of you."

Naked teeth grinned sardonically. "As is my wise master."

I narrowed my eyes. "I'm the master of no one."

"Then free me."

"Once we get Connor."

The Spaniard leaned forward. "If you release me, I give you my word. I will fight the jinn beside you."

My jaw twitched. I didn't respond.

The apparition nodded. "You deny being my master, yet you do not deny being afraid of me."

I faced forward, avoiding his dark gaze. "What did Chevalier mean? About you eating the power of necromancers?" Milena flashed a worried glance in the rearview mirror.

The wraith's breath scraped against his throat. "The bokor speaks the truth," he answered. "But it is only one truth. Is it the sword's fault when it kills?"

"I'm not talking about what you are now. I'm talking about what kind of person you were in life. How many Taíno did you enslave? How many necromancers did you steal power from? What, exactly, was your endgame?"

He watched me with amused curiosity. "Brujo, you speak of the past as if it can be changed."

"We're too deep in shit to get philosophical, Spaniard."

"And we're almost there," added Milena, directing some sharpness to me as well. "Do you think we might wanna... I don't know... discuss an actual plan at some point?"

I stretched my neck. Squeezing into the cramped car was getting to me. And right now I wasn't too sure how I felt about working with the wraith. But he was spot on about being a weapon. That was exactly what I needed right now.

I exhaled long and slow and got to it. "Back at the Port, I noticed Connor lowered himself by fighting a zombie. Like, actually got down and dirty with it. At first I thought he was making a point. But then I ran into a witch who threw me around with spellcraft. She had trouble against the zombie too. Later on she kicked spectral-wolf ass, so it wasn't only the living that she worked against."

Milena finished my thought. "It was the dead that gave her trouble."

I nodded.

The wraith cocked his skull. "You wish to strike down the jinn with my hand."

"The dead have a different kind of power," I asserted. "Necromancy is a separate art. A forbidden one. Connor's used his blink magic to avoid my best attacks, but the zombie grabbed him. Maybe the undead interfere with his spellcraft."

"It is a dangerous assumption that I can hurt him."

"But it's a serious possibility. Connor can be hurt by the dead. *That's* why he wants the Horn. The undead are his weakness. With the Horn, he holds the weapon that can hurt him while also subjugating the animist population that are his biggest threat."

I thought of Tunji Malu, the vampire. As far as I knew, he was the only member of the Covey not under the spell of the heartstone. He'd served Connor willingly, but cautiously. He knew of the jinn's wrath. "That's why Tunji created me. The dead man. He strengthened my skin, gave me tattoos of protection. I wasn't just his personal hit man—I was his insurance against Connor Hatch."

"Oh," said Milena, rolling her eyes. "Well at least you don't have a persecution complex or anything."

"It's not crazy if it's true."

The Spanish conquistador leaned between us. "You are forgetting one thing, brujo. Until now, you have used my power judiciously. You have never exposed me to the jinn for fear that he might usurp that power. And now you ask me to confront him."

I licked my lips. "It's a risk."

"It doesn't have to be."

I locked eyes with him.

"Despite your protests, brujo, I am a slave. Not to you, perhaps, but to the Horn. It limits my spellcraft. It binds me to service. If you truly want the best shot at defeating the jinn, you must release me from the Horn's embrace." The apparition's shriveled fingers shook with anticipation. "I will grant you power unimaginable. I will instruct you in the lost arts. I will stand beside you against your greatest enemy."

I clenched my jaw. I'll give the Spaniard one thing. He was persistent. It was a tempting offer, made more so by the realization that the wraith was the perfect ally against Connor.

It was obvious now why so many wanted the Horn of Subjugation. Even if it had more nefarious purposes than I'd consider using, there were other gains as well. The Spaniard was wise beyond his years. A formidable necromancer in life, even more so in death. He could teach me a lot.

I wondered how much I could force out of him with a more draconian hand. But that was the temptation of power talking. That wasn't me.

Milena pulled the car along the Miami River. Its black water reflected the city lights like stars.

I steadied my voice. "What you're offering sounds like a long-term proposition. Training. Planning. Working hand in hand. We don't have time for that."

The apparition hissed. "We cannot face the jinn tonight. We are not ready. We will lose."

"We have no choice," I snapped. "We're going in there together. We're gonna do this."

"And so you crack the whip."

I grunted. "They have my daughter. Right here, right now. There's no time for anything else."

"Daughter?" The conquistador cocked his skull. The red fires within burned evenly. I wondered what thoughts drove him. Was it possible to retain any semblance of humanity in that state of undeath?

The wraith and I had made a deal fair and square. So far, for all his offers and objections, he was living up to his end of the bargain. I didn't know what kind of person he'd been, but I knew what kind of person I was. I would live up to my side of the bargain as well. When the time came, I would set him free, even if I wasn't sure it was the right thing to do.

"You see what this means, brujo?" asked the wraith somberly. "By attacking his powder trade, we had hoped to force the jinn into a corner. But he has turned the tables. He is forcing you to act in desperation."

I swallowed. It couldn't be helped.

The Spaniard leaned back in the seat and faded out. "Then the jinn has already won."

Chapter 41

We parked behind a line of police cruisers on South River Drive. A thin row of trees and a waist-high wall were all that separated the sidewalk from the marina. Multiple concrete platforms protruded into the river, some ending in narrow docks and crowded by small skiffs. A squad of police officers with DROP team uniforms held binoculars to a distant building on the largest platform.

"Where's Evan?" I asked, coming up behind them. They flinched. It probably wasn't the best idea to surprise heavily armed SWAT units, but I was full of bad ideas.

Most of the men went back to their surveillance, but one broke it down for me. "No tangos outside the building. No activity either, but we don't have eyes inside yet. The lieutenant is breaching with Drop 1."

"He's already inside?" I cursed and headed down the street.

"Hey. You can't go in there," warned the officer.

"Try and stop me," I said, not bothering to turn around. Nobody tackled me so I figured I was fine.

I cut into the property and circled the building to find Evan and three cops standing flush with the wall, weapons drawn. He did a double take when he saw me.

I patted him on the shoulder. "What do you got?"

"Movement inside. We're getting a closer look."

"Is it them?"

"We're getting a closer look," he repeated through clenched teeth.

Evan pointed to two of his men and directed them around the corner with hand signals. One held a small battering ram and the other a flash grenade. They positioned themselves on either side of the door. Evan counted with his fingers. One, two, three.

They smashed the door open, flung the flashbang inside, and took cover against the wall. I looked away. White light reflected off the ground. By the time I picked my head up, two of the officers were already breaching. Evan spun to the door.

"Miami Police!" they yelled. "Nobody move! Guns down!"

Despite the sensible instructions, chaos overtook the quiet marina warehouse. Gunfire erupted within. I thrust my arm over Evan's shoulder and sparked my shield just in time to deflect a round.

SWAT rifles returned fire. Peeking inside, I saw the problem. The warehouse was littered with metal crates. Not a maze of shipping container walls like at the Port, but plenty of cover nonetheless. Men with weapons were scattered throughout the room, hunkered down. The obstructions were good news for the officers that had already taken position, but it meant this could be an extended firefight.

"Returning fire!" yelled Evan into his radio. "DROP 2 is go!"

A door on the opposite wall crashed open. The two officers already inside crouched down behind their cover. Evan turned to me and said, "Eyes down," and then ran inside. I chased after him, shield up, watching the floor as a second grenade went off.

Panic surged through the ranks of gunmen as they realized they were surrounded. Evan and I slid into position behind a crate. I surveyed the warehouse.

"These guys are Russians," I told him.

Evan nodded and gritted his teeth. Then we both noticed Milena hunching down next to us.

"What are you doing here?" I asked.

"I clearly have no idea," she said, squeezing her eyes shut.

Errant shots went over our heads and we all ducked further.

"Screw you, pigs!" came a familiar voice. It was the Ukrainian muscle-shake junkie, at an elevated position with two other men. Between a crate and the corner of the wall, they were entrenched.

"Flash!" called out someone in DROP 2. One officer suppressed the elevated position while another lobbed a grenade across the width of the room. It came up short and popped on the near side of the wall. A couple of us, myself included, caught some of the backlash. I had to sit back to recover.

"We gotta get over there," I said.

"Negative," replied Evan. "Drop 1 is handling the center of the room. We're pinned down here. There's not enough cover to flank that position."

I growled. He was right. We were sitting ducks if we

tried anything. DROP 2 engaged the fortified position. The problem was, they couldn't advance without exposing themselves either.

"Say hello to my little friend!" screamed the Ukrainian in an offensive Cuban accent. His heart was in the right place, though. He hefted a giant military-grade cannon over his cover. I had no idea what kind of gun it was, but if video games had taught me anything, it was a BFG: a Big Fucking Gun.

Boom. Boom. Boom.

Everybody ducked as the deafening reports echoed throughout the warehouse. Holes the size of silver dollars punched into distant crates. The fire was directed at DROP 2, stemming their advance. With both teams suppressed, the Russians in the center of the warehouse had free reign to take potshots at us.

I slipped my hand from the shadow and aimed my sawed-off shotgun. The birdshot clanged against the crate protecting the elevated position. They were too far. Barring a direct hit, my shotgun was next to useless against this kind of weaponry.

Evan and another Drop 1 member suppressed the BFG with automatic fire. Now we were talking. Except there were a lot of loud bangs and sparks but not many actual hits.

Brilliant white glittered over the fortified men. At first I thought it was another stun grenade, but it was too slow and sparkly. I checked the area and saw Emily poking her head into the doorway we had breached.

Within seconds, the Ukrainian's fortified gun nest was too bright to look at. Anybody within must've been struggling. The BFG fired frantically, but the shots strayed from their targets. The Ukrainian was firing blind.

"Cover me!" I yelled. I skipped to my feet before they could talk me out of it.

Drop 1 turned their fire to the Russians on the ground. With the high ground suppressed, I was in more danger of getting shot from the side. As the enemy ducked, I ran full speed ahead at the bright corner, turning to Emily and exchanging a wordless message. I could only hope she had an idea of what I needed.

I sprinted and loaded another shell into my sawed off. A battlefront was one thing, but close combat was my jam. I leapt onto a crate, vaulted onto the box the men cowered behind, and dove into the air.

Emily had gotten the message loud and clear. At the height of my leap, the dazzling light in the area vanished. Beneath me, three mobsters huddled together. I came down on top of one and turned my weapon on the other two. I fired.

A cone of glue plastered the two men and the BFG to the side of the crate.

"That's more consideration than they gave Scarface," I noted.

DROP 2 turned their attention back to the main group of gunmen. At this point, sandwiched between two elite teams, the Russians quickly threw down their weapons. It took some time to clear the warehouse and advance on them, but everything was in hand. I watched while keeping my gun on the joker lucky enough to have escaped the glue. Well, lucky was relative. He'd traded it for an alligator boot to the face.

Eventually, nine Russian mobsters were zip-tied and

lined up on their stomachs. Two more were dead. The DROP team zip-tied them too, just in case.

Evan set to work quickly. His training and discipline impressed me, to be honest. Within minutes the raid had transitioned into a search-and-rescue op. Evan shook his head while surveying the damage. "I have no choice but to call this in."

"Is that gonna be a problem?" I asked.

"It depends what I say."

Milena walked up and down the line of mobsters twice. "I don't get it," she complained. "Nikolai's not here."

Evan turned to her. "Nikolai?"

"The owner of Pop Stars," I explained. I turned to Milena. "That has-been sent underlings to do his dirty work. I doubt he made an appearance."

She hissed. "Would've been nice to see him go down too."

"If he was giving the orders," said Evan, "we can still charge him as an accomplice."

Milena hiked a shoulder. "If not I can always kick him in the balls again."

Evan and I instinctively grimaced. A few DROP team members reported their progress. The dock was clear. The building was clear. The Russians were in custody, their weapons locked down, but no signs of a boat or drugs or other contraband.

"Check every crate," ordered Evan. "There has to be something here." He turned to me slowly. "You might as well help out. But I think we've been misled. We're too late."

We called out to Fran and checked the containers. We

found piping, joints, and a lot of industrial rubber supplies. No people, thankfully, but that was a mixed blessing.

I went outside to the platform on the water. This was a relatively large marina considering it was on the River. Really it was a series of smaller docks. Not too many buildings, but there were a lot of small boats parked along the piers. Here, though, on the platform the Russians had been guarding, there was nothing of note.

Emily came to my side as I stared into the water. "She was here," she said, grasping her crystal ball. "But that was a while ago."

"Is she close, at least?"

She took a measured breath. "I don't know, Cisco. There's no recent trace of her at all. It's like she... vanished."

Emily leaned her head on my shoulder. I put my arm around her.

The bad men had come and taken my little girl. They'd put her on a boat and somehow taken her out of range of Emily's scrying. Salt water would've been my go-to theory for magic interference, but this was a freshwater channel.

"Money!" called out an officer from DROP 2. We turned to the warehouse. A false floor had been uncovered. Apparently I hadn't seen enough bags of cash today because several more were hauled out. The sheer amount of money hidden underground put what I'd stolen today to shame.

I stood by the water, watching the officers through the open loading doors. One by one, the DROP team stacked bags on top of each other. They laughed and high-fived. Not a bad score for them. It was gonna make a hell of a photo shoot.

Something didn't sit well with me, though. This was the right place. Fran had been here. There had been a real deal. The Russians were still hanging around with a bunch of guns and hidden money.

I stepped toward the building, eyes darting over my allies. The wetwork was over with, but there was an eerie tension in the air.

"Connor's still here," I whispered.

Emily perked up. I studied her a moment. When the police had breached the door, the gunfire came back too quickly for it to have been a surprise. The Russians were spread out and ready. Whatever deal Connor had going, we'd interrupted it. He'd vanished into thin air while the Russians had braced for a raid.

I marched toward the warehouse. "Connor's still here!" I announced.

Some of the officers turned to me casually, weapons locked and over their shoulders. Evan's eyes widened. That was troubling considering he was looking right next to me instead of at me. I turned, and Connor Hatch smiled.

"Bravo," said the jinn. "The Port was supposed to get messy. I admit I didn't think you'd get anywhere near the Russians. Then again, they've fulfilled their purpose."

Drop 1 raised their guns and stormed outside in formation.

He ignored them and laughed. "I suppose all that money I gave them won't be spent."

"Don't shoot," ordered Evan.

The rest of the police realized what was happening and snapped into formation. Milena held her pistol on the Russians in custody while ten officers in SWAT gear formed a circle around Connor and me. Emily fixated on the jinn, terrified of his presence.

"Connor Hatch," barked Evan. "Hands behind your head."

"I will do nothing of the sort," he stated calmly.

Nobody moved for a beat.

"Well," said the jinn, "aren't you even going to ask?"

I clenched my fists. "Where's Fran?"

"Thank you," he said, amused with himself.

A dollop of air burst from the water. Half the team jumped and pointed rifles at the River. More bubbles burst to the surface. A dark mass came into view underneath.

The DROP team shuffled nervously. They'd cleared the waterfront and the shipyard. This was a surprise. And they didn't like surprises.

The underwater mass was large. Wide. But it was made of metal.

White foam crashed through the bubbles. A leviathan breached the surface. As it rose, water cascaded down its sides. The entire plane of water broke and rolled toward the edges of the River, splashing onto the platform and washing over our shoes.

The DROP team broke the circle, choosing to pin Connor against the water rather than keep their backs to the monstrosity. Evan pulled Emily behind them and stepped away. He kept his weapon on Connor.

Besides the drug lord, I was the only one who didn't move. Water misted against our faces as the sloshing cleared away. All of us watched in awe. Towering above us and taking up the width of the River was a juggernaut of technology and engineering.

Connor Hatch had bought himself a Russian submarine.

Chapter 42

The gargantuan submersible rose like a wall. The sail of the submarine. When the deck breached the surface, it rocked to a halt. It swayed steadily in the calm Miami River, hiding its true size underwater.

I'd heard about drug smugglers using submersibles built under the canopy of the Amazon jungles, sold to whatever mercenary outfit bid the highest. But those were sad imitations of the real thing, in many cases unable to fully submerge without flooding their diesel engines.

This was the real deal. A decommissioned military vessel. Top of the line, if a bit outdated. Seeing a sub of this magnitude made everyone hesitate. Suddenly ten elite SWAT officers were worried about being undergunned.

"This is an illegal vessel," stated Evan, as if that wasn't obvious.

Connor's eyes flashed. "Isn't it magnificent? Kilo-class. Diesel-electric. Quieter than a nuclear sub. This slipped right under the Coast Guard's nose." He turned to admire his new purchase. "It's a bit gaudy to bring it right up the River, but I had to know it could be done."

This was definitely a new one in my book. This sub could dive deeper and longer than anything utilized by a drug lord before. No need for go-fast boats to race radar under the cover of night. No need to smuggle on casino cruises. With a full-fledged submarine under his control, the jinn could transport a monster amount of cargo completely undetected. And if he could sneak it into the River, he could unload his drugs practically anywhere.

"Can you guess who's inside?" asked Connor, savoring every word.

I immediately got it. No wonder Fran had fallen off Emily's radar. It had nothing to do with salt or distance. It was depth.

"I'll kill you for this," I said.

The jinn laughed boldly. A man untouchable in the Earthly Steppe. And he knew it. The growth of his power over the years had made him audacious. Dealing with the Russians and acquiring a decommissioned Soviet vessel was just another rung up the ladder. Connor Hatch didn't just dominate the Caribbean powder trade—he *was* the Caribbean powder trade.

So what was I? The Port. The beating and kidnapping of friends and family. Cisco Suarez was just a sideshow.

I clenched my fist. Time to get the show on the road, then.

The voice of the wraith came to me as clear as if he stood with us, except he was invisible to all and only I heard him. "I will strike while he gloats."

I hardened my features and stared down the jinn. I wanted nothing more than to take my best shot at him, but I couldn't do it yet. Without eyes on Fran, it was too risky.

"Not yet," I whispered.

Connor studied me curiously.

"Where's my daughter?" demanded Evan, rifle trained.

"Now, now." Connor turned to my friend with aplomb. Then his eyes narrowed and fell on Emily. He hadn't expected her here. "You should know, my dear, that I didn't want it to come to this. Despite all your faults."

Emily squared her shoulders at her old master. "Fuck off, Connor."

The Spaniard chimed in again. Anxious. "He is preoccupied, brujo. Make your move."

My alligator boot twisted on the concrete. I needed to wait for Connor's play. I needed to see what he had planned. I reminded myself: killing Connor didn't get Fran back.

"I wanna see her," I insisted.

The drug lord bit his lip, annoyed he could savor this moment only so long. He nodded to his submarine. The top hatch squeaked and flipped open. All eyes were on deck. Who climbed out of the hatch sent some murmuring through the police.

A long skull that looked like a bull with canines. I knew it now to be some twisted giant wolf. The mask of the Vucari. Did they wear the heads of dead comrades?

A gaunt man stretched lanky arms to the sky. One held an oversized wooden club. He tossed it to the foot of the platform. Then he hopped from the submarine tower himself. A twenty-foot drop and he stuck the landing. The police moved away in a line. Their rifles were raised like a firing squad, except they were now uncertain who to aim at.

I wasn't sure myself. What I was seeing should've been impossible. The man's face was hidden, but I knew him all too well.

"Milena..." I warned.

She had left her post over the Russians to back us up. She stood further away on the dock, watching in shock. "It's Darko," she said. Her pistol fell to her side.

The little methhead cocked his skull-head. "In the flesh," he snarled.

I wanted to tell Milena she was free and clear. That she hadn't killed anyone. But more Vucari skulls breached the hatch. One by one, men donning tactical gear and holding crude weapons hopped down. Some of them I thought I recognized from the dock. Others were new. It was hard to tell with the ceremonial skulls.

The last man wore no mask. He wanted his identity known. He was short, broad, and hairy. Bald, with a robust beard, and a symbol tattooed on his face. Vukasin Petrovic landed on the dock and took place ahead of his men. Like Darko, he was not only alive but uninjured.

The Gray Lady had said the Sons of Van were the descendants of Death. Was it possible dear old mother still watched over them?

"Get on the ground, motherfucker!" ordered an especially bold police officer. He gestured forcefully with his weapon.

"Hold your fire," commanded Evan.

"He's the one," called Milena. "He's the one who beat up my *abuelo*."

Emily nodded. "He's the one that came into our house. He's the one that took our little girl."

Evan sneered. He marched right up to Petrovic. Vukasin was short but he was an intimidating figure. His shoulders spanned the width of three men. He also had a team of supernatural zealots backing him up. Evan didn't care. "Where's my daughter, asshole?"

Petrovic stared down my friend. Then he glanced aside at his men and cracked a smile.

Evan slammed the butt of his rifle into the man's nose.

The blow spun his head, but that was all. Vukasin was too large to nudge. The head of the Vucari returned Evan's sneer, baring large canines.

"That," he growled, "was not nice."

Evan squared his jaw and spoke firmly. "You're outnumbered. You have automatic weapons held by Miami's elite trained on you. And you have my daughter. Do I look like I give a shit?"

Vukasin silently considered the odds. He flashed another smirk to his brothers. "Take off your masks, comrades."

One by one, the skulls rattled to the ground. Each face held a scowl worthy of maximum security prison. Each was unrepentant. These bastards were bullies. Far as I could tell, they were also invincible. Here they were, staring down ten assault rifles, and they hadn't even flinched.

"Evan?" I called out softly. "Maybe you shouldn't piss off the subhumans."

"*Sub*humans?" spat the Serbian. "I hate that word." A clamor broke out from their ranks, infecting the Vucari until they all boomed with laughter. "I think you find we are *more* than human."

The Sons of Van howled viciously at the sky, baying together. Long wolf snouts pushed out of their mouths. Their human jaws cracked open. Blood sprayed from twisted flesh. Fur sprouted.

"What the hell?" cried an officer, tripping backward over

his heels.

The ranks of the police broke. Not into rampant chaos, but close enough. A couple of the men abandoned trigger discipline and opened fire on the creatures.

"Don't shoot!" cried Evan, but it was too late. Fran was a variable that didn't come into play anymore. Other lives were on the line. Once the gunpowder sparked, it became a chemical reaction that couldn't be stopped.

Chapter 43

The Sons of Van took immediate hits. Some writhed and fell back into the water. The others recovered, and they seemed quicker than bullets.

Vukasin Petrovic lunged. He swung a backhand at Evan. I phased into position between them, raising my arm bar and taking his blow. It was a sweeping strike that hit my arm high. The tattoo flared and left me unhurt, but the force sent me flying.

Evan fired his assault rifle. The wolf somersaulted under the spray. He came up with his hands on the weapon and ripped it away.

A bright pin of energy spawned between Petrovic's eyes. He cowered from the spellcraft, moving so quick that Emily's magic couldn't track him. The Serbian zeroed in on her, framed in the shipyard's floodlights. He raised Evan's rifle and cut her down.

"No!" screamed Evan and I together.

But the image of Emily flickered. The light around her bent like a prism and revealed her true position a few yards away. Son of a bitch. She could refract the light around her. Not as versatile as Shen's illusions, maybe, but the same result.

Vukasin snarled and spun to her new position, but his scanning eyes instead fell on the tip of my short-barreled shotgun.

I pulled the trigger as he battered my hand upward. The spark powder exploded just over the wolf's head, lighting the battlefield in an orange glow. Damn. I'd done nothing more than singe his hair.

He used his rifle as a club. I took to the shadow and slid to his flank, careful to keep away from the floodlight coronas on the cement. Instead of going in for a blow, I pulled my last fire round from my belt pouch and cracked my shotgun in half.

Emily's light returned. This time Petrovic ignored her. He pointed the assault rifle at me and pulled the trigger. I fell down into the floor, becoming a dark mass, waiting as lead rounds chipped away the concrete beneath me.

When the magazine clicked empty, Evan jumped. He grabbed his rifle with both hands and rammed it into Petrovic's face again. The wolf released it and slapped my friend down. Evan crumpled on the ground beneath him.

Luckily, he'd given me enough time to reload my shotty. The barrel snapped closed. Petrovic turned. A cone of fire lit up the shipyard again. It glanced off the wolf as he rolled away, but his body twisted and tumbled. He'd avoided taking the full brunt of the blast, but half his head was a smoking pulp all the same. Vukasin Petrovic fell to the ground in a lifeless heap.

Evan retreated with his weapon, reloading and planting himself between the wolves and his wife. I wasn't sure Emily needed the protection, but I couldn't fault his instincts. Together they drew closer to the warehouse.

The square dock platform was a chaotic jumble of Vucari and SWAT officers. Say what you want about the strength of spellcraft, but the assault weapons held the wolves at bay. Still, the Sons of Van were so fast it made shooting them difficult. Worse, the two that had taken the initial spill into the river crawled out, bleeding but ready to fight again.

"Form a perimeter!" directed Evan, pulling his men away from the water's edge. If they could gather side by side, forming a line, it would increase their damage potential and limit the chances of crossfire, leaving the Vucari with precious little space to run.

They dragged two wounded officers by their shoulders. Milena came up behind them and emptied her pistol. Then she tossed it to the floor and scooped up one of the downed officer's rifles. She braced the weapon against her shoulder and fired short bursts into a charging Vucari.

His evasive maneuver sent him into a zigzag pattern. He gained ground. I pulled out an egg of white powder and threw it in his path, sending him into a coughing fit and slowing him down enough for Milena to empty the magazine into him. The wolf howled and toppled. These dogs were tough, but it looked like they could be put down after all.

Someone tackled me from the side and my neck nearly snapped. I was scooped into the air and tossed down hard. Darko. I phased into the darkness, sinking deeper than the surface, and came up behind the puzzled creature.

Shadow flared up my arm and enveloped me. Just as Darko spun around, my fist found his stomach. He yelped and launched halfway across the River, disappearing in a splash.

Score a point for shadow magic. I grimaced and stumbled to a knee. But damn had that tackle hurt.

Connor Hatch calmly threaded through the swarm of gunfire and rushing wolves. The police were set in formation now, their perimeter established. The unorganized Vucari were having trouble with the onslaught. Connor witnessed the tide turning and approached the center of the command structure. He lifted his arm and a gout of flames twenty feet long rocketed toward the DROP team.

Flamethrowers don't just hurt. They're demoralizing as hell. The police line broke in half instantly. The men scattered. They rolled and patted down their clothes and checked each other in disbelief that they hadn't been hit. They thought they were lucky. I knew better.

"He can't hurt you!" I screamed. "Connor's fire can't hurt you!"

For some inescapable reason, the police officers believed their eyes over me. They fired at the newest threat, automatic rounds finding only air as Connor casually vanished.

"Evan!" I called. "Get your men back in formation. Don't waste your ammo on Connor!"

My friend nodded. He tried reforming the line but, in the chaos of combat, it was only half effective. In the meantime, the Vucari had the breather they needed. They regrouped. They pulled in their wounded. They howled and drew strength from their patron, Van.

The jinn continued spewing erratic bursts of flame to panic the crowd. To maintain the charade, he orchestrated each attack to barely miss its target.

"He can't hurt you!" I yelled, this time running into the path of Connor's fire. The jet of orange and red gushed over me, barely warmer than the Miami night. When the flames extinguished, the DROP team marveled at the illusory attack. They shook away their fear and began hearing their lieutenant's orders again. They moved to reestablish the line.

But it was too late. The Sons of Van charged the center of the formation, where the ranks were thinnest. Unlike the jinn, the wolves were an actual, tangible threat. The only way for the police to survive the encounter was to avoid getting close. The wedge assault split the DROP team in half. Now, with the Vucari sandwiched between, the police lost their firing angles.

This was bad, and quickly devolving to worse. I could almost hear the wrestling announcer on the echoing PA system: "King of the ring! Rage in the cage! Every man for himself!" I cursed. The cops wouldn't last long in a supernatural melee.

Luckily, they had Emily on their side. She dithered her attention from one wolf to the next. Blinding them before their attacks struck. Refracting the warehouse light and bending the positions of their targets. For a single woman it was madness to keep track of. Even then, she was falling a step behind.

Connor scowled. "I may not be able to harm them, Cisco, but they're not all untouchable."

He sent a spear of flame to Emily. My arm flashed up with his. I manifested a small shadow wall to shield her.

Except Connor's spear had purposely missed the white witch. He'd aimed for her but at an angle. The fire javelin roared wide past my wall and missed everybody.

"Ugh!" cried Emily. Her true position shimmered in. Connor's fire had glanced through her side. She buckled to the floor.

"No!" I swiped uselessly at Connor. He blinked to the other side of me.

Emily clutched her blackened side and rolled in pain.

"Son of a bitch!" hollered Evan, sprinting to his wife's side.

"It is fitting," said the jinn softly. "You being here for this. You can hold her while she dies."

The flamethrower roared from his hand again, bearing down on the couple. This time Emily had no strength to refract her position. This time Connor had a clear, unmolested shot at her. But this time, so did I. My shadow wall solidified into position just in time.

The fire bombarded the shadow. My spellcraft ate it like a black hole. But the darkness wasn't all powerful. The light from the flames licked at it. Withered it. The black shied away from the light.

I bit down and forced more darkness into the construct, replacing the shadow as it was dissolved. Connor snarled and doubled down, both hands sending his blaze forward.

I'd never tried this before, but I was desperate. My spellcraft isn't like Emily's. Light is a presence. It's sourced by something. It can be spawned in a void.

Shadow doesn't work like that. Shadow can't be created at will. It just is. Shadow is an absence, existing only where light isn't. I can play with it, thicken it, but I can't very well go against the laws of the universe.

Except, somehow, my defense was holding. Even if only

for pitiful moments. The fire devoured my wall but the shadow returned behind it, slowly giving way to the inevitable. The distance between searing oblivion and Emily Cross dwindled.

The white witch produced an aerosol can. She sprayed white paint on the floor around her. Meanwhile, I begged Opiyel for more. To open the faucet even if it burned me alive. To give Emily the time she needed.

The Intrinsics flowed through me with a raging current. Too much, too fast. I could only give Emily a few more seconds. By then, her circle of protection was complete. A coil of white paint surrounded Evan and Emily, my shadow disintegrated, and Connor's fire spread over them. The flames curved around the invisible orb. It was a beautiful sight. The most metal snow globe ever.

But the effort took its toll on me. My legs gave way. My arms barely kept my face off the cement. I was suddenly dizzy and weak. My head spun.

Spellcraft isn't meant to be pushed. That's why so many fairy tales and legends lecture on the temptation of magic and the fear of dooming your soul. My take? It isn't anything as moralistic as all that. The simple truth is there's only so much punishment the human body can handle.

Even though Evan and Emily were safe, the DROP team was a different story. Half of them had retreated to the warehouse. The other half were convincing Evan to do the same. Emily tried to shove him away for his sake, but he wouldn't leave her. He ordered his men to fall back. They took up what fortified positions they could.

As a necromancer, any circles I'd used were for blocking spirits. Magical attacks, not so much. I couldn't tell what kind of protection Emily was running, but I watched the Vucari pound on her dome like frustrated mimes. Somehow, she managed to block evocative magic and sheer force.

"You've been studying in secret," noted Connor in mild annoyance.

Emily was in too much pain to snap back. She was focused on the circle, probably scared out of her mind. For all I knew, this was her first real firefight, her first real experience with her life on the line. She had told me she wasn't built for this kind of thing, that she was only here for her daughter.

Well, damn. Given the odds, I thought she was doing just fine.

I groaned and steadied on my hands and knees. The Spaniard's voice rasped in my head. Shouting about missed opportunities. Wary of falling into the jinn's hands. I could've set him loose, but the image of my daughter drowned out his pleas. This was for Fran, I reminded myself. I couldn't reveal the Horn and make my move until I could ensure her safety.

I forced my limbs into a shell-shocked crawl. Through the swimming haze in my head, I heard the gunfire slow and the calls of the DROP team to conserve ammo. I hadn't considered that the Sons of Van could take more bullets than the officers had. Too bad I hadn't been able to outfit them with better weaponry. A supernatural edge. If we ever lived through the night, I told myself I would fix that.

"Cisco Suarez," laughed Connor. He strolled alongside my feeble attempt to crawl. "It's time for a deal. You've lost here."

I grunted. "What battle are you looking at?"

Finally, I pulled myself to my target. I leaned on the twitching body of Vukasin Petrovic.

Connor raised an eyebrow. "Whatever are you doing?"

I coughed. "That thing at the docks you did. With the zombie. I realized how to hurt you." I put the silver whistle to my mouth and blew.

A tremor went through Petrovic's body. A grunt escaped his snout. The wolf picked his head off the floor and fixed on me. Half his face looked like a skinned tomato that was on the grill too long, courtesy of my fireshot.

I smirked and turned to Connor. "The dead."

The corpse's hairy hand clamped around my throat.

Wait. That wasn't supposed to happen.

"Eep," I cried, struggling to slink into the shadow. Too late. We were stuck on the ground, immobile. I couldn't slip out.

My mind raced. This wasn't normal. My thralls had never attacked me before. That could only mean...

Vukasin Petrovic wasn't dead.

Chapter 44

"You're supposed to be dead," I snarled.

The Vucari's wolf jaw opened in a smile. "Little man, death is afraid of Vucari."

"Watch who you call little," I warned.

His grip on my neck tightened. He stood, hefting me high. My alligator boots swung wildly, searching for ground. I pulled my sawed off, loaded a shell of regular birdshot, and fired into his belly. He didn't let go, but he wavered enough to set me down.

It was still difficult to breathe with him crushing my neck.

I dropped the shotgun and pulled at his hand, giving me sweet relief. I knew I didn't have the juice to break out, though.

Vukasin Petrovic smiled and said, "I told you I'd come for you."

I tugged but it was no good. I pulled my right hand to my side and drew shadow over it. Immediately, I felt woozy.

"This isn't about old man," said Petrovic. "This isn't about little girl. Though she was fun to steal."

I growled. This guy was right here, in my face, taunting me with my daughter's kidnapping. I didn't care how much more my body could take. I used the anger to call the shadow to me. I turned off all the warning alarms in my brain. Ignored all the muscle spasms that tried to shut me down. My blood seared with rage and I fed it with everything I had. And when Opiyel warned me down, I cursed him too.

A mass of darkness dripped from my palm. I folded it into itself. Again. And again.

"I know what you think," said Petrovic, gloating. "You kick yourself for not killing me back at Port. For not finishing me here on ground." He squeezed his hand. "But I have bad news for you, Cisco. Even if you did kill me, I only come back for you again."

Petrovic boomed with laughter. His massive frame heaved with amusement. I hardened my shadow as he laughed. I fed my rage and sharpened it into a prison shiv.

"You forget, Petrovic," I rasped. "You're not the only one who's been dead before."

I shanked him right between his man-boobs. He gasped and released me. Tree-trunk legs shook the floor as he stumbled backward. But he righted himself before the fall. I couldn't say the same.

The shadow fled me. I dropped to my knees. I squinted, trying to see straight. I was exhausted and the fucker was still laughing.

Right up until his head exploded.

I turned my head weakly. Milena had also fallen to the floor. She regained her feet, lugging the BFG over her shoulder. The thing was so big it had knocked her over when fired.

"I don't give a shit about killing that guy," she said

triumphantly. She stood at a lean because of the heavy gun.

I massaged my throat. "I'm pretty sure you're supposed to brace that thing on top of something," I squeaked out.

She shrugged with her free shoulder.

Right about that time we noticed everything had gone silent around us. Connor was watching, of course, but the Vucari had stopped their assault as well. Each subhuman reverently scrutinized their fearless leader.

I turned back to him. Vukasin Petrovic was still on his feet, if that was possible. He was deader than a doornail, though. His head was missing. It wasn't on his body or the floor or anywhere, really. It had just exploded into giblets from the anti-vehicle round.

Kinda made me feel like a wimp. I had a perfectly working head and I still couldn't manage to stand up. Petrovic was just showing off.

The Sons of Van collectively howled when their leader didn't stir. It was a raucous lament. Maybe they realized they would die here as well.

Connor scrambled to mollify their ranks. I kept wondering why nobody was fighting. But we were spent. Emily wounded. The DROP team nearly out of bullets. My body betraying me. This battle had become more about attrition than strength. And here I was, unable to manifest a single shadow. Hell, I couldn't even get a solid foot beneath me.

But I wasn't done by a long shot. Never let it be said that Cisco Suarez is a one-trick pony.

I put the whistle to my mouth again. This time I tapped the High Baron and Opiyel both at once. I called on the Spaniard to assist me. I wormed my way into the dead subhuman's husk. Usually it wasn't reliable to play this fast and loose with zombie preparation, but I was between a submarine and a hard place.

I closed my eyes. Suddenly I was standing again. No longer writhing on the floor, I was now an oak tree of a man, all hair and fat and muscles. (No head, though.) I took a heavy step forward. I was more Jeep than Bentley, but I was undoubtedly mobile. The body was mine. I paced ahead, one target in mind.

Connor arched his eyebrow and turned to the headless corpse.

"Vukasin?" he asked.

I swung my log of an arm without hesitation. The blow slammed into the startled jinn's chest and knocked him on his ass.

Connor rolled over, his eyes wide with disbelief. An audible gasp escaped the crowd.

Back on the floor, I opened my eyes and smiled. "Connor Hatch," I called out. "If you don't fear the living, let's see how you do against the dead."

The jinn swung an arc of fire at the standing corpse. Flames danced over the body. The zombie caught fire, but he didn't melt or explode or turn to ash. The magic powering the husk didn't extinguish.

For once I laughed at the power of the Sons of Van, near immortal and able to absorb obscene amounts of damage. I laughed like a madman and dove back into the Vucari's body. Petrovic stomped ahead.

Connor was never one for a fight. As soon as I lumbered near, he tried to blink away. But something curious happened. His magic failed him. The dead *did* interfere with his magic. What was clearly an attempt to escape left the jinn standing idly.

I clasped strong arms around him, picked him up, and crushed him to the ground. My fist came down but he caught it. Connor pushed up at me. Impressive, but I was stronger than him. Petrovic was stronger than him. I shoved his hand down slowly. Then I lifted a foot and curb-stomped him in the stomach.

The jinn folded into a fetal position. Before I could get another blow in, he stabbed my knee with a sword of fire. I tumbled to my hands. Connor rolled away and tried to blink again. No dice. From a crouch, I lunged at him. He bounded away. Capitalizing on my diminished mobility, he fired a lance at my other knee.

Pain seared through my being. I caught myself on the ground again, enraged. He was getting away. Not with magic, but on foot. He sprinted toward his submarine.

I wanted to tell the Spaniard to strike, but I couldn't feel his presence from Petrovic's husk. I ignored the pain and pushed to my feet. Connor raced to the edge of the dock, dove forward, and blinked out.

I returned to my body, eyes jerking open. My head swiveled over the docks. Damn it. Connor Hatch was gone.

"Coward!" yelled one of the Vucari. "Stay and fight!"

A soaking wet Darko surveyed the dock in a panic. "Screw this," he grumbled. He pulled several of the Sons of Van away toward the street. The DROP team held back, happy to watch them scurry away.

"Stay and fight," repeated the first subhuman. The ugly one. "They are wounded." His allies hesitated.

I snarled. The Vucari couldn't even retreat properly. I

closed my eyes and jumped into Petrovic again. I lowered my shoulder and charged.

"We will not die!" yelled the rallying Vucari.

With a crash, I bowled him over.

The sight was too much for some of them. Connor running. Their fearless leader attacking as their enemy. The mass of Vucari fled. Only two retained the bloodlust to fight at the ugly one's side. The odds had irrevocably turned.

The DROP team focused all their fire on a single unlucky foe. The rifles discharged until clicking empty. Milena downed another with the BFG.

Vukasin was stronger than the others, but he was missing a head. Not a normal head, mind you, but a mean pagan wolf head with giant fangs. I didn't realize the disability until the Vucari grappling me chewed at my arm and gained the upper hand. He forced me to my back. I worked my strength. He worked his leverage. It was a stalemate.

Evan Cross put a rifle to the base of the subhuman's skull and fired. Multiple rounds shredded his head. One of the bullets popped through the neck and found Petrovic.

"Ouch!" I screamed, snapping back into my own body. "That hurt!"

Evan gazed at me flatly. "No one likes a whiny necromancer, Cisco."

I rubbed the imaginary wound on my chest and pouted.

Milena dropped the BFG to the ground. She ran over and smothered me with a hug. The battlefield was clear.

All said and done, five dead Vucari were all that remained, including Petrovic. The real kills had only come at the end of the skirmish, when their numbers were vastly overwhelmed. Tough sons of bitches, I give them that. Evan checked each of the bodies and made sure they were down for good.

He ordered his men to assess the wounded while he tended to Emily. Half the DROP team was hurt with varying degrees of severity. One of them looked dead. The chaos of the battle had worked out in their favor, though. The Vucari were damage sponges, but the bullets and squad tactics had mostly kept them at bay.

Still, five hurt officers was gonna raise a lot of eyebrows. And the men had now seen more than most did in a lifetime. Their ideas—their beliefs—would be forever altered.

I hope I didn't just ruin my best friend's police unit. But mostly, I hoped Emily was okay.

I struggled to my feet. Milena helped me over to Emily.

"I'm fine," she asserted, before I even reached her. Her dress was burned open, the skin on her side blackened. Her hand covered in blood. Emily pressed it to the wound and tried to stand. Every bit as stubborn as I was.

"Stay on the ground," said Evan, kneeling by her. "You need medical attention. Fire Rescue's on the way.

"We're not done yet," she protested.

"I know," he said.

"Um, Cisco?" chimed in Milena, pointing to my thrall. "Your zombie's on fire."

Vukasin was doing an admirable job of ignoring the continued flames. By now much of his skin was blackened, but it hadn't crisped away yet.

"Get in the water, Wolfman," I commanded.

Without me driving, the thrall mindlessly stomped toward the River.

Milena cocked her head. "If the only wolf part of him was his head and he's decapitated, is he still a wolfman?"

"Philosophy 101," I muttered. "Classic use of the half man, half wolf, half zombie paradox."

"I'm pretty sure you can't have three halves," noted Emily, piling on through gritted teeth.

Milena smirked. "Plus, technically, wolfmen have humanoid faces."

I gave them both a patronizing smile. "It's great to see you ladies finally getting along."

We watched my zombie extinguish himself in the water.

"I don't like that vile thing," confessed Connor from above. All eyes went up to where he protruded from the submarine's top hatch. In one arm he held my little girl, and with the other he pointed a pistol at her head.

"Don't do it!" cried Evan hysterically.

I clenched my jaw and made my way to the platform's edge. Evan checked his rifle, dropped it on the ground, then pulled off his jacket to reveal a pair of Colt Diamondback revolvers in shoulder holsters.

"What can I do?" asked Milena.

"Stay close to Petrovic," I answered.

This was it. Connor's endgame. Everything else had been a prelude.

I was weak. I could barely walk. It physically hurt to channel the shadow. But I was ready.

Without a word to the others, I waded into the water and climbed onto the deck of the Soviet sub, pulling my zombie up behind me.

Chapter 45

"I'm gonna have to ask you to stop right there," said Connor, giving Fran a forceful shake.

I paused on the deck of the submarine.

Fran was a frightened doe in his arms. Lean frame and wide eyes. Despite her fear, her outward appearance remained calm. Good girl.

"I want my daughter back," said Evan, drawing a revolver and moving to the edge of the concrete dock. Connor's vantage was a good twenty feet above us.

"Would you really risk her life with such a reckless move?" asked the jinn.

"He's bluffing," I said. "Jinns can only hurt people who've made deals with them. He can't touch Fran."

Connor flashed a sly grin. "Very well, Cisco. I didn't want to be so heartless, but it appears you require a demonstration."

Connor reared the grip of the pistol and smacked the side of Fran's head. She yelped and tried to scramble away, but the jinn kept her pinned to his body.

"Bastard!" I yelled. Evan raised his gun.

Connor used the girl as a body shield and laughed boldly. "Put your weapon away, Detective," he ordered. "I won't ask twice."

The muscles in Evan's arms and shoulders were wound as tight as possible. He worked his jaw but holstered the pistol.

"Thank you," said the jinn. He pointed at my friend and fired once. Evan clutched his chest and fell. Fran screamed hysterically.

Milena grabbed the collar of Evan's vest to drag him away. She had trouble with the weight, but Evan kicked his feet to help her. They pulled back to Emily and the DROP team.

"Oh, relax," said the jinn, rolling his eyes. "Lieutenant Cross hasn't entered any bargains with me so I can't hurt him."

"Get off me," grumbled Evan, shrugging them away. He wiped the slug from his bulletproof vest.

Connor turned to me. "Doesn't anybody listen to you?" His gaze strayed to my thrall beside me. "Beside your pet, that is." He considered Petrovic. "Now this one is a different story. You turned my ally against me. Clever."

The jinn fired three rounds at him. The zombie took two in the chest. Another ricocheted off the deck by my foot. I never flinched. My pet didn't look the worse for wear either.

Connor twisted his jaw in amusement. "A subhuman zombie. An impressive gambit, Cisco." His face suddenly went straight, like he was bored with the act. "Now lose the pet. Dispel it."

I didn't move.

The jinn pressed the pistol into my daughter's head. "Dispel it."

My allies huddled on the dock, watching. Emily was seriously wounded, waiting on the paramedics. Evan and Milena had their hands tied. The rest of the DROP team was in no shape to continue either. Petrovic was my only weapon against Connor.

No, not my only weapon. Not even the best one.

With a wordless command, Vukasin Petrovic went limp. He crumpled to deck, slid down the rounded surface of the sub, and plopped into the water. Gone for good.

"Excellent," said Connor with renewed satisfaction. "Now, follow me. If you don't, I kill the girl. If anyone else enters, I kill the girl. Understood?"

I ground my teeth and nodded. The jinn made a show of checking with all the spectators, in case they wanted to object. Then he pulled Fran down the hatch with him.

I loosened the cloth wrapping on the Horn that hung at my belt. I felt the familiar thrum of its power. Then I hopped onto the ladder, climbed to the hatch, and descended inside.

I didn't know a damn thing about submarines or military vessels. I had no idea what to expect within. I climbed down silently. At the foot of the ladder, my feet echoed on the grated floor. A long metal hall stretched in two directions.

A few members of the *Agua Fuego* cartel stood at a distance. Mercenaries, like the ones I'd infiltrated earlier. It made sense. Something this size couldn't be crewed by one man, jinn or no. Connor had probably rented himself a bunch of South American and Russian ex-soldiers to operate his shiny purchase.

It was a good thing I hadn't gotten the best of Connor on the dock. In my bloodlust, I'd almost lost sight of my goal. Fran. Alone in here, with the mercenaries. If I had successfully defeated Connor, there was no doubt they would've killed my daughter and split.

I took a heavy breath, then chose a path. My alligator boots rang out on the grill. The mercenaries backed away, staying on the fringes of my vision. They were afraid of me.

The hallway was narrow, the roof low, the atmosphere claustrophobic. No place to maneuver in this sardine can, but there was nothing for it. I stomped ahead, making a racket the entire way. Connor waited at the end of the hall beside an open hatch. My insides tightened at the sight of my daughter in the jinn's hands.

"It's stifling in here," he said, his voice tinny against the walls. "Being surrounded by water instead of air. I feel like a pathetic Nether creature. This is what I'm forced into."

"You made a mistake," I told him. "You might be able to blink around in here, but you can't run to the Aether. Not without contacting the open sky."

His lip curled. "So you wish to end this. That's what you're saying?"

I growled. "You messed with my family."

Connor was nonplussed. "You have it backwards, Cisco. Emily was never your family. She never loved you. She was engineered for you. Manufactured. Her light to your shadow. Fake from the beginning."

I sneered. "My love was never fake. I don't care that it was built on a lie. *I built it.* That means something to me."

He chuckled dismissively at the entire human race.

"Please," squeaked Fran. "Let me go."

Connor's face went dark. He rapped her head with the gun. Not too hard, this time. "What did I say about talking, dear?"

The girl buttoned her lips and held her breath.

Connor turned to me and flinched away in time for my bronze knife to clatter against the wall directly behind him. He shook for a moment and pulled Fran up to cover his face.

"Are you crazy?" he asked.

I kept my voice low and steady so he wouldn't miss a thing. "If you ever hit her again, it'll be the last time you do anything."

Connor watched me strangely. Unsure. He stood straighter and rested the pistol against her head. He didn't want a fight, I reminded myself.

Poor Fran didn't have any such confidence. Each of her whimpers was a dagger in my side.

"It's okay," I assured her. She didn't seem to hear me. "Fran," I said softly. "Look at me. It's going to be okay."

The poor girl barely acknowledged me. She was frozen in terror.

"What did you do to her?" I spat. "How could you make a deal with a kid?"

He shrugged like it was nothing. "The little one and I struck a bargain on her seventh birthday," he revealed. He looked into her eyes. "I told her magic was real and I would teach it to her, as long as she didn't tell anyone. She couldn't agree fast enough."

I clenched my fists. He'd gotten Emily the same way, more or less. Passing through family members like a cold. Except once he had his hooks in them, they were stuck with him forever. I couldn't bear the thought of a nine-year-old being doomed to that fate.

The jinn saw the rage burning on my face. He taunted me further, his voice light and feathery. "Well, I needed a backup, Cisco. I needed your lineage to find the Horn. I might need it to access its power."

My lineage. That's why Connor had looked into my family's genealogy. He was looking for more relatives. More backups. Once everything with me had gone pear-shaped and he lost the Horn, his plans evolved. Except I didn't have any siblings or relatives. Tunji had made sure of that too.

That meant all of Connor's plans now hinged on Fran. Now and in the future.

I unwrapped the artifact and let the cloth covering fall to the floor.

"I have the Horn," I said firmly.

And with that, the Spaniard materialized between us.

Chapter 46

Connor Hatch admired the wraith. The breastplate. The side-sword. The gnarled fingers, skull, and glowing red eyes. Connor looked upon what would make most men shudder without so much as a blink.

"The Spaniard," he said reverently. "A man who escaped the limits of his humanity. You surprise me again, Cisco." Connor's hold on Fran loosened as he admired the apparition. "It is a pleasure to make your acquaintance after all these decades."

Holy crap. Decades? Connor had been searching for the Horn for a long time. It must be powerful for a jinn to sacrifice so much. And I'd done what the Spaniard feared: I'd brought the Horn right to him. I hoped this wasn't a huge mistake.

The Spaniard clasped his hands behind his back and hovered closer to the jinn. "Connor Hatch," he rasped inquisitively. "For all intents and purposes, a higher being. The pleasure is mine. I have long waited for this moment as well."

Connor flicked his eyes to me cautiously. I swallowed.

The Spaniard didn't waste time. "I seek my freedom, jinn."

Uh... What?

Connor's beard and lips pulled away from his teeth. He laughed. "Then we have similar goals, Spaniard. Kill Cisco Suarez, let me assume the Horn, and assist me in a single pursuit. Do these things and I will set you free, whether I succeed or fail. You have my word."

I narrowed my eyes. Connor was overeager to strike a deal. For a jinn, one so bound to terms, it seemed careless.

"He is the bearer of the Horn," stated the wraith evenly. "I am unable to harm him or work counter to his interests."

"Could've fooled me," I warned.

His red eyes smoldered without passion and flicked back to Connor. "However, if you agree to free me, I will guide you through your needs."

The jinn's face tightened. "What worth are your words without the Horn? If I assume the artifact then you'll listen to my commands regardless."

"Perhaps. But I am the only one who can persuade the bearer to hand it over in the first place."

"Fat chance," I said. They ignored me, locked in their own negotiations. I eyed Fran, wondering how many seconds it would take to charge the jinn and yank her free.

Connor pursed his lips and studied the phantom. The jinn was a master of manipulation. He had to be aware of more angles than I was. Trusting the wraith was obviously a risk. Yet Connor took only a handful of seconds before nodding in satisfaction. "We have a bargain, then."

If I was supposed to feel something accompanying the words—a presence of binding energy or a pact taking hold—I didn't. Were the jinn's bargains so easy to make?

"How about it, Cisco?" asked Connor, wagging his

pistol. "You know all I want is the Horn."

I frowned. I had no intention of handing it over. To be honest, I wasn't sure whether the wraith was acting or not, but I had to play my part. "I'm open to the possibility. But I need some assurances."

Connor smiled pleasantly. "Like what?"

I had to be careful here. He couldn't hurt me, but he could hurt Fran. Theoretically the wraith was now susceptible as well, but I doubted Connor could affect the spirit. He wasn't a necromancer, after all.

I took measured steps toward the jinn. He made a reciprocal movement. Circumspect. Still shielding himself with my daughter. The wraith stepped from between us and let Connor pass.

"You can't touch Fran," I said firmly. "Forever. Not now. Not ten years from now. She'll never be a part of your schemes. Never hurt by your actions. Ever."

Connor looked into the child's eyes, almost as if he would regret making that promise.

Behind the jinn, the Spaniard opened his bony hand. The bronze knife scratched the floor grating as it whisked through the air and into his gloved palm.

Connor cocked his ear to the sound and started to turn.

I stepped forward quickly, regaining the jinn's attention. "The same goes for Emily. She served you faithfully for over ten years. You've used her enough. You can't touch them, directly or otherwise."

Connor lifted his chin to consider.

"For that matter," I added, "you'll agree to leave their families alone. Emily's husband. Her son. Any other kids they might spit out. And their kids too."

The jinn opened his mouth to object. But I wasn't done.

"You know what?" I spoke over him, just getting started. "That's not enough. *This* can't happen again." I shoved a finger toward the jinn. "You're not allowed to come at me through other people. Beating up old men and kidnapping children. You're not allowed to twist my arm by threatening my friends. I don't care if it's my soul mate or the old lady who sells me *café con leche* every morning."

Connor stood fifteen feet from me, not wanting to approach further. There was enough shadow to slide close, but I wasn't sure I had the juice. Behind him, the wraith hovered near with the ceremonial knife, looking to me for the word. Now if I could only get Fran away.

"That would limit me greatly," said Connor. "Those are expensive terms."

I couldn't believe Connor was actually considering the offer. It was a stall tactic. The wraith's eyes flared in anticipation. I ignored him and took in the image of Fran in Connor's arms. Her cute cheeks. Her crooked smile that ended in dimples.

"In potential cost," I admitted. "Maybe. But the actual cost to you is nothing: Spare one life, right here, right now. For decades you plotted to find the Horn. For years you desired the power it holds. You can get everything you sought with a simple nod of your head, all for the cost of handing an innocent girl over. It's a simple trade."

Connor ruffled a hand through his beard. He turned to my companion. The Spaniard backed away and deftly hid the knife.

"I saw your library at the island compound," I said, raising the Horn. "I know you're a collector above all others. I know you can't turn this piece down."

From a distance, Connor studied the artifact. This was going better than I'd dreamed. But he was hedging now. Considering an alternate strategy where he didn't need to sign so much opportunity away.

I cleared my throat. I had to sweeten the offer.

"And don't forget what else you get," I added. Connor waited greedily. I lifted my index finger to the air, commanding his full attention. Then I rolled my wrist and pointed to myself. "A deal from me. Once we agree to terms, I'm not untouchable anymore. You can hurt me."

Connor Hatch showed his teeth, and I knew I had him.

"Fine," he said. "But I can defend myself against them, with deadly force, if they come at me or conspire against me." His voice dropped a few notes to emphasize the point. "Their protection is contingent upon them staying out of my business. They forget about me, I forget about them."

Well, he wasn't a complete idiot. He wouldn't agree to combat invincible chess pieces. Instead he was taking them off the board entirely. It suited his interests. I wasn't so sure it didn't suit mine either.

"But you can't trick them into confronting you," I said. "You can't seek their attention, directly or otherwise. Any ancillary conflicts resulting from normal police duties don't count either."

He nodded.

"To honor the terms," I stipulated, "you'll let us go. You'll leave me alone long enough to get Fran back home. We need to get everyone out of here safely. Only after that can we resume our business."

The Spaniard's eyes flared. He advanced on Connor

again. I remembered what he'd revealed to me before, that he could only affect the physical world through my will, whether subconscious or not. The mind tricks he played, the attacks he carried out—as the bearer of the Horn, they only happened with my consent.

I forced my will into him. Full stop. I no longer considered it a healthy risk.

Here's the thing. The Spaniard didn't really know whether he could kill Connor or not. It was a gamble. Admittedly, this was a damn better chance than I'd ever had, but I wasn't sure that was good enough.

I hadn't planned for this eventuality. It just sort of happened. A last-second inspiration after thinking of Emily outside, wounded. After seeing the fear in my daughter's eyes. After slamming headfirst into the limits of my own shadow magic.

I was so close to victory, but I was just as close to defeat. If Fran were hurt, if Connor twitched a single finger and blew her brains out, then I would've failed in everything right and just.

No, this wasn't the plan. But I had to consider what victory really meant to me. Killing Connor? Protecting the wraith and others from his ends? Or was it doing the one thing I'd sworn myself to since returning to life?

My only job was keeping family and friends out of danger.

And I could do that now. With a simple agreement. Without making another move. Hell, it was practically done. I'd already won.

"Brujo..." warned the Spaniard. Connor ignored him.

All I needed to do was give the wraith the okay, to

silently wish him to attack the jinn, and he would strike. But then my bargain would be lost, my daughter's future uncertain.

I kneeled and placed the Horn of Subjugation on the metal floor between us. My boot kicked it toward the jinn. "You have a deal," I said.

Connor Hatch's smile stretched from ear to ear. He released the girl and stooped before the Horn.

Fran ran for me. I caught her in open arms. She wanted to run, to keep running, but she didn't need to anymore. I clasped my arms around her and held her tight. She tucked her face into my shoulder and breathed muffled sobs of relief.

"The Horn," pronounced Connor as he held it in reverent palms. "The Horn of Subjugation is mine!"

The Spaniard's heavy voice rasped through his bones. "Yes, Master."

Chapter 47

A chill ran through me at the sight of the jinn and the wraith standing side by side. I didn't know who the Spaniard was in life, but I'd witnessed glimpses of a conscience within him. Now, bound to serve Connor because of the Horn, it didn't matter what the conquistador thought of the jinn. He would do his bidding. They were allies now.

With Fran in my arms, it was hard to care about anything else. The moment seemed like everything to me, but I hadn't made a deal with the devil for a single moment. It was for everything. Everyone. Now, and in the future. They would all be safe.

Fran lifted her head and wiped tears from her eyes. "Daddy!" she squeaked.

My heart stopped. I paused, unsure how to respond. I pulled Fran away. Gave her a startled look, half confused, half elated. But she didn't meet my eyes. She was fixated behind me. Fran shook out of my grip and ran to meet Evan approaching at my rear. My friend hugged her with one arm and spun sideways to position her behind his body.

I breathed again. For a moment I'd thought...

"Sorry, buddy," said Evan. "It's not that I don't trust you, but I couldn't sit out there doing squat."

I nodded absently. Then he raised his Colt Diamondback to Connor.

"Evan!" I snapped. "No!"

"Get behind me, Cisco."

"Don't do it," I urged. I turned my back to Connor and the Spaniard and held my arms across Evan's path. "You're safe—*she's* safe—as long as you back down."

Connor Hatch crossed his arms calmly. He stood unimpressed, in cocky challenge. The bastard wanted Evan to fire, to cancel the terms. If that happened, it would've all been for nothing.

Evan remained in a firing pose but allowed my words to sink in. He lowered the gun a hair and darted his eyes to me. Thank God.

"He's letting Fran off the hook," I said softly. "And you. And Emily. You're all free of Connor Hatch forever."

His brow furrowed. He wasn't sure it was true.

Connor shrugged in disappointment. "A deal's a deal, Lieutenant. Give my regards to your wife."

Evan checked his daughter in his arm and then considered me again.

"I told her I'd do anything to get her back." I sighed heavily. "You're my family." Then, "Get out of here, Evan."

My friend clenched his jaw. "You too, Cisco. Let's go. Don't die down here for nothing."

"He won't," remarked Connor. "Not tonight anyhow. Such are the terms of the truce. But it is odd, Cisco, that you would sell one family out for another."

The jinn waved the Horn to me in a taunt. It took me a few seconds to catch his meaning. I swiveled to meet the Spaniard's eyes, but he glumly dropped his head.

Suddenly, I understood why I had been the one to find the Horn in the first place. Why the Covey had chosen me for the task. Why Fran was the backup. In a rush of clarity, I answered the question I had never bothered to ask: why my lineage was important.

The fucking Spanish necromancer, the subjugator of the Taíno people, was my great great copy paste great great rinse repeat grandfather.

Connor casually turned away and made for the end of the hallway. For him, there was nothing else of interest here. The Spaniard stood silently, head down, allowing the jinn to pass.

Connor ordered the wraith without a passing glance. "Escort them off the vessel." When the jinn crossed the far hatch, he turned around in triumph.

"Sleep, Cisco. You'll have peace tonight." His eyes flared even as his face darkened. "After that, you'll never again know what it's like to be safe. You'll always look over your shoulder, wondering when Connor Hatch will come for you." He sneered. "And trust me, I *will* come."

The hatch shut and twisted closed. The Spaniard hovered listlessly and nodded for the exit. Evan was only too happy to get Fran out of there. My steps were less driven. Once I made sure they were on the ladder above me, I paused and turned to my old companion, at a loss for words.

The engines of the submarine kicked on. The interior whirred around us.

"Ten years ago," said the Spaniard hollowly, "I convinced you not to hand me over to them. Now you have done so willingly."

I swallowed. "My whole world has changed since then."

"More is changing still," he countered. "Next time we meet, it will be as enemies." He placed the ceremonial knife in my palm. "You have made a grave miscalculation."

"Why didn't you tell me?"

The burning eyes and raspy voice betrayed no emotion. "It was not relevant."

"The hell it wasn't." I watched Fran clear the hatch. "She's my daughter," I said plainly.

"That is exactly why I held my tongue. Family matters disturb your judgment."

"Is that so wrong?" I asked indignantly. "You know, considering our relationship, Fran's your family too."

He looked after her wistfully, but she was already gone. Evan, too, disappeared outside. "It is not your heart that I fault."

I swallowed again. The taste of what I had done was bitter in my mouth. "Could you have done it?" I asked. "Could you have killed Connor?"

"I am confident I could have triumphed." His helmeted head cocked to the side. "But I was confident right up until I was bound to the Horn as well."

I nodded. That told me I'd made the right move.

I gripped the rung of the ladder but remained at the bottom. I couldn't pull myself up yet.

"I'm sorry," I said. "I'll find a way to get you out."

"That is no longer in your hands, brujo."

"The hell it isn't. I'm free to fight Connor without my friends and family getting hurt now. I won't stop."

The apparition scolded me harshly. "You have given away your best weapon against the jinn. I will make short work of any thralls you send his way. I, his greatest fear, am also his greatest defense."

I scoffed. "I made you a promise, and I intend to keep it."

The wraith considered me without pretense. "You do not know what you've done."

Water rushed into the ballast tanks. The vessel listed slightly. I held the ladder tight for balance. The Spaniard had no need for the precaution. He hovered wordlessly and nodded his skull upward.

The submarine was beginning its descent. It was time to go. I climbed up and out. As I stepped down the sail tower, the top hatch flipped closed by itself.

That was pretty cool. Why hadn't I used the wraith for dramatic stuff like that?

Then again, I'd used the wraith very sparingly, out of fear that he was a corrupting power. Whether or not he was, Connor Hatch would have no such reservations.

Waves of bubbles flooded the surface along the submarine's length. The vessel rocked. Jets of water misted the air. Before I could fully make it down, water rushed over the deck, submerging it. I jumped directly from the ladder to the shipyard platform.

Milena hurried to my side. Evan brought his daughter to Emily. She lay next to the other wounded DROP team officers, crying tears of joy. Even the Drop 2 member I thought was dead looked like he was gonna pull through. The Fire Rescue vehicles lighting up South River Drive were a promising sight.

It was over.

I watched as Connor's sub disappeared under the surface of the Miami River. It was anticlimactic. But maybe that was because I'd been gunning for the wrong climax. It was a good day, all things considered. Maybe I hadn't secured a victory, but I'd prevented a debilitating loss. All these people that I cared about, they wouldn't be in harm's way anymore. They wouldn't live in fear. All because of one simple powder trade.

I rejoined the crowd. I shared their smiles. We all had made it against stacked odds. Everyone was happy and relieved and full of adrenaline.

That would wear off. The pretty makeup would flake away and reveal the scars underneath. Fran had lived through a nightmare ordeal. Emily and others were injured. Evan's eyes were open to his wife's power now, and that wasn't even considering whatever Fran knew. I would need to follow up with her one day. Then there was the DROP team. Onetime enemies, full of bravado and camaraderie. They'd seen things today they'd never soon forget.

Everybody would change after this. I wasn't scared about that. Change is good. Change is the only way to grow. To prove you're alive.

Evan returned and pulled me and Milena aside as the crews of paramedics entered the marina. "You guys should get out of here," he said. "My team will take care of the rest."

The sub was gone, but the Russians were still secured in the warehouse. The bags of money and weapons were on display.

"What're you gonna tell them?" I asked.

He smiled. "I'll let you know when I figure that out." He shoved us toward the edge of the property, where we could slip down the street before the police arrived.

"Emily?" I asked.

"She'll be fine."

"I mean you and her."

He bit his lip. "She'll be fine."

I grunted. Milena and I hurried away.

"Hey, Cisco," he said, watching me over his shoulder. "What I said before, about operating outside the law..."

"I know," was all I said.

We traded a wordless glance, like it was us against the world. It reminded me of our days in middle school. Then he went back to the cleanup.

"Let's go," said Milena, leaning into my shoulder. "After firing that artillery cannon, I think I need a massage."

"It's gotta be two in the morning," I protested.

She smiled coyly. "I'm sure you'll manage." Milena pulled me to the street where we skirted the incoming emergency vehicles.

Everything was a blur. I felt different, somehow. Either the adrenaline was wearing off or I was in shock. The burden of the Horn was gone, but I carried a larger load now. I was personally responsible for unleashing an unknown threat on the city of Miami. My city. I tried not to think about Chevalier's disappointment or the Society's wrath. Hell, I forced myself not to consider how and when Connor Hatch would come for me next.

With the Spaniard as his ally, the jinn now knew where I lived.

But I had one night, damn it. One night I could enjoy, per the terms of the bargain. And seeing Fran in her mom's arms had made up for everything else.

I won't apologize for my decision. I would, however, do

everything in my power to set it right. My family was now safe, but my city wasn't. No way, no how was I gonna let that slide.

-Finn

About the Author

I'm Domino Finn, hardened urban fantasy author, media rebel, and espresso junkie. (Pro Tip: Sugar is your friend.)

Black Magic Outlaw isn't done yet. Join my reader group at DominoFinn.com to get the first word on sequels and cover reveals.

If *Powder Trade* was your jam, give others a chance to hear about it too. Please leave a review where you made your purchase, even if it's only a line or two.

Finally, don't forget to keep in touch. You can contact me, connect on social media, and see my complete book catalog at DominoFinn.com.

Made in the USA
San Bernardino, CA
30 April 2017